Group

By C.G. Buswell

Also by C.G. Buswell

Novels

The Grey Lady Ghost of the Cambridge Military Hospital: Grey and Scarlet 1

The Drummer Boy: Grey and Scarlet 2

Buried in Grief

One Last War

Short Stories

Christmas at Erskine

Halloween Treat

Angelic Gift

Burnt Vengeance

The Release

Christmas Presence

Torturous Grief

For Ray and Katherine, the dearest of friends.

Monica

'I hate you for taking your own life,' whispered Monica across the empty room. She was sitting on her sofa, hands worrying over a duster. A can of polish was on the low table beside her. 'And so violently too.' She looked up, turned on her seat, and stared at the alcove, 'How could you let me find you that way?' She stood up and jutted out her chin defiantly, 'I was your mother, no mum should see their child like that,' she shouted as she walked across the room. She reached for the photo frame that was laid on its front, glass side down. A layer of dust had settled over the back of the frame. Several spider webs were criss-crossed across the shelf and upon the edges of the neglected gilt edge. Her hands hovered over the frame, one set to grasp it, the other poised to wipe the years of dust away. 'Not today, I'm sorry, Josephine. I still love you, but I can't look at you, it's just too painful.' Several tears fell from Monica's face. Some landed on the duster and were absorbed; others fell on the neglected shelf, causing some of the fragile web network to crumble.

After a few minutes, she composed herself, wiped away her tears with the fingers of her left hand, and absently dried them on the duster. She then walked across the room, picked up the spray can, and began her cleaning.

The room was tastefully decorated with soothing pastel coloured paintwork and adorned with pictures of the local area; several were watercolours by a local artist who specialised in capturing the wild

1

ruggedness of the Scottish coast. Monica had opted to purchase the gentler scenes, hoping to bring some peace to her rented cottage. She had moved here a year after losing her daughter to suicide. She had tried to live in the family house, but it was a constant reminder of her loss. She experienced flashbacks to finding her daughter's body in the bath every time she walked into the bathroom. The images would overwhelm her each time, though she tried to keep them hidden from her husband, to lessen his pain. They had tried to work on their marriage, but their grief and guilt caused too many arguments and they had amicably split. They sold their house, neither wanting to live on, alone in a house where their daughter had violently taken her own life; and went their separate ways. She never heard from him again until his solicitor informed her of his death and private funeral. His ashes had been scattered at the grave of his daughter, and his estate, most of the money from the sale of his share of their home, had been bequeathed to Monica, along with a letter expressing his sorrow at the loss of their daughter and the breakdown of their marriage. He too had taken his own life, alone in a forest, hanging in a tree for an early morning jogger to find.

This semi-detached cottage, in the oldest part of the city, was rented from her closest friend, who lived next door. It had proven to be a healing blessing. Their friendship had grown even closer and Robyn had been and continued to be a superb listener. Monica fell in love with the low-beamed ceilings and roughly plastered walls. She loved that she could look out of her windows and see the North-East sandy beach. She liked to watch the deep-sea trawlers and container ships navigate their way into the narrow harbour to offload their cargo. She delighted in hearing the gulls and catching occasional glimpses of seals and dolphins swimming around the harbour, looking for easy catches. She called it her mindfulness moments. Best of all, she loved that Robyn would leave her with Judy, her playful Yorkshire Terrier.

Monica continued to spray and polish the few ornaments that were in the opposite alcove to where she had been crying. The shelves here were dust free and looked gleaming when compared to the opposite area. Like everything else in this room, and every room in the cottage, the objects and furniture were all brand new when she had moved in four years ago. She couldn't bear to have any reminders of what she had lost, except for the neglected photo frame. She looked back at it, 'One day, I promise, sweetheart. I'll be able to look at you and smile and remember all the fun we had. Well, until your heart was broken, and you felt you couldn't go on without your first girlfriend.' She sighed. 'I see her now and again, you know. I don't say hello. I don't trust myself, not yet. I think I'd lose my temper with her. I know I shouldn't blame her. You were both so young. She has a child of her own, I know that I should have told you this before, but I found that painful. I think he's about two. I couldn't see a wedding ring.' She smiled, 'Yes, I know, I'm old-fashioned. You'd probably tell me to get with the times if you were still,' she broke off the sentence, unable to finish it as her thoughts went down a dark path. She picked up another ornament and furiously rubbed at some invisible dust.

Robyn whistled and a small dog, dark brown, with lighter patches, padded boldly through from her basket in the kitchen. In a well-rehearsed ritual, it jumped onto a low stool set by the sofa and then leapt up onto her blanket, placed in the centre seat. Robyn laughed and sat beside her, 'We'll have a quick cuddle before seeing your best friend forever.'

Judy's ear pricked up at the mention of her friend next door. Her small face seemed to light up, and she looked from her owner and then across to the wooden front door. She looked back to Robyn and yielded to the strokes across her back. She laid down and turned over, exposing her belly as she received tummy rubs. She kicked up her feet playfully in the air. She was in dog heaven as Robyn ruffled her stomach several times and then gave a firm pat to show that she should now sit up.

Robyn placed the tartan jacket over Judy's back, covering her lighter patches, which almost looked saddle shaped. She clipped it on securely, ruffled Judy's face and stroked down her moustache and beard-like area and ended on an ear tickle. 'You do a magnificent job of looking after our friend, don't you girl.'

Judy waggled her small tail several times in agreement. It tapped gently against a lilac cushion.

'You be good for her and I'll be home after my shift at the supermarket. I've a busy day today, lots of interviews. I just hope there is a wee gem amongst them who will join our happy team. I wish I could take you with me, but we can't have you running around the food aisles, can we?'

Judy, impatient, jumped back down to her stool, waited for her back legs to catch up, and then bounced off and onto the oak flooring and trotted off to the front door. She waited patiently by the coat rack and looked up longingly at her leash.

Robyn laughed, 'Well, I guess you won't be yearning after me at all, will you? I can't compete with Monica, can I?'

Judy marked her agreement by turning around on the spot and jumping into the air, snout just missing the dangling ornate leash.

'Okay, okay, I can take a hint, let's get you on your best leash for Aunty Monica.' She reached for a dark green leash that was interspersed with varying shades of yellow, a Christmas present from her friend. She then knelt and attached her canine chum, gave her another ear tickle, and clicked her tongue for their 'Let's go!' command and the pair left their front door, locked up, and walked the few yards to the adjoining cottage.

Judy trotted obediently at heel and then stopped whilst Robyn took a few minutes to embrace the unexpected sunshine from the early September morning. The seagulls were already shrieking, and several had settled on the taller house roof to the left of their home. This was an old warehouse that had been tastefully converted into an executive style spacious home, well beyond the purses of the two friends. There were parking restrictions in this neighbourhood, and it was rumoured that the Porsche parked in the residents' bay at the end of the cobbled streets belonged to the man who lived in the big house.

Neither of the friends had met him. Robyn worked too many shifts to help pay her mortgages for the two buildings to have any spare time to devote to snooping, and her friend, who worked part-time for one of the oil companies, had no inclination to pry on others' concerns. She was still too deep in her grief to worry about anyone else. Judy sighed as she wondered if her pal would ever find happiness again. She replaced her frown with a false smile, wanting to convey warmth into her chum's life. She knocked gently on the lavender door.

Monica opened the door after a few seconds, 'Och, you shouldn't be knocking on your own door, I've told you before,' she gently berated her pal as she hugged her good morning. She felt a frantic clawing at her legs, broke off the greeting and bent over to ruffle Judy's beard, 'Hello gorgeous, yes I know I should make a fuss of you first, but I'll have you all day and your mummy will go in a few minutes.' She took possession of the leash.

'Thanks for looking after her, I should be home at six tonight, all being well.'

'It's no bother, I love her company. We'll go for a walk along the beach and then have a cup of coffee at our favourite dog-friendly café along the promenade. They always make her welcome there and I'll treat her to one of their doggy ice-cream sundaes, she loves them.'

'You spoil her rotten!' laughed Robyn until a fresh beam of sunshine broke through from the clouds and lit up the doorway. She looked at the dark, sunken red stained eyes of her friend, hidden during their hug. She knew that she'd been crying again and probably hadn't slept the whole night.

'I've no one else to spoil,' replied Monica, downcast.

Robyn reached for her friend's hand and gave it a gentle squeeze, 'I'll bring home a bottle of your favourite wine and come for dinner?'

'That sounds lovely, shall I cook?'

'How about we get a pizza delivered?'

'That sounds great,' replied Monica, planting a false smile on her narrow face.

Robyn nodded, though she saw how thin her pal was. She barely ate, just picked at her food, surviving on many cups of coffee throughout the day and night. She'd rarely bought any new outfits since the death of her only child, and her clothes hung from her, highlighting her withered frame. She'd made no effort with her hair again. It hung down to her neck like tangled bits of string, when once it would have been brushed and straightened with hair-straighteners every morning. It had lost all lustre, was grey streaked, and though they were the same age, Monica now looked ten years older than her thirty-five years. She no longer wore make-up, not even a touch of lipstick that would have brought some colour to her ashen face.

In contrast, Robyn had bouncy hair that was curled around her face, giving her a youthful, fun appearance. Her false eyelashes gave her an exaggerated coy look that drew you in to her mesmerising eyes, her dark liner hinting at a playful character. Her red lipstick was enticing, put on deliberately to attract the attention of the new man on the tills. She'd dressed in her skirt and matching jacket, an outfit she nicknamed her head teacher uniform, because she was expecting a visit from the head office later in the afternoon.

'I'll be off then. My bus will be here any minute.' She reached down to give Judy one last stroke of the ear, but she had trotted through to Monica's kitchen, in search of her favourite squeaky toy that she knew she'd left buried under the table yesterday. 'Oh well, at least I don't have to worry about her missing me. I'll catch you later.' She reluctantly turned and walked as briskly as her new high heels would allow. She'd wanted to appear taller than her interviewees, she believed it gave her an edge over them, though they soon saw past her stern bluster, falsely there to wheedle out the wheat from the chaff so that she could find a candidate who would stand up to demanding customers and keep a cool head in a busy store.

Monica watched her friend until she turned the corner. She hoped she wouldn't be too disappointed when she discovered that the new man on the till had a steady girlfriend and two small children. Her friends at the oil company office knew him from University and she'd overheard them chatting about how Liam wasn't putting his degree to good use, going from one supermarket job to the next. She looked up at the Victorian lamp posts whose ornate tops proved a prized resting place for several gulls. She made a mental note to keep a good eye on them as she'd read in the newspaper that along the coast, one had swooped down and tried to take away a Yorkshire Terrier that had been off its leash on the beach.

Robyn crossed the road and was rewarded with the sight of the golden sand shimmering in the September sun and envied the dog walkers with their pets. She was looking forward to her day off on Thursday when she and Monica would go for afternoon tea at a hotel in the city. She might even treat them to a taxi there and back, though the two mortgage payments would be tight this month. She still couldn't bring herself to charge her pal a normal rental price. She hadn't expected her to stay long in the cottage. Though she loved her company and would be sad to see her go, she'd hoped that she might find love again, and perhaps even have another child with a new partner. She was still young enough; they both were in her eyes. She walked the few paces to the bus shelter, idly watching a cargo ship sail towards the harbour.

'Morning love.'

Robyn smiled at the man perched on the thin bench running parallel with the back of the bus shelter, 'Oh, hi Graham, how are you this morning?'

'Can't complain,' he nodded to the small screen, high to his left, alight with red writing. 'The bus will be here in a few minutes.'

'I'm glad I didn't miss it; I'm having to walk slower until I get used to these new heels.'

Graham took the opportunity to look down at her shoes, discretely admiring her legs on the way down and up. He nodded to his highly polished shoes, 'I'd rather be wearing comfy trainers, but they don't go with my suits.'

'Your manager would complain?' she enquired. They were still nodding acquaintances. She only knew his name, having only met two weeks ago. They were still on the talking weather stage.

'He's a lovely manager, the best, so handsome, strong and with a sparkling personality, you'd like him if you got to know him.'

Robyn grinned, 'It's you, isn't it, you're the boss?'

'Busted! Yes, I own the financial advice firm, our clients expect to see me highly dressed, it gives them reassurance that their finances are in expert hands.'

She still hadn't realised that Graham had subtly asked her on a date. 'Wouldn't they wonder why you take the bus then?'

'No, I think that makes them see that I'm frugal with money and that their hard-earned cash is being invested wisely. Besides, I like the nostalgia of buses, you know the smell of them.'

'But this route isn't diesel anymore, it's hydrogen now.'

'Busted again! I enjoy meeting and getting to know people. For instance, I know you are my neighbour, but that's all. I don't even know where you work.'

'I'm the manager of the supermarket four stops away, I love it, we've a fun team, you should see us on our nights out!'

'I'd like that.'

Robyn looked at him properly, taken aback at his proposition so early in the morning. He was well-proportioned, fitting snugly into his smart blue suit, clean shaven with immaculate short hair. The fringe was waxed back and to the side. 'Wait, do you live in the big house, the old warehouse?'

'That's me! I know it's too big for me, but I just love the spaciousness of it, I can have my music loud without bothering anyone, and I don't need to leave for the gym, I've my equipment in one of my rooms. Perhaps you'd like to come over for a drink one night?'

The bus pulled up beside them, quietly like a stealthy commando, no noisy air brakes released on this modern fleet. The opening swoosh of its doors interrupted the duo.

Graham beckoned with his hand that Robyn should go first. She obliged and as she entered the bus, she tapped her bus pass on the scanner and waited for the beep before moving to the third row of seats, hoping that Graham would follow. Her mind was now free from the new bloke on the tills.

Judy trotted along past a row of closed restaurants that would only spring open for the hectic lunch hour and roaring evening trade. They had the pavement to themselves. The Council workers had done an outstanding job of picking up the discarded pizza boxes and fish and chips wrappers from the weekend that the seagulls hadn't shredded during their scavenge for food. The squawking birds had rapidly devoured any, though the occasional sticky stain remained. She sniffed at every doorway, recognising her favourite male dog's scent. She hoped to make new pals and see old friends at the café that her best friend forever took her to. Her small tongue darted out in anticipation of her cold treat that helped cool her down. She wouldn't have long to wait; they always served the canines first.

Monica looked down at her charge, smiling as they continued their short walk for her morning coffee, the third that day. She gave a cheery 'Good morning,' to a couple walking past with a stunning-looking dalmatian, though deep-down in her heart, she was full of sorrow. Tomorrow was the night of her support group and though she looked forward to seeing Oliver and Isobel, she dreaded any new members. Not because she wanted her friends all to herself, but because it meant that someone's loved one had taken their own life and those left behind had raw emotions and unanswered questions. Lots of unanswered questions. And guilt. Too much to carry sometimes. She knew the group was an immense comfort to people, but they rarely found the answers they sought. 'If only Oliver and Isobel knew what I thought deep-down. Oh!' Monica regretted the words the moment she had spoken them aloud to herself. She bit down on her lower lip and tugged at it with her teeth, as if trying to take back the sentence.

Judy ceased her stroll, causing Monica to halt. The dog looked up towards her, as if checking in, making sure that her BFF was okay.

'Sorry girl, I was getting maudlin again, wasn't I?'

A black snout creased within its bearded face, as if showing agreement and concern. She gave a few yelping barks and then settled.

'The secrets I tell you. I'm glad you can't speak, otherwise you'd let Robyn know what I secretly yearn for, and that wouldn't do at all, would it?'

Judy wagged her short tail tentatively.

'Let's go Judy, you've an ice-cream to eat,' announced Monica, cutting short her monologue.

The duo walked on towards the next building with the huge paw print signage on the facade.

The bus drove along the row of flats to the right, modern three-story apartments with rounded facades with individual balconies which sat alongside a row of linear double-storied flats built in the sixties and showing signs of age such as peeling paintwork on the rusting metalwork and harsh bitumen flat roofs. Robyn ignored the buildings; she'd normally people watch through their windows, but today she was too fascinated by Graham. 'So how many people work for you?'

'There are a dozen of us, an accountant, five other financial advisors and three secretaries, though they are part time, juggling their family life. I think they get a good balance of work and home life.'

'I'm no counting wizard, but with you included, that only makes ten. Is there a Mrs Graham who works there too?'

'There was, not that she worked there, God no!' he chuckled. 'She'd have driven me up the wall even more. I hadn't realised how insular and selfish she was until I'd married her. We soon drifted apart. She liked social events, the classier the better. I enjoy relaxing at home with my music. She soon found an older man who was richer than me. I'm glad. She's happy.'

'I'm sorry. Though that still leaves ten at your work.'

'I keep forgetting the two part-time cleaners, the most important of our team. They keep our offices spotless. I rarely see them. They juggle other jobs, so either come in early o'clock, or late in the evening. I trust them to work their own hours between them, they've never let me down. It's another reason that I leave the car at home. It's only a short drive and car parking is expensive and difficult. Our clients always come to the office; we rarely go to their homes. By taking the bus, I save a fortune and always have an excuse to leave on time.' He winked at her, 'Though sometimes I'm naughty and I walk up to the vinyl shop and treat myself. I love the homely smell there and often find a bargain.'

Robyn was about to ask about his taste in music when he suddenly stood up.

'That's me then,' he declared as he pressed the bell for the driver to stop at the approaching bus stop now that they'd negotiated the busy roundabout, already hectic with parents in their cars journeying to the nearby school. 'It's been lovely getting to know you better Robyn, I hope we can chat again soon.'

Robyn flashed him what she hoped was her winning smile and nodded as he departed.

'Hello gorgeous!' shouted the barista from behind his burbling coffee machine. He leant over the counter, looked at the floor and was rewarded with a short stubby tail attempting to sweep the floor furiously in its delight. He left his equipment, came around from the counter and crouched down and tickled Judy under her chin, 'And how is the best-looking dog in town?'

'She's fine,' answered Monica. 'How are you today, Mathew? Keeping busy?'

'I'm great, the café is great, everything is great! We've finished our breakfast rush. You'd be surprised at the number of dog owners who can't resist a sneaky bacon or square sausage butty after their walks along the beach. I always leave the rind on so that they can share with their four-legged friends. Can I tempt you today?' He looked up, concerned, knowing that his favourite customer never ate here, but needed to. She looked ever so thin.

'Not for me thanks, just our usual please.'

'A bowl of delight for madam coming right up then,' he patted Judy on the head and stood up. 'And a cup of our finest coffee for you.' He turned and walked back behind his counter, getting busy with a shiny metal dog bowl. He always served them first.

Monica looked down at Judy, 'Let's go to our favourite spot.' They walked to the table on the central side wall, far enough away from the back row of assorted sized cages and blankets for those dogs who needed some alone time and away from the hustle and bustle of the till area. On the way, she took this morning's local newspaper from the rack. The headline announced another fatal car crash, and she felt for the family left behind.

Oliver

'I'm popping over to the café for a bite to eat, can I get you something?' asked Oliver to his secretary.

'No, I'll finish this report and head on over myself, probably in thirty minutes,' replied Mitch. 'Mum's cooking my favourite lentil Dall, it's great with their spinach and mixed leaf salad.' He stood up from his computer chair and leaned over to his boss, 'I'll get told off if I don't correct this.' He pulled a tissue from a box and lightly brushed at a stain on Oliver's tie.

'Cool, thanks. If you leave it on my desk, I'll refresh myself with it before the conference call.' He looked down, 'I hadn't spotted that, I couldn't refuse a doughnut earlier. Your parent's café is just so irresistible!'

'No bother, have something tasty!'

Oliver nodded his agreement; he couldn't resist the home-cooking from the enterprising couple who had set up their catering business on the ground floor of the vast office complex. It had been several months before Oliver realised they were Mitch's parents. He thought it was sweet that they all worked in the same building. They were skilled cooks and a savvy business duo. They served a mixture of hot and cold drinks and snacks from seven in the morning until they closed at six in the evening. In-between times they tempted the many businesses that worked there with freshly made quick hot meals, salads, sandwiches, wraps, and more. Their hard work ethic had rubbed off on their son, and Oliver knew he'd miss Mitch if ever a rival company sought him out. Not just because he always corrected his messy stains, missed patches of shaving, or unruly hair. Mitch was an efficient diary-keeper and report-maker. He walked down the corridor, his thoughts already turning to tomorrow night, when he'd meet up with his pals at the support group. As he pressed the button for one of the three lifts that served the complex, he wondered if he'd have to help console any freshly grieving mum, dad, or sibling. Occasionally it would be a friend, rarely a grandparent or uncle and aunt. He didn't mind, he just knew that any words didn't succour. No amount of hugging could take the intense grief away. He stifled a yawn with his palm.

The lift made a casual dinging noise to announce its arrival, and he entered as the doors automatically opened. He walked in, nodded hello to the occupants, and noted that the ground floor button was already lit. He joined the others in staring at the LED countdown high above, like a small group of zombies awaiting passing victims. As the doors opened once more, he was hit with the aroma of fresh coffee and the tang of something simmering away. He heard his stomach growl its emptiness, though its noise was soon absorbed by the hustle and bustle of the café ahead of him. Several servers were already clearing tables, empty plates were evident of the satisfied eaters who had returned to their busy offices. His quality assurance company shared a floor with an insurance call centre and an oil company. Expert soundproofing and panelling ensured their suites kept a dignified silence. Though the clever architects had omitted this down here so that an ambience was created, and Mitch's parents were the beneficiaries, there was seldom a table empty for long.

Oliver walked across to the café and went straight to the till area, he'd only allowed thirty minutes for lunch, he really needed to refresh his mind about that report. He knew it would be waiting on his desk upon his return.

'Hello Oliver, what can I tempt you with today?' Harriet looked up at the wall clock. 'You are early today. I hope my Mitch is behaving himself?'

'He's working hard on a special report. We are hoping to secure a new contract with a drilling company. But he's recommended your special Dall and salad.'

'Coming right up, along with your pot of green tea.' She made to turn to the hotplates but stopped as Oliver continued.

'It's my support group tomorrow, could I please order two dozen of your homemade biscuits, those chunky ones went down a treat last month. Nothing fancy, it seems frivolous to bring extravagant cakes or biscuits to a bereavement group.'

Harriet nodded, her son had told her a few months back to look out for her boss and give him special status and a generous portion. He rarely cooked properly for himself, not since his wife had taken her own life two years ago. She'd taken an overdose soon after losing yet another baby by miscarriage. Though Harriet had heard that this one went full-term. Oliver had taken several months off and his assistant manager had carried the company during this time and for many months after. It took over a year before Oliver could work full time and even then; he wasn't attentive enough. Harriet wasn't surprised, she often wondered how someone could go on after something like that. She hugged Mitch tight the night she learned about his boss. 'I'll bake them myself and have them ready for you to collect when you come for your lunch.'

'Thank you, Harriet, you're a real asset to this HQ, you're the heart of it.'

She blushed, her hot flush was even more apparent because she'd tied her long hair into a tight bun and it fully exposed her cheeks. 'Och, away with you. Pay my lump of a husband and I'll get one of the lads or girls to bring your meal to you.'

Oliver grinned at her and continued along the queue towards Jude, a stout jolly faced man whose booming voice cut through the hustle and bustle of the café as he directed his other customers to use the contactless machine by the enticing rack of ethically sourced chocolate bars made by a local artisan chocolatier.

Two tiny feet went bounding along the central aisle, intent for one of the open cages. She had spied a potential hiding place from her mother. She was dressed in an all-in-one padded white suit, which gave her petite frame the appearance of the Ghostbusters Stay Puft Marshmallow man. The little girl's legs were going too fast for her small feet to handle and she fell to her face beside the table occupied by Monica and Judy. She began an ear-piercing cry, more from shock than pain since her jacket and trousers absorbed the impact.

Judy continued to lap at her ice-cream, pausing only to see if the girl was coming over to refill her bowl.

Monica instinctively rose, intent on helping and comforting the child. She saw the child's mother rush towards her and left the expert to it. She smiled at the mother, 'They are a handful at that age.'

'Tell me about it,' replied the mother as she reached down and scooped up her child, checking her for injuries and making soothing noises to placate her. The crying soon eased as they cuddled. 'You have family?' she politely asked.

The smile fell from Monica's face and dark worry lines creased her forehead and at the edges of her eyes. She lied and said, 'Yes, my daughter was always falling over at that age. She ran faster than her legs could cope with.'

'My one can't resist hiding in the cages. We come here because she loves the dogs. We can't have one because my older daughter is allergic. When she goes to school, we come here for a drink and cake and then enjoy some time on the beach, she loves splashing in the sea. You've a beautiful dog. Your child must spoil her rotten.'

Monica couldn't trust her voice, and the stranger couldn't see the sorrow upon her face. She merely nodded.

'Well, I'll leave you in peace, it was nice meeting you.'

Monica nodded again and held herself together until the stranger left her. She picked up the paper, opened it out and held it in front of her face, as if reading small words close. Only then did she allow her tears to fall. She always felt a rush of emotions whenever she heard a child cry. It was a sharp reminder that she hadn't realised how much emotional pain her daughter had been in the months leading up to her suicide. She felt she had failed her daughter.

'I've been told by Harriet that I should sit at your table.' The young woman looked around her at the empty tables as if excusing her behaviour in bothering Oliver.

He put down his fork and smiled a welcome. 'She does that. It's best not to make a scene and just sit down.' He rose to his feet as he gentlemanly acknowledged her and waited for her to sit down. 'I'm Oliver, pleased to meet you. Harriet is motherly towards me; she hates to see me eat alone. She always sends a new friend my way. I work on the third floor, with her son, he's my PA, I'd be lost without him, he's the most efficient personal assistant that I've ever had.'

She laughed, 'That's so sweet. I've seen him behind the till sometimes. Mitch, isn't it?'

'That's right. He often gives up his lunch hour to help his parents if someone has phoned in sick. If he comes back late, he always brings up some snacks to make up for it.'

She sat down, 'I'm Rachel, fourth floor, asset management, nice to meet you too.'

Oliver smiled. She was far too young to be interested in chatting to him, what was Harriet thinking. Though he guessed, correctly, that she'd rather be sitting next to his PA. 'Mitch recommended the Dall, it's thick with lentils. I hate to think what it'll do once digested.'

Rachel gave an embarrassed laugh, 'It's what I'm having. I'm a vegan.'

'I try. Eating here helps. I miss it on weekends. I'll let Mitch know you loved it too.'

Her eyes lit up, 'What time is his lunch hour?'

'Normally at one, but I'm afraid that I'm being a hard taskmaster and have him working until he finishes a report. You'll probably have to be back to your office by then?'

She nodded; her disappointment was etched on her face.

'I'll make sure he has an early lunch tomorrow.'

Her face radiated warmth and her eyes twinkled.

Oliver grinned at her, Harriet would be pleased and perhaps a bit surprised it was he who had done the match-making this time.

Mathew carefully carried the cup and saucer across the café. He'd waited a few minutes before preparing another coffee, this time a decaffeinated one, though it would look and smell like his regular caffeine hit. He placed it on Monica's table. 'On the house. It'll prepare you to face the day. You're my favourite customer,' he looked down at Judy, 'Both of you.' He patted Monica on the shoulder, 'You've done well to face the world today.'

Monica had composed herself and was still grasping the napkin she'd used to dry her tears. She tucked it into her pocket, not wanting her precious tears to be exposed to another. It wasn't fair for others to clean up after her. 'Some days I just want to pull the duvet back over me, say no thank you to the world, and fall back into a deep sleep, though I can't seem to manage that most nights.'

'I know, the nights are the longest when you know your child can no longer experience a new dawn.'

Monica nodded. She knew Mathew had experienced the loss of a child too. A hit-and-run driver had killed him, joyriding through the streets in a stolen car. His son, David, had been walking home from Scouts and had almost reached the safety of their home when the car spun out of control during the police chase and crashed into him. He was killed outright. The youth behind the wheel ran off but was later caught by another team of police. He'd escaped a manslaughter charge and was given a two-year sentence for the motoring offences. Mathew and his wife had rebuilt their lives and gave up their jobs in the city and followed their passion for dogs and built this thriving business. They were proof that grief would not dominate the lives of those left behind. 'It catches me unawares sometimes. Thank you for being a good friend and listener.'

'I know I keep saying this to you whenever I see you, but counselling helped us to move forward, to forgive and to heal. Perhaps it's time for you to find someone professional?'

Monica thought back to the website she had visited a few nights back. 'Yes, I think it is. You are one of the few people who would understand this. I've been thinking of going on a retreat.'

Mathew looked puzzled, 'You mean like with nuns?'

Monica burst out laughing, tears now forgotten. 'Never change Mathew, you come out with some howlers. Can you imagine me as a nun? Dressed in a habit! Hair tucked harshly back in a veil!'

He laughed with her, imagining the sight, 'Maybe not! Do nuns even drink coffee?'

'I certainly wouldn't be allowed my nightly wine. No, it's called a retreat, but it's more like a conference or study weekend. A charity runs it. It's for parents who have lost a child and they have counsellors and fellow bereaved mums and dads who are specially trained to offer comfort and support day and night. They even run poetry and craft classes. All meals are provided, and you stay for two nights. I think it's come at the right time for me.'

'Yes, I've heard of these retreats, now I come to think about it. Our counsellor gave us a leaflet, it's in a drawer somewhere. Our other children needed us at home though, and Birmingham seemed a long way to go. Pity, they held it in the mansion that the first Cadbury's owner lived in. I've heard that the grounds are magnificent.'

Monica nodded, 'This one is in Perth, so I can hop on a bus. Perhaps even a train. I haven't researched that bit yet.'

Mathew looked back to his till and saw a couple with a boxer dog sat between them, 'I'd better get on. Enjoy the coffee and let me know how you get on with the retreat.' He reached into his apron pocket, took out several small packages and placed them on the table. 'A rep gave me these freebies. They are instant coffee samples. I won't use them. I thought you could take them to your support group. I know you are not supposed to use the church's supply.'

'No, we get rude messages from the congregation tea ladies if we do! Thank you so much, Mathew.'

He reached down and tickled Judy on the neck, she'd been patiently waiting for him to refill her bowl and was disappointed to see him walk away.

Oliver flicked through the report, impressed with the layout of the pie charts and graphs, the forecast of costs and projected revenue savings for the French company. Mitch had sent them an updated copy by e-mail, and their Zoom chat link was set up for him. He closed the folder and reached for a pencil, ready for any notes, though he was confident that he and Mitch had foreseen any possible questions. He sat back in his chair and let his thoughts drift away to Monica and the group. He often thought of calling it a day, but he enjoyed their company, especially Monica's. Though he could see the hurt in her eyes, he loved her smile. It didn't happen often, but it was like a ray of sunshine peeking out in-between showery rain. It lit up the church hall and touched his heart. He knew little about her, just what she revealed during each meeting, the first Thursday of a month, except if it fell on Christmas Day, not that many of them would celebrate that special day. He always tried to catch her for a chat afterwards or offer her a lift home. He was sure that they could be great mates outside of the group. He'd love to have a ten-pin bowling or cinema buddy again. He'd asked Mitch, but he'd always seemed to be on another failed date.

A brief tune came from his laptop, interrupting his thoughts. He reached forward, clicked his mouse, and smiled to his webcam, 'Bonjour!'

Monica hopped on the bus which her friend had taken earlier. She had Judy tucked safely within the breast of her jacket, the zipper pulled halfway.

'Hello sweetie!' declared the burly driver, his biceps bulging from his uniform short-sleeved shirt. The words, in a high-pitched tone, seemed incongruous from his lips, spoken to the small dog peeking out. He continued to speak, as if to a baby or toddler, 'I saw your mummy this morning, yes I did. And where is aunty taking you today?'

'Hello Len. We're off to the building society.' Monica leant in closer to him, towards his Perspex screen and whispered conspiratorially, 'I'll sneak Judy in under my jacket, they'll never know she's there.'

Len winked at her, 'So long as you're not going to hold it up, I'd miss you if the police catch you, you're my favourite passenger.'

Monica tapped her bus pass on the scanner and looked around the bus, 'I'm your only passenger.'

Len chortled to himself as he watched her walk to a seat and waited until she'd safely settled down with Judy before driving off.

Monica looked out the window, thinking of the retreat, knowing that she could easily afford it. She was off to the building society to increase a standing order, rather than to check her funds. Her husband had left her well provided, though she didn't think she deserved to benefit financially from his death. That caused her sleepless nights too, despite giving chunks of it to the bereavement support group and the Samaritans. She still had the capital from her half of the house sale, and other than wine, she had no vices to spend it on. It was the worry of being on her own at the retreat, though the charity had responded to her e-mail saying that many were on their own and soon made new friends. Deep down, she knew this. Many parents divorced after the death of a child and some, sadly, took their own lives too, the pain being too much for them to carry.

Judy pawed at the zipper, gently easing herself out and in the process interrupting, once again, her friend's morose thoughts. She felt herself lifted and placed into a lap and a gentle, rhythmic, reassuring hand began stroking her. She got herself comfy, laid down and succumbed to sleep.

Isobel

Isobel giggled like a teenager, almost conspiratorially, with her great-granddaughter as she splashed warm water over her tiny stomach. 'You cheer me up Lindsay, you are such fun.'

Eight-week old Lindsay gurgled with delight as her nana continued to bathe her, not fully understanding, but mirroring the sounds from the adult.

'Oh yes, you are!' cooed Isobel as she now sponged down her charge's back. 'You have brought fun back into our lives, oh yes you have!' She leant over the bath and kissed her great-granddaughter on her head, breathing in the lovely baby smell she had missed for nineteen years. A blob of bubble bath perched on the end of Isobel's nose as she leant back. She looked at Lindsay, cross-eyed as she then focused on the soapsuds at the end of her nose, and then blew them away. Fresh laughter erupted from the duo as the bubbles floated off.

It hadn't worried her when her granddaughter, Wendy, had announced one day that she was pregnant. It was a bit of a shock; she'd only been dating Darren for six months. He was a nice enough lad, had a secure job at the local fish factory, but Isobel wanted more for her granddaughter, especially given that she'd lost her mum, Paula, her dad Aaron, and grandfather in the space of a year, when she was only twelve. She'd gone off the rails, had fallen in with a bad crowd, failed her exams four years later and had been passed from one NHS psychologist to another, then through a series of psychiatrists and psychotherapists and then cut loose from the child support and protection team at eighteen, with no further psychological support, until she fell in love with Darren. The news of their pregnancy hadn't shocked Isobel at all, they were so in love and why shouldn't they share that love with their own child. They were adults, and Wendy had lost so much in her brief life. She needed happiness now.

Wendy called him her rock, and now, aged nineteen, she had his baby and had moved out from the family home and into their own flat. Though they were only several streets away, which was a fine walk with the pram. Wendy had gone back to college, at Darren's insistence, and Isobel had eagerly babysat Lindsay day and night when needed. Her husband's life insurance had paid out handsomely after he lost his struggle with cancer, and she'd never needed to work again. Roy's diagnosis had shocked them all, he'd been fit and active, aged only fifty-nine, no excess fat on him, a non-smoker and very occasional drinker. Life didn't seem fair, especially for Wendy, who loved and worshipped her grandfather. The man who sat with her each night after her mother had taken her life after another schizophrenic episode and her father, Aaron, Roy, and Isobel's son, later took his own life from grief.

Roy had been so patient and gentle, even though his pain and own grief for Aaron and Paula troubled him deeply. His only thoughts had been for Wendy and Isobel. He'd have loved to have been a great-grandpapa. He hadn't lived long enough to even hear the news or see the first scan image. Ironically, Isobel, who had enjoyed a nightly gin and smoked a packet of cigarettes a day, remained fit into her late fifties. She'd given up the fags and booze the night after Roy's stoical reaction to the news of his diagnosis at the cancer unit. The consultant had been so kind, offered a treatment regime, which Roy dutifully obeyed, but the radiotherapy and consequent chemotherapy couldn't halt the advance of the rapidly growing cancer. It had spread to his brain and bones after just six months, and he'd died peacefully at home, another six months later. He was buried with Aaron, in the lair they'd bought from the Council, thinking that in a decade or two, they could join their son at rest in the cemetery. Paula's family had insisted on a cremation, and they had scattered her ashes over her favourite beach. Roy and Isobel hadn't been invited to attend the scattering and had no contact with Paula's family since.

Isobel had wanted to scream at the injustice of it all, but had to be calm for the sake of Wendy. Her life, since the deaths of Aaron and Paula, had been Isobel's focus, and now she had Lindsay to centre her maternal instincts on. She pulled the bath plug, all the time ensuring that her left hand continued to support Lindsay's head and neck, and reached over for the fluffy bath towel. 'It's a juggling act, oh yes, it is my lovely,' she fussed as she wrapped the towel around the baby. She lifted her out and snuggled her to her chest whilst drying her off with gentle movements, not caring that some water was seeping through to her blouse. She walked through to the spare room and gently placed Lindsay on the raised changing mat unit. She winked at her great-granddaughter, 'Don't tell mummy, I know she doesn't believe in it, but it never did my dear Aaron any harm.' She took out the small bottle of talcum powder from the shelf above. It was tucked behind an assortment of baby creams and spare shampoo. She fiddled with the opening and then gave Lindsay a liberal dusting. This elicited a fresh gurgle of delight from Lindsay as she watched the fine white clouds rise above her eyes and then settle over her body. Her nana reached for a disposable nappy whilst wishfully thinking how much better for Lindsay's skin and the environment a terry-towelling washable nappy and cloth liner would be. She missed having a row of newly washed whites on the washing line, smelling freshly of Napisan, and flapping like sails on a boat on a breezy day.

Suitably protected from bodily functions, Isobel then wrestled Lindsay into her babygrow as the baby kicked out energetically with her legs. She was soon fully clothed and attired for her mummy getting home from her studies. Isobel announced to baby Lindsay, 'Let's get you fed with your mummies milk and belched and burped before she gets home.'

As she picked up her little one, she marvelled at all the advances in childcare since she had her Aaron, especially the discrete, quick, and pain-free breast pump that Wendy occasionally used in her presence. She felt old sometimes, but then again, she felt rejuvenated once more whenever in Lindsay's presence. It almost halted the pain of grief at her own loss of first a child, and then a husband. But looking after her grand and great-granddaughters had always taken priority, even over her own feelings and emotions. 'I'll miss you tomorrow, but Wendy won't let me miss my group, not even for you my darling.'

She scooped up Lindsay once more, leaving the talc still open and the wet towel draped over the edge of the bathmat. She'd tidy up later, after they'd gone home, and before Corrie. 'I've never missed an episode of my favourite soap,' she boasted to Lindsay. 'Not even when Roy, your great-grandpapa was ill. He always asked if it was still on series record on the disc recorder. You'd have loved him lass, he always put others first and had a heart of gold. I know that you've Darren's side of the family for manly relatives, but I'd have loved for you to have known Roy.' Isobel sighed as she clung on tighter to her great-granddaughter whilst the pair left the room and walked down the stairs to the kitchen.

'Okay Judy, I'll need you to settle down and not to bark out like you did last time.' Monica was speaking to her jacket, drawing in some strange looks from the two elderly ladies at the bus stop on this busy main street of the city. She placed an arm across her stomach to support Judy in her hiding place. She was about to step into the building society but waited a moment whilst she quickly stuffed her leash into her trouser pocket.

The automatic doors opened as she approached them and she smiled at the assistant whose job it was to meet, greet and direct customers to the various tellers, desks, and cash machines. Monica walked confidently towards the nearest teller, but froze when another member of staff blurted out, 'Dog!'

Monica looked down at her jacket, not seeing any movement or sticking out bits of tell-tale fur.

The other assistant walked past Monica saying, 'I know I shouldn't, but can I say hello to your dog?'

Puzzled, Monica turned around and was rewarded with the sight of a beautiful golden retriever. A young girl of primary school age held its leash. She held the hand of a giant of a man who overshadowed what must have been his daughter; they had the same piercing blue eyes.

'You shouldn't. It distracts Ruby from looking after my daddy. He's a hero, you know,' scolded the young girl.

The tall man grinned, 'They look after me, and my daughter is right, I'm afraid that it distracts Ruby from her duties. It's all right this time, I'm keeping calm, I saw you coming, it's the people who come from behind that I explode with. My temper can erupt so easily these days. I've learnt that it's best to do as Annabelle says, she's the boss of us both. Please don't make a fuss of my assistance dog, Ruby.' He looked down at the animal with fondness lighting up his face. The leash was still held proprietorially by the youngster, 'Sit,' they both commanded at the same time. The dog dutifully sat down and looked from the girl and then back to the big man, repeating the head turning, seeking a fresh command. The trio were partially blocking the entrance and exit from the building, and other customers were squeezing past them, obeying the 'Do not distract or stroke' signage on the dog's harness and jacket.

Monica stared for a bit longer, wanting to read the printing on the jacket. She knew it couldn't be a guide dog. The towering man seemed to have his eyesight. She read the word 'Bravehound' and made a mental note to look this up on the internet when she had a spare moment. Judy gave a wriggle within her jacket, acting as a timely reminder to her she shouldn't have her friend's dog in here. She turned away from the trio and continued her way to the nearest cashier to change a standing order and transfer some money to someone else's account.

Isobel paced her lounge whilst gently bouncing baby Lindsay, who was cuddling into her shoulder. She gently patted Lindsay's back, encouraging her to burp. Lindsay cried out with discomfort from an overfull stomach from her latest feed. Isobel sang a song from her motherhood when she'd done something similar for Aaron. She surprised herself as she sang out the words; she'd found music and the emotions it brought out, painful to listen to since the suicide of her son. She never had the radio on in the car, she had put away the house stereo unit up in the loft, and never, ever, hummed or sang, until now. She stood in front of the blocked-off fireplace, where the artificial floral display sat in an ornate vase. She knew that this too would have to go into storage in her loft when Lindsay learnt to crawl. It would be too much of a temptation and a source of danger. She didn't mind, all that mattered was the happiness and safety of her great-granddaughter. As she sang, she looked up at the portrait of her son and daughter-in-law, taken between Paula's spells in the local mental health unit, often in the secure wing for her and others protection until more new medicines could be tried and a therapeutic dose achieved and she was stable once more.

She looked into the eyes of her long dead son and daughter-in-law, the photo's faces not revealing the pain and turmoil she had endured. Isobel had failed to see it when she was alive and she blamed herself for years, until her new friends at the group, Nancy, the group facilitator in particular, had helped her see that she'd done all she could, as had the health care professionals. No one was to blame, certainly not her Roy either, he'd been the model father and husband, learning all he could about his daughter-in-law's illness. This was in the days before the internet. He'd bought expensive medical books from the local bookshop, one after another, making notes in the margins, filling up notebooks with ideas and possible treatments, seeking a miracle pill or therapy that could ease her suffering.

Isobel broke off her stare and looked lovingly at the baby she was soothing. She leant down and kissed the top of her head, 'You'd have adored your grandfather and grandmother. They were kind souls, well when she was well. They would have been proud of your mother and would have loved to have taken you for long strolls in your pram, especially in the local park and along the old railway line. That pathway was his favourite walk, especially in the summer when he could pick and bring home the brambles.' Isobel's eyes lit up at the memories. 'Though he ate more there than he brought home.' She gave Lindsay another few gentle taps on her back and ended the movements with a rub. She was rewarded with a belch and a wet, warm feeling soaked through from the towel draped over her shoulder. 'He'd often have a tummy ache, just like you, from eating all the fruit. He had a sweet tooth and a mouthful of iron fillings to prove it.' She brought Lindsay from her shoulder and into a cradle in one effortless movement, muscle memory from two other babies, spaced about eighteen years apart, aiding the deft action. She gently rocked Lindsay whilst repeating the mantra, 'And I'm going to love you three times as much as everyone else, once for your grandfather and grandmother, twice for your great-grandpapa and thrice for me, the biggest of all!' She lifted Lindsay up to her face, so that their noses gave the gentlest of touches, and finished her songs with a gentle nose rub.

Trudie, from head office, sat sternly to attention and gave off a malevolent presence across the desk from Robyn. She was primly dressed in a dark blue trouser and jacket with a startling white blouse. Her hair was tied back tightly in a bun, almost forcing her highbrow backwards. She made Robyn feel like she was a pupil awaiting lashes of a cane by a strict head teacher from a 1950s boarding school. Especially when she'd asked for the July figures, though Robyn knew that she'd already received and analysed them at head office.

'Why didn't you push the barbeque range, other stores were shifting enormous amounts of the farmhouse branded sausages, burgers and pre-made kebabs?' quizzed Trudie.

'Perhaps in England, but we don't get the fine weather up here, at least not every day. We had the special section in the fridges, and the displays of barbeque utensils and charcoal. But who wants those when it's raining? We even cooked some and had samples for customers to try.'

Trudie's eyebrows arched at the mention of giving away stock and gave a brisk tut with her tongue.

Robyn smiled, not to disarm her superior, but at the distracting thought of whether Graham would be on the bus home if she could get rid of madam here.

'I guess that could have worked, if only you'd have had the sunshine.'

Robyn shrugged, as if taking reluctant responsibility for the weather.

'Your sales of tanning lotion have fallen compared to last year too.'

Robyn tried not to look at the clock on the wall. She hoped Graham would go to the music shop and catch a later bus. That would be the one she'd have to take now. She pointed to the screen with the nib of her pen, 'The range of indoor games sold well, far more than the other branches. In fact, we had to request an urgent resupply from the stores throughout the UK.' She sat back in her chair, winning this round, and basking in the celebration. The card game where the children had to battle out with points with their friends and win or lose each other's decks had been the latest craze, driven by local social media. Her supermarket had been the sole stockist for the six-week run of this year's school holidays. It brought desperate mums, dads, aunts, uncles, and grandparents into her store with laden trollies and had changed the shopping habits of many families, especially when they saw how fresh their fruit and vegetables section was, thanks to punnets of tempting strawberries from the adjacent county of Angus.

Robyn tapped the mouse with a flourish and revealed the August figures, a tremendous increase when compared to last year. It had topped the sales chart for all the UK stores, earning her a tidy bonus that helped with that month's mortgage payments.

Trudie relented, 'Yes, I was going to thank you for those, well done,' she begrudgingly offered through pursed lips. 'And your staff turnover?'

'One of the best, I'm sure you'll agree. We've a happy team here and have an almost unheard of one hundred percent retention rate for the last two years, with only one member, Kelly, off long-term sick, though we are putting in place a special ergonomically correct till area so that she can return to work after her brain haemorrhage. It'll have a specially designed alcove for her speech machine, discreetly out of eyeshot of customers and with a hidden speaker. Her physiotherapy is helping with her slight limp, where her right foot drags a bit. Sadly, her mother told me she won't regain the use of her right arm. She supports it in a special sling. Kelly is confident she'll return to work by October. She's a firm favourite with our older customers. You should see the number of cards they sent to the hospital.'

Trudie almost broke into a smile which to Robyn looked like a grimace, revealing her too white and perfectly-aligned teeth, which she was sure were veneers. She let her mind wander again. Perhaps the iron lady had a weakness for dental cosmetic surgery. She thought back to Graham's smile and how carefree he seemed. Trudie interrupted her happy thoughts with, 'And the man on the tills, with the black hair?'

'That'll be Liam. He's new, on a zero-hour contract, for the build-up to Christmas. Our older customers shop early and start stocking up their cupboards and buying gifts from early September. He's great. He's worked in a couple of our competitor stores over the years and brings a wealth of experience. He needed little training and is no longer supervised. He's a hit with our younger generation and has a vast circle of friends.' This time Robyn looked at the clock. She hoped Graham would make several purchases at the music shop and would listen to a few tracks there. Perhaps, she hoped, he'd be on the even later bus.

There was a sharp intake of breath, 'You don't mean that he spends a lot of time chatting? It wouldn't do if his throughput were slow, and you had to open another till to stop long queues forming. Have you timed his rate of scanning?'

'Sorry, no, that's not what I meant. His friends now shop here just so they can say a quick hello as they shop. You'll see that last week's figures show about a ten per cent rise.' Robyn gave a few more clicks of her mouse, glad that she'd had the foresight to see this line of questioning; her homework had paid off.

Trudie gathered up her paperwork, making a show of straightening the sheets of paper by tapping their edges on the desk, only stopping when they were perfectly aligned. She placed them into her padded leather folder and zipped it up. 'Well. Thank you, that's all satisfactory, keep up the excellent work. Let's hope for a sun-filled summer next year.'

'And a Merry Christmas for all our spending customers,' beamed Robyn.

Trudie looked at her, 'Indeed,' was all that she said as she marched off.

Mitch shut down his computer for the night and walked over to Oliver's open door. He tapped respectfully on the door anyway and loitered by the frame. 'I'll be off then, boss; unless you need me for anything else?' He began folding up his shirt sleeves.

Oliver looked up from his desk, familiar with the garment action, it signalled that his PA was getting ready to go downstairs and help his parents load up the last of the dishwasher loads and clean down the tables and chairs. Mitch was a dab hand with the mop whizzing around the concourse at double the speed of his father and mother. 'No, I'm just finishing as well. Thanks so much again for working late through lunch to get the report finished. I'm glad that your mum saved you some Dall, it was superb.' He patted his stomach in exaggeration. 'But I want you to have first lunch tomorrow, so have a light breakfast.'

'Oh, okay,' a frown crossed Mitch's forehead. It wasn't like Oliver to worry about mealtimes, he was normally too busy. 'You okay, boss?'

Oliver grinned like a schoolboy who'd won a conkers challenge in the playground. 'Your mum and I have a pleasant surprise for you. I'm owed you a few hours, so don't rush back if you don't need too.'

Mitch nodded, though with a hint of uncertainty across his innocent face. 'I know I don't need to remind you, but I thought I'd check. It's your group tomorrow, have you ordered your biscuits? If not, I'll ask mum.'

'Already done mate, thanks. You have a good evening. Is it the gym tonight?'

'Afraid so, I've no date tonight. Pity though, there is a vegan pop-up restaurant on the Brae until Sunday. I'd have liked to have taken someone there. The menu sounds enticing.'

Oliver's smile widened and he bit down on a knowing laugh, 'I'm sure a handsome lad like you will have a new date by Saturday, one worth waiting for.'

Nancy

The train gave a warning toot as it approached the last bend that led to the station. Its speed was reducing and after a minute it slowly came to a halt in front of the signals light. The driver waited patiently for the sign to change in his favour. He idly looked out to the gorse on either side of the carriage.

Nancy, facing forward and sat on a table of four with three strangers who were busy on their phones and tablets, took out a gold crucifix from around her neck. She'd had to delve under the folds of her jumper which, being relatively new, was still tight around her neckline. She unfurled the chain and let it rest on the outside of her top.

The train gave a slight jolt as their journey progressed once more, taking them to the approach of a tunnel, the underpass having been built over the principal thoroughfare of the busy city street above. The high, soot-blackened arches of solid granite hung over the track, like the legs of a giant.

Nancy's hand shot up from her lap and to her crucifix. She gave it a reassuring rub and then took it to her lips, kissed it, closed her eyes, and mouthed a familiar prayer. She didn't need to open her eyes to tell that the carriage was now in the depths of the tunnel. She kept her eyes closed, and her prayer going, until daylight once more burst upon the passengers and the tunnel was long behind them. She opened her eyes, tucked away her necklace, and did the sign of the cross over her chest.

The middle-aged woman sat across from her, put down her tablet and made eye contact with Nancy, 'There's nothing to be nervous about. Our country has the highest rail safety records. A crash or derailment is rare. I'm Mae. Are you getting off this stop too?'

'No. I've come down from the Highlands and am going down to Dundee,' replied Nancy, glad of the distraction. 'I'm Nancy.' She looked up and saw the approaching station platform 'Nice to have met you. I travel on this line often; we may meet again.'

'That would be nice,' she picked up her tablet and shut the screen down. 'It would be nice to have a conversation with an actual person, instead of on this. Is it business that causes you the travel?'

Nancy willed the train forward faster. She never knew what to reveal to people. It was always a conversation stopper if she over-shared. Though her son, Roland, told his mum that she should get talking to as many people as possible. That's what he did, and he always left them with a business card. so that they could phone, text, or e-mail at any time. It was good for his business. He'd found many clients this way. 'I run several support groups throughout Scotland and two in the North of England. That's what I'm doing tonight.'

The other two passengers on their table rose and left the train without a word or acknowledgement of their existence. The train was now stationary and was sitting patiently at the platform, engine idling over as its human cargo offloaded.

Mae looked at her newfound friend and briefly considered her. She could see kindness in her rare deep green eyes, and a motherly, almost grandmotherly appearance that would make people trust her and probably speak openly to her. She looked like someone's favourite elderly aunt or nana. Her mousy, curly hair gave her a younger appearance, and was probably dyed, knocking a decade or even two from her correct age, though her wrinkled hands gave her away. 'That sounds interesting, and so rewarding, I imagine. It's a conversation for another time, though. Be seeing you.' She rose and left the train, wondering what the groups all had in common. She hadn't liked to have asked, but she could envisage her new pal running a cancer support group network. That must be it. Good for her.

Nancy leant back in her chair and stretched out her legs, grateful for the extra space. She was pleased to see that no new passengers joined her table. She could now be left alone with her thoughts, which were directed to her other child.

Robyn gave the bus driver a cheery goodbye and stepped off the vehicle, embracing the fresh air after being stuck in the office all day. She'd be glad to get home and take off these heels and her good outfit, and especially her bra. The straps were digging in something awful. She'd had a lonely journey home. Her eager eyes had scanned for Graham, but it was just the usual commuters on the seats. She walked around the corner, past the car park. The gleaming Porsche was not there, and onto the familiar cobbled street. She slowed down and developed a careful tread; Victorian pavements were not designed for killer heels. She'd just pop home and change into her comfy pyjamas before going next door to her baby and Monica. They were well used to seeing each other in their night attire; they were like an old married couple sometimes. She swung her bag gayly, the two bottles of wine clinking cheerfully as she trotted home.

Nancy took out her phone and tapped out a message to her son, letting him know that she'd made a new friend and would pass on his business card, and another to her husband, reminding him to reheat the dinner she'd left him for the full four minutes in the microwave. He'd complained that the last one was cold. He was her second husband and so understanding of her need to be with other parents and families who had been affected by suicide. He'd always drive her to their nearby train station, see her safely onboard, and would be there waiting for her when she came home, often on the last train at one in the morning. Her two children's father had been a tormented soul, and a taunting father and husband. All three of them had been on the wrong end of his quick temper far too often, and she wasn't sorry when he'd been found slumped dead over a table in his favourite bar. The pub staff had thought that he'd fallen asleep again in a drunken stupor and had left him until last orders. It had certainly been last orders for him; he was stone cold dead. The frightened barman wasn't sad either, the dead man had been an abusive drunk and had caused trouble at the pub for years and was a nightly nuisance. The regulars had secretly breathed a collective sigh of relief at his passing.

None came to his funeral. The barman had even begrudged his late night, dealing with the police and forensic team.

Nancy slipped her phone back into her pocket, slumped further down the seat, closed her eyes, and drifted off into a pleasant nap. Yesterday had been a busy day of travel and an emotionally exhausting group, with a new member who was in a fragile state.

Robyn, carefully balancing her goodies, locked her front door and walked over to her other house. Her chunky padded footwear, part sock and part slipper, was ideal on the cobbles and caused her no problems in balance nor discomfort. She was wearing her favourite cartoon character pyjamas. She hoped Graham wouldn't see her; she was braless and didn't have the upwards thrust support that she knew men found alluring. She rang the doorbell.

The door opened and a rush of light brown with dark patches ran out and circled around Robyn, like a protective security guard. Only this one was yelping as it then got over excited and belted off and ran around the open square, weaving around the lamp posts and jumping over the ornate drain gully covers. Robyn momentarily ignored her dog, letting it run off its energy, carried aloft her two bottles of wine, like an Olympic torch bearer, and declared to Monica, 'It's wine o'clock!'

Her friend surreptitiously eyed the wine labels and nodded her approval, 'How's your day been?'

'It got off to a brilliant start, I met someone interesting and found a wee gem during my interviews, but then the dragon from

46

head office spoilt it all. But let's not dwell on her.' She looked over to the big house, 'Let's get in off the square before he sees me in my tatty, comfy clothes.' She was about to whistle for Judy, until she looked down and saw her exhausted chum, tongue thrust out, panting away by her feet. She clucked her tongue, and the trio went indoors. Judy made straight for her water bowl.

A puzzled Monica asked, 'Who are you worried about seeing you?'

'Oh, you'll never guess who I saw?' teased Robyn as she followed her friend through to the kitchen. She placed one bottle of wine on the table, by the two wine glasses and a corkscrew, and put the other in the fridge.

'Is it the new man on the till?'

'Liam, he's in most days, no.'

Monica did a double-take to her friend, forgetting about picking up the corkscrew. 'Someone new?' she asked with an excited rise to her voice.

'Only the man in the big house!' revealed her friend with breathless enthusiasm.

'Where was he, in the supermarket?'

'No, we caught the bus together.'

'The bus!' blurted out Monica in surprise, 'But I thought he owned the Porsche,' she offered, now puzzled. 'Why would he be catching the bus?'

Robyn opened the drawer below the unit that housed the microwave. 'He reckons it saves him money, he works as a financial advisor, well owns the business and has a dozen staff working for him, he must be well off. You should have seen him,' she drifted off into a wistful daze as she took out the pizza delivery leaflet. Though they always ordered the same thing, it was heavily circled in bold red biro. She handed it to her pal.

'Oh, that's frugal, I suppose. I'll have the same as last time. It's my treat. What about you?' She took out her phone and opened the food delivery app.

Robyn then noticed the five pounds note Monica had also taken out of her pocket and had tucked under her phone. She always tipped generously.

'That's what he said. He reckons his clients like to see him being thrifty, and it'll make them trust him with their money. I wonder if any of the local footballers use him. I bet he knows many famous and rich folk. The usual for me too, please.' She nudged Monica gently with her elbow, 'We really are like an old married couple, aren't we? Perhaps Graham can introduce you to someone?'

Monica pretended not to hear this last part as she concentrated on ordering their dinner and tapped away at her phone.

Water was gently dripping down on Robyn's feet, soaking through the deep wool of her footwear. She bent down and scooped up Judy, who had now stopped dribbling the water she'd carried in her mouth from her bowl. A line of water drops was on the floor, narrowing down the further they were from the bowl. 'Have you missed your mummy? How much have you missed your mummy?'

Judy's little tail was furiously thrusting from side to side. Her little tongue darted out, and she began licking her mum's face, as if tackling another illicit ice-cream treat.

'I bet you've been spoilt rotten by your favourite aunty.'

'She's had a lovely walk, then we went for coffee and caught the bus into town.'

'No doggie treat in the café?'

Monica gave a small laugh, 'As if Judy or Mathew would let me not give her anything. She had an ice-cream, but she's worked it off whilst walking around town.'

'At nine in the morning, aren't you a spoilt madam,' she kissed her dog, not caring that the little animal was slurping all over her mouth in return.

A mild plop sounded the uncorking of the wine and Monica poured two generous glasses. 'Did you get the bus back with Graham?'

Robyn looked downcast, 'No, the dragon took longer to breathe her vile disapproval. I reckon Graham either got home in good time, or he went to the music shop for more vinyl.'

'Ah, yes, I've heard Jazz coming from the big house when his windows were open during that heatwave.' The friends looked at each other and burst out laughing. 'Well, no one's perfect!'

They clinked glasses in agreement and Robyn joined her pal in taking several generous drinks of their wine, she with her Yorkshire Terrier cradled like a babe in arms. She then put down her glass, gave a satisfied sigh, and put her pet on the floor. She walked over to the cupboards, opened the door, and took out a small box of dog food.

'Was she very harsh? Your job is secure, right?'

'I think it's all an act with her. I bet she's a real pussycat when you get to know her. Yes. don't you fret about me, you've enough to worry about.'

'Okay, that's good to hear. I'll do that if you promise me, you'll stop ringing the doorbell, and just walk in. It's your house, after all.'

Robyn shook her head, 'No, that wouldn't be right. You need your privacy. You might have a guest. Perhaps a male friend?'

Monica joined her friend in head shaking, 'No, it's just me and Judy, she's the only close friend, other than you, that I need.' She picked up her glass and walked through to the lounge.

Robyn quickly filled up Judy's food bowl, put away the dog food, and followed her friend through to the lounge: glass and wine bottle in her hands. She glanced over to the dusty alcove with the neglected photo frame, still picture side down. 'Nobody would blame you. I think you deserve a bit of happiness.'

Monica pretended not to hear her pal as she was looking out of the window, as if in early expectation of the food delivery. She quickly changed the subject, 'Don't be cross, but I've transferred some money into your bank account, and increased the rent payments, you've been undercharging me for far too long.'

'You didn't need to do that, I'm managing, but thank you, it will be handy. I always thought that you'd move somewhere better, you know, into a larger house in the main part of the city again, with your own car in the driveway, and a garden.'

'I'm no trouble here though, am I?' Monica bit her lip at the thought of being a nuisance.

'Not at all. I feel selfish, having my best friend next door. It's been great for Judy. She loves your company and your walks. And especially the ice-cream!'

'I like not having a car. The walking takes my mind off things. I like not having grass to cut or borders to weed. The park walks fulfils that side of things, without the responsibilities. Can I stay, please?'

Robyn put down her glass on the table and her friend unconsciously mirrored her actions. She reached over to the fragile bereaved mother and divorcee and hugged her tight. 'You can stay here forever. I just want to see you happy again. You've lost so much, and I'll always be here for you.'

Tears fell from Monica's eyes as she hugged her friend tight, 'Thank you,' she whispered.

The duo held each other for a few minutes. The gentle tick tock of an old-fashioned clock on the wall was the only sound interrupting their embrace. Until two pairs of small legs came scampering through from the kitchen, jumped up onto her stool set by the sofa, and snuggled between the women, trying to reach her blanket on the sofa.

The women unclasped and simultaneously reached for the comfort of their wine glass, each wiping away teardrops with the sleeve of their pyjama top.

'I'm going on a retreat, in November. I paid for it today.'

Robyn quickly put down her wine glass, 'Like, with monks?'

Monica spurted out her wine, back into the glass. She took a few breaths to recover and then looked at her pal. They broke into fits of giggles, like two teenagers enthralled over a dreamy pop star magazine. Monica recovered first, 'I knew you'd say that!' She explained about the other charity which supported bereaved parents, keeping it brief, as they waited for their pizza. She really wanted to know more about Graham and of her pal's plans.

Oliver walked along his short path, brushing lightly against the overgrown bushes and undergrowth, searching his pockets for his keys and found them in the last pocket he felt, took them out slowly, and unlocked his front door. He took a breath in and stood momentarily on his doorstep, not wanting to go into the already darkened house. He always kept the blinds shut when he woke up on workdays, and sometimes at weekends. He stepped into the darkened lobby and shut the outside world out with a firm push of the door. A wall of silence confronted him.

His house was detached, in a quiet cul-de-sac, and set back from the main road. His garden was extensive and rambling, the lawns overgrown with patches of withered wildflowers still clear if seen in the daylight. No neighbours disturbed his peace. He was isolated and felt alone. He sighed deeply as he broke the silence by placing his keys in a ceramic bowl and braced himself. His ears felt like they would pop. The silence threatened to perversely deafen him. He took several more breaths as a dizzy spell clouded his vision, causing him to reach out and grasp at the wall. He leaned against the wallpaper, hand brushing on a towel draped over a framed object, and forced himself to take several steps forward, towards the shut lounge door. He attempted to grip the handle, but pulled his hand back, as if he'd touched a hot surface. He shook his head, 'Not tonight, sorry Emma. I just can't bring myself to go back into the room, not where you died.'

Tears fell unashamedly from his eyes, soaking into the carpet, leaving a trail as he walked into the kitchen and switched the light on. The one chair by the table had its seat facing the doorway, as if awaiting its captive. Oliver had hated sitting by himself, staring at the other empty chairs, willing Emma to suddenly appear on one. He'd taken the other three and put them in the small spare bedroom. He'd moved his clothes, bedside cabinet, and bedding into the larger of the spare bedrooms. He couldn't face returning to the marital bed, not without his beloved Emma.

He'd awaken several times through the night, on those rare nights when he got some sleep, to feel over to what had been her side of the bed. His heart always sank when he felt cold, bare sheeting.

His tears dried up as he recalled the horror of finding her in their lounge. They had gone to bed at ten in the evening, ready to face another working day. But she had gone downstairs, written a note to him declaring her love for him, but describing the pain of losing baby after baby, and took a fatal overdose of the anti-depressants given to her by their kindly GP, along with several packets of over-the-counter painkillers. She had died within the hour and was cold and blue when

Oliver had awoken at one in the morning, found the bed empty and went downstairs to check that she was okay.

The police had ordered him to find alternative accommodation, for at least five days, whilst they carried out their due diligence, treating Emma and their home as evidence. They even went so far as putting a deadlock on his front and back door, ensuring that no one, but them, entered the property until the local pathologist carried out a post-mortem.

That was the last time that Oliver stayed with his parents. They provided no emotional support. They were too worried about what their friends would say about a suicide in the family. He hadn't spoken to them since. Nor to Emma's side of the family, they were highly vocal in their scathing comments about him and his inability to keep their beloved daughter, their only child, alive.

He could no longer sleep until one in the morning had been and gone. The last words spoken aloud before he tried to sleep were always an apology to his wife, though in her letter she had thanked him for being a supportive husband and making her happy. He blamed himself. She clearly wasn't happy, and he had failed to see it. He knew it was the last pregnancy that had broken her, almost broken him too. She had to carry this foetus full-term and delivered it naturally. The midwives had been brilliant, so supportive and caring, but their child had died a day before delivery. Emma had felt no movement for several hours and the midwives found no heartbeat and tried to explain what happened, but neither could take in the terminology. All they knew was that they had lost another child, and it devastated them.

He ignored the chair, walked around it and to the fridge. He opened it and the light revealed its almost empty shelves. There were just a few bottles of various salad creams and ketchup, a tub of margarine and several cans. There was no milk, he didn't need hot drinks; he needed the succour of the lager, and sometimes he topped this up, when he could be bothered rinsing out a clean glass, with a generous tot of whisky. He took out a can, pulled the ring, threw this on a pile by the sink, and gulped a deep draught before sitting down at the chair, leaving it facing the door. He stared through the doorway and to the lounge door and began his vigil.

Nancy left the train station and was surprised to find that the evening was now darkening. The nights were fair drawing in; she realised. She'd been so busy going from one support group to the other, that she hadn't realised that it was early September and that here in Scotland the nights were soon darkening. She looked up and was relieved to see the Uber driver waiting patiently. Her son had taught her how to use the app, and soon she had a regular driver who knew all about her and Roland and was even using her son's services. The business card she left in the back seat had proved fruitful.

She gave a cheery wave as she neared Blake's car and continued hurrying to it and opened the front passenger seat. She hated sitting regally in the back seat; they had become friends after all, and she always left him a glowing review on the app to help him find more satisfied customers. She also liked that he knew why she was here, about her loss and how she helps other bereft parents, husbands, wives and sometimes friends and other relations. She didn't need to have that awkward revelation to a strange taxi driver that always stemmed the flow of conversation when they didn't know how to respond. She wasn't ashamed of her daughter and what she did, she just couldn't get herself off the hard drugs and fell into debt with her dealer and saw no other way out. Fortunately, no trains had gone past as she leapt from the bridge, despite their high railings and signs for the Samaritans. She had died instantly from the fall, and shocked passers-by had alerted the police, who had alerted ScotRail to halt their trains. There were hundreds of unhappy commuters that evening, and a devasted brother, mum, and dad, though the latter took the brunt of the blame for failing his daughter and causing her unhappiness. His drinking became heavier, and he was soon gone from their lives, no longer inflicting violence to his grieving wife.

'How's your month been Blake?' she cheerfully enquired as she sat down in the car and closed the door, ready for the off.

Blake checked his mirror, signalled and drove off before answering, 'Not too bad, thanks for booking me again. I'll be waiting at ten for you, as usual. That'll get you on the last train, you'll have plenty of time, so don't you worry, you just help those families.' He gave a silent prayer of thanks that his partner and their young children were healthy and happy.

'Thank you, Blake, you are kind. Roland sends his regards.'

'Right back at him! He's been brilliant with Janice; she looks forward to their chats on the phone or Skype. Thank him for the discount.'

Nancy grinned, she loved to know that her Roland was doing so well in his business that he'd set up a few months after losing his sister. It was good to know that she sent work his way. He deserved to be busy, and what he was doing was so important.

'You look all wrapped up for winter,' Blake observed as he glanced her way to check the turning was clear.

'I have to be. The church hall doesn't put their radiators on until next month. The old building seems to leach heat, I don't think they have any insulation at all, we hear the gulls settling for the night or fighting over food, and the traffic. But we can't complain, they are the cheapest place to rent for the few hours that we are there.'

'I guess that even churches must be run as businesses and can't afford to rent out their halls for free. That's what I liked about your Roland; he gave his initial hour consultation for free. With no pressure to continue his services. Janice finds the easy payments by instalment via PayPal so effortless, just that one or two taps on her phone a few months ago and they are all set. Like with you and my Uber.'

'He's a clever lad, is my Roland, I'm proud of him.'

He nodded his head vigorously in agreement as he pulled alongside the church hall. 'It's amazing what you both do, each in your own way. I hope it goes well and I'll see you in a few hours.'

Nancy thanked him and left the car, taking the few steps to the church hall door with some trepidation, she'd be consoling two new mums and one father tonight, and that was only the tip of the iceberg, she knew. Those who ended their lives by suicide always affected a huge circle of family and friends who would go through the awful grieving steps of anger, shock, denial and bargaining before, often several years later, coming to accept their loss and slowly rebuilding their lives in a new way. Though she and Roland helped as many as they could along the way.

Adam and Corrina

Dr Munro stretched over to the passenger seat and lifted her medical bag, a gift from her proud parents on graduation day, but now battered and showing signs of age. She exited her car, wondering if she should replace the bag soon before she had an embarrassing accident where everything fell out whilst on a home visit. She'd been putting this chore off because it would be another link lost to her mum and dad, both gone for five years now. She locked her car for the day and walked across to the disabled ramp that took her into her surgery.

She looked absently through the windows as she walked. She could see Adam and Corrina waiting in the surgery, always punctual for appointments, usually ten minutes early. Neither saw her, Adam had his head slumped forward, palms clasping it, staring at the floor whilst his wife of thirty years was busy rubbing his back in support. Dr Munro didn't waste her time in waving to them. Nothing could bring them cheer. They had lost their son four weeks ago, and she'd asked them to come to the surgery every week. She was worried about them. After an initial home visit, the day that the surgery had been alerted to the suicide of their boy, Fraser, Dr Munro, and her medical partners, had decided that they should give the family priority appointments without notice needed. The couple didn't choose this option, they never liked to be any trouble to folk, and instead had booked a Thursday morning double appointment and had kept each session, this being their third.

The automatic doors gently opened, and the doctor stepped through to reception, 'Morning. All good?' she asked of her receptionist, who was tucked safely behind a glass partition that could be easily closed when they were talking about sensitive issues on the phone. It also gave them protection from the more aggressive and abusive patients.

Dominic gave his boss his winning smile and the thumbs up sign and handed the doctor a sheet of paper. In a sensitive whisper he informed her, 'Adam and Corrina are ready for you, though they are early. Shall I make you a coffee?'

'Yes, please Dominic, though, could you bring it after they've seen me? I'll just sign into my computer and then I'll see them straight away. There's nothing urgent for me?'

'It can all wait until you've a space between appointments.'

'Thank you, Dominic.'

Dr Munro walked past the waiting area and tried to catch the attention of the couple. Corrina was still consoling her husband. Now that she was closer, she could see that he was crying. She gave them more privacy and walked on to her consulting room. She'd use the announcing system that would flash their names and tell them to which room they should go. She hoped that they'd be looking up to the waiting room screen.

She entered her room, switched on the lights because there was not enough natural light filtering through from the small frosted panes of the windows set high upon the rear wall, privacy being more important, and turned on her computer and printer. The fans whirred into life as she settled herself in front of the screen and she then swiped her identity card along the top of the keyboard, barcode facing the various numbers, letters, and symbols. She quickly scanned her list of appointments and then gave a few clicks of her mouse and found the couple's files, though she'd remembered vividly their previous appointments. She clicked away on the announcements tab and rose from her chair and walked to the door. There was a polite knock just as she was reaching for the handle. She opened the door and ushered the couple in, 'Come away in Adam and Corrina and sit yourselves down.'

Corrina took her husband by the hand and motioned for him to sit on the left of the two chairs. He dried his eyes on a tissue as he came into the room and sat down obediently. Corrina then sat down and reached for her husband's hand. They both looked to their doctor in expectation of a miracle cure that could take away their pain or bring back their son.

'I won't ask how you've both been, that seems rather superfluous. Are you getting some sleep?'

'A little,' offered Corrina. 'The tablets have helped.'

'You'll have run out of them?'

The couple simultaneously nodded, 'Last night,' said Adam quietly. 'Trying to get some sleep is a problem. We keep wondering what we did wrong, or what we could have done better. I keep thinking of all the times I told Fraser off. I should have been a better father.'

Corrina gave his hand a gentle, loving squeeze.

The doctor gave a firm shake of her head in disagreement. 'You've nothing to feel guilty about, I could tell you were a good, loving family. I know we've spoken about this last week, I'd like to try you on another tablet, it's called Mirtazapine, these are less addictive, the Temazepam should only be used for a week at a time, otherwise your body gets addicted to them and when you come off them, you'll have horrible side-effects.' She gave a few clicks of her mouse and the printer whirred and whilst she waited for the prescriptions, she gently asked, 'The people I spoke about on our first appointment, have they tried to make contact?'

'No,' replied Corrina with a narrowing of the eyes, 'Don't you worry, if they come to our door, I'll send them away with a flea in their ear.'

The doctor stifled a laugh. She knew how stern Corrina could be when it came to protecting her family, and good for her. 'I'm sorry that I've had to talk about this distressing thing, but we're powerless to stop these charlatans.' She handed the printouts to Corrina as she could see that Adam was trying to keep his tears at bay and had his tissue to his eyes again. 'They fleeced one widow out of thousands of pounds and they just kept coming back for more. Anyway, I know you are more sensible and you're such a strong couple.' She pointed to the prescriptions, 'This will help as a short-term measure. You need to sleep. What you are experiencing is an extreme grief, and there are no answers, and you mustn't blame yourselves.'

'But I do,' interrupted Adam, 'I should have been a better father,' he repeated.

'You were, I could see that whenever you came to see me, you'd always be worrying about your family, instead of putting your own health first. I highly recommend that you both take these tablets, it's a low dose, each night, about an hour before you want to sleep. Don't be put off that they are anti-depressants, I'm giving you them for a few months to help you sleep, because the low dose shouldn't give you side-effects and we can quickly build up to the strength you need to get some sleep, they have the beneficial effect of giving most folk at least six hours deep and refreshing sleep. I want you to keep seeing me every week, to make sure you are sleeping, eating and that you are safe and well.'

'I feel like ending it all, but I won't, we've our other children to think about,' stated Adam flatly.

The doctor nodded, 'They need you; we call them the protective factors. There are several organisations that can help you, but the main one I'd like you to see, won't allow referrals until six months have passed. They say that it allows the raw emotions to settle somewhat. Then they can offer counselling when you have a clearer headspace. They can help your children too; it'll be additional support after the help they are getting from their school. You still have the list of phone helplines that offer immediate counselling?' She waited until both nodded and then slipped across a business card. 'This is a support group that meets up once a month, tonight I think, and is run by other bereaved families who have been specially trained by the charity. They have all lost a loved one to suicide. They meet up in one of the church halls nearby. Will you please promise me you'll phone this morning and go to at least three meetings?' She was pleased to see Corrina take the card and nod. 'I haven't had to refer anyone to them for several months, so my information is a little dated. Perhaps you'll tell me about the meetings at one of our later appointments?' She looked to the couple, taking the time to assess their gauntness and their sunken, red eyes. She hoped they would keep their weekly appointments. They looked highly vulnerable. Once the couple were nodding their agreement, she continued with, 'Do you need a sick line for work?'

Adam and Corrina shook their heads, and Corrina answered, 'We own the business, we don't really do much, we leave our managers to do the day-to-day running and they are fully informed. We'll not return to work for several weeks, maybe even a month or two. It doesn't seem that important, not anymore. Our staff practically run everything for us, they are a great bunch.'

'I'm so sorry that you are going through this, Fraser was such a gentle boy. The crime he experienced was dreadful, he just couldn't live with what happened to him. I know that it's no comfort, but he was a credit to you, and you must take one day at a time. Have friends supported you?'

'Oh yes, doctor, they have been fantastic. They've made us meals and ensured we ate, and they've been great company. You certainly learn who your loyal friends are when something like this happens. And thank you for looking after us, we're sorry to be such a bother.'

'You're no trouble at all, let me get the door for you and I'll see you next week and please ring the number.'

The duo nodded solemnly as they left the room and walked out of the surgery, both still processing the information from the GP.

Robyn tottered along to the bus stop, killer heels on again, with a freshly dry-cleaned matching skirt and jacket, wearing her best nylons. She was pleased to see Graham waiting patiently at the bus shelter, for her, she assumed, rather than the bus. 'Hiya,' she cheerfully announced as she perched on the bench next to him. She hoped that the allure of her new perfume would entice him. 'I missed you last night, I had to work late, but I'll be home early tonight, my friend has a day off and is babysitting. She's got her group tonight, so I'll be on the five o'clock bus.'

Graham quickly absorbed this information dump and prioritised his questioning, 'I didn't realise you had children?'

'Oh, no, me, goodness, no. That isn't to say that with the right person, I would, you know,' she flustered.

Graham patiently waited for her to compose herself.

'She's my dog,' quickly corrected Robyn.

'I've seen her, she's gorgeous, my gran had a Yorkie.' It was his turn to quickly correct himself, 'Not that I look at you and think of my gran, blimey, no.' He quickly looked her up and down, 'You are so young and beautiful,' he blurted out. A reddening spread to his cheeks and he adjusted his tie and then altered his shirt collar button.

'That's good to know!' She bumped shoulders playfully with him.

He quickly changed the subject, 'What's the group, is it like a band?'

Laughter broke the ice between them, Graham hesitantly laughed along, unsure why she found his question so funny.

Robyn recovered, 'Oh that's priceless, wait until I see Monica.' She noticed his cheeks getting redder and stopped her laughter and a sombre look fell upon her face, 'It's a support group. Her daughter took her own life.'

'Oh, that's so sad. My partner took his life, several years ago. I felt so powerless.'

Robyn reeled from this revelation and blurted out, 'I'm so sorry. I didn't realise you were gay; you must miss him terribly.' It surprised her to see Graham double over with amusement.

'I'm so sorry, I couldn't help it, you misunderstood me. Yes, I miss him, but he was my business partner in the law firm. I'm a solicitor by trade, I folded up the practice after his death, I couldn't face doing all the surveying and conveyancing for houses, though I still do some for clients and good friends. That's why I set up the financial advisor team. I wanted a job which was flexible, so I put in place various experts and left them to it. I pay them a higher rate than my competitors, bonuses too, even the cleaners, and now I can choose my hours. It leaves me more time to take my car out, he's a beauty, you should see him. I love getting out in the country with him and going for picnics and pub lunches.'

'That sounds nice, but lonely on your own?'

'Yes, sometimes.' He left this statement dangling in the air, drew up his chest with courage, reached for her hand and was delighted by its soft, warm returned grip and offered, 'Come with me tomorrow, I know this lovely cottage on the banks of a river that opens up its conservatory for afternoon teas. We'll take my car and make a day of it.'

'That sounds perfect, it's my day off too,' she purred as their bus pulled up. They hopped onboard, still holding hands.

The phone vibrated and rang in Nancy's handbag as she reached the till of the newsagent in her home village. She put down her intended purchase and shrugged her shoulders to the young assistant, 'Sorry, I'd better take this, it could be one of my groups.' She went outside, walking and rummaging in her bag.

The assistant put Nancy's mints and newspaper behind the counter. She knew she'd be back after her call. Most folk in the village knew about her and Roland and what they did. Though they saw little of Roland now that he'd moved to the main city.

Nancy perched on the low wall alongside the shop. Behind it was a row of neat gas cylinders with a caged and locked fence. Some folks in the rural homes still used these for cooking and for heating and would swap their empties periodically. She put the phone to her ear, not wanting to use the speaker in case it was a delicate subject.

'Hello,' said a gruff voice. 'Our doctor gave me your number. Is this the support group?'

'Yes, it is. I'm Nancy. How can I help?'

Adam described the recent events of Fraser's suicide and where they lived.

'I'm so sorry that your son is no longer with you, we've a meeting tonight, the church hall is two streets away from you.' She gave him brief directions.

'Thank you. Yes, we know where it is. We've never been to a support group before.'

'That's okay, we are mostly mums and dads who have lost a child too. In my case, I lost my daughter.'

'I'm sorry to hear that,' mumbled Adam.

'Thank you. Just come along at seven thirty tonight and we'll be in the hall at the back of the church. We provide teas, coffees and biscuits, Oliver does all that. He lost his wife. We chat for an hour, have a break, and then chat some more. There is about a dozen of us.'

'Okay, thank you Nancy, see you tonight.'

'Bye then Adam.' She slid her phone back into her handbag and then returned to the shop. She would stay overnight at Roland's flat and he did like her to take the local papers for him.

The alarm buzzed on Oliver's phone, reminding him it was ten to twelve. He waited patiently for Nick, his immaculately dressed deputy, to finish his sentence. They were assessing if they could afford to shave a further five percent off the French contract and wondering if they could go back to them with a three percent offer. 'Let's mull it over Nick, over our lunches. I'll be straight back. I want Mitch to have an early lunch. I've bought a sandwich up from the café, so I'll take mine in the office and man the phones, though I might pop down later for a coffee.' He swiftly exited Nick's office, leaving his friend to smooth down his waistcoat and fiddle in the small pocket for his lucky charm. He liked to play it along his fingers when he needed some thinking time. Oliver was confident that they'd reach a mutual choice, as they always did. He strode up to Mitch's desk and their eyes met at his approach.

'Mum didn't know what you are hatching, she says, whatever it is, it's nothing to do with her.'

Oliver grinned back, 'It most certainly is. You take your lunch now, and no helping your parents today. Nick and I have some mulling over to do, so don't rush back.' It was all he could do to stop himself from giving a conspiratorial wink.

Mitch's head tilted, as if assessing his boss. He saw Oliver stifle a yawn and hoped that he'd mull over his decision whilst in his recliner chair; he looked like he could do with forty winks. 'Okay, pumpkin rice for me today. Can I bring you something, or ask mum to lay aside something?'

'No, I've a sandwich I bought earlier. I'll go down later for the biscuits and grab a coffee, I've a late night tonight. I'll be going off early so that I can open the hall and prepare the teas and coffees. Perhaps you'll want to finish early too?'

'That'll be nice, I can help mum and dad.'

Oliver nodded, though he knew his PA wouldn't be doing that tonight. He watched, almost paternally, as Mitch grabbed his magazine and walked off. Oliver knew that he'd not be doing much reading either.

The sea flowed up to the beach, chasing Judy off its territory as she snapped at the foaming water whilst the sand and shingle tried to absorb its journey until it was ready to recede. Monica walked along the deserted beach, bare-footed, enjoying the sensation of delicate wet sand intermingled with the rough texture of the tiny pebbles. She made occasional encouraging noises to her canine pal, interspersed with laughs at the enjoyment of her antics. The dog would boldly follow the ebbing tide, until fresh surges of tidal water turned back upon her, forcing the dog to turn tail and flee. Unlike her human friend, she hated getting her paws wet. They continued like this for another three hundred yards and then Monica said the magic words, 'Ice-cream time!'

Judy instantly sprang alert, her ears stood proud, and she immediately turned from the ocean and ran to heel by Monica. Her tiny front paws scrabbled about Monica's naked feet, trying to find purchase to climb higher. Her claws scraped against the bare skin from where Monica had rolled up her jeans.

It was a familiar sensation for Monica. She seemed to enjoy the scratching feeling as much as she enjoyed getting closer to the ground she walked on. She held her shoes and socks in her left hand and juggled moving the dog's leash from hand to hand, so that her right side could scoop down and pick up the jumping dog. She knew it would tire Judy. This was their second walk of the day and would be a return visit to their favourite café. She hoped it wouldn't be too busy with the lunchtime crowd, all she wanted was another coffee, she couldn't face any food. Not today, not on a group day. The fresh grief from new families always hit her hard and was a sharp reminder of how she had been, and still was, over the loss of her daughter. The anticipation of this anxiety was enough to curb her already reduced appetite.

Judy, sensing a change in mood, leant further into her pal's embrace, and snuggled into Monica's neck and showered her with doggy licks and kisses.

Monica giggled like a contented child at the tickling, wet sensation. 'You certainly know how to distract me when I'm feeling down, let's get you another treat, but don't tell your mum that you had two, it'll be our little secret.'

Judy gave a conspiratorial soft bark.

'I'll hold the lift for you,' announced Rachel as she firmly pressed the shiny button at the side of the door to the chagrin of the two suited impatient older men. She ignored their tuts and gave Mitch a dazzling smile as he gave a half run to reach the elevator.

'Thanks, I should really take the stairs and get some exercise, but I was at the gym last night and I'm still aching.'

71

'That's okay,' replied Rachel in a soft voice. She watched as he strode confidently in, turned in front of the two men and gave her a returned smile. 'Mitch isn't it?'

'Yes,' he replied in surprise. He arched his eyebrows as he wondered how she knew him, he'd only seen her twice, from afar. He'd never been able to catch up with her and introduce himself.

'Your mum sent me to have lunch with your boss yesterday.'

'Ah! She does that. She doesn't like him to be on his own. How was it? Dall, I think?'

'It was delicious. It's so nice to have a vegan café with such a choice.' She glanced at the two men behind them and whispered, 'He's a bit old for me!'

The ding of the bell and the herald of the ground floor by the lift announcer was not enough to drown out the young couple's innocent and carefree laughter as they exited the lift and walked in unison towards Harriet and her café of delights.

His mother had been on alert for the last fifteen minutes, like a meerkat looking out for predators. She had been glancing over each time the lift opened and spilt out its human cargo. Oliver had been down earlier and asked her to hand her son two portions of their special. He'd paid for them in advance, despite her protests, her son always ate for free. She'd assumed that her son's boss wanted them to have a quick lunch together, whilst his deputy was in the office that day. Her vigil had been rewarded, and she lifted two plates of prepared pumpkin rice with coconut, onions, and cabbage. She walked from around the counter and met her son before he could join the queue. She handed the plates to him, but was looking approvingly at Rachel. She liked how she was dressed in a yellow flowering dress, flat, sensible shoes, bare, slender legs, and hair tied in a playful ponytail. Most of all, she loved how her eyes lit up in the company of her son, and the carefree smile. She hadn't looked this way when she was dining with Oliver yesterday.

Mother and son locked eyes as the lunches were handed over and in unison they said, 'Oliver!'

Isobel switched on the light to the loft space as she carefully climbed the ladder. This used to be Roy's duty, but, like many things, she'd had to learn to fend for herself. She stood up straight. The high roofline made this possible, as did her five feet six inches height. She scanned the area, eyes targeting the gadget that she'd put away years earlier. She bent down and lifted it off the dust-laden floor, wiped it down with the duster from her pocket and tucked the cloth away and placed the object under her arm, ready for the ladder descent. She knew baby Lindsay would love this, as would she now that the time was right for her.

'I have to confess that I've seen you help your mum and dad often, so I knew a bit about you. I hadn't realised that you are a fellow vegan. There are more and more of us about in the building, thanks largely to your parents.' Rachel moved the Scotch bonnet chilli sliver carefully to the edge of her plate and then placed another chunk of pumpkin in her mouth as she looked across to Mitch.

'Yes, they work ever so hard. We travel in together, so it makes sense for me to help them, otherwise I'd just be sat around.'

'No girlfriend then?' she tentatively asked. She gently fingered her fine hair that fell across her fringe and then gathered up her ponytail and ran her hands through it, as if checking it was still in place.

'No, not for a while. No one serious. How about you?'

'No, I've been waiting for the right man to ask me out.' She left the statement hanging and was pleased when Mitch continued the thread.

'Mum is a bit of a matchmaker for poor Oliver. If she sees a single female, she sends her his way. Though I think she's given up on the not-so-subtle matchmaking as I've seen her send men over in the recent weeks.'

Rachel frowned, not liking the direction the conversation was going. She stopped her nervous hair stroking, leant forward, and whispered conspiratorially, 'He's a good bit older than me.'

Oliver nodded thoughtfully, 'He's aged since his wife died, it's taken its toll. My other boss, Nick, he thought he'd never pull through, but he's rebuilt his life and seems to enjoy work again.'

'That's so sad, I can't imagine losing someone you really love.' Tears formed in her eyes as she looked to Oliver.

Without thinking, he pulled out a napkin from the container in the middle of their table, reached forward and gently dried her eyes.

'Thank you, Mitch,' she sighed as she gently stroked his free hand.

Harriet, hovering in the background, about to bring the couple a pot of turmeric tea to share, turned around and placed it on a nearby table and said to the surprised three men having an informal business meeting in a mutual place, 'On the house, I'll bring another cup and saucer.' She walked away, a satisfied smile upon her face.

Barry

'Fancy meeting you again!' declared Mae as she sat down on the train seat and placed a magazine on the table.

Nancy looked up at hearing the familiar voice, not quite placing the face to the voice. She expressed her puzzlement, 'Oh, hello, er?'

'It is Nancy, isn't it? We met on this train, yesterday, wasn't it? You were going to Dundee? How was it? I'm Mae.'

'Sorry, yes,' realised Nancy. 'It went well, I was late home, but up early to get the papers for my boy. That's where I'm going, I'll stay in his flat tonight, after another group session in the city.'

'Gosh, you get kept busy, especially with all the travel.'

A brisk whistle announced the imminent departure of the train, 'Yes, but it's all worthwhile, I think I provide some comfort, you know.'

Mae nodded, though she wasn't entirely sure what the groups all had in common. She was about to ask, when a tune broke from within Nancy's pocket and her new friend took out her phone and said, 'Hello, Nancy speaking, I'm on a train,' announcing to the caller that the conversation would not be private.

'I found her, I found my girl, there was so much blood. I've never seen so much blood,' uttered a fraught and breathless voice.

Nancy inhaled deeply, preparing herself, 'Take a couple of deep breaths love, that's it, try to calm yourself.' She spoke slowly and deliberately, hoping that this would convey a feeling of calm, and waited patiently whilst her caller composed himself. 'That's it, now what's your name?'

'Barry. I found my daughter, it was awful.'

'I'm so sorry Barry, when was this?' she expected to hear that it was recent, given how distressed the caller was.

'Two months ago. The church minister gave me your number.'

'Bless you, Barry,' Nancy instinctively said, mirroring what a vicar may have said. 'Are you wanting to come to one of our meetings?' She glanced up, shocked to see where they were already, cradled her phone closer to her ear, held it there in the crook of her neck and scrabbled to take her crucifix from under her jumper. She kissed it, but reluctantly failed to say her ritualistic prayer. But she closed her eyes, not bearing to look at the track sides, or towards the tunnel. In a wavering voice she said, 'We are going in a tunnel, the phone reception may cut out. Will you promise to call me straight back Barry, will you do that?' she almost pleaded. She did not want to lose a soul.

'I will. I can hear you fine, Nancy. Sorry if I upset you, but it's almost like I'm reliving it again and again. I'm sat where she did it. I can still see the blood. The police arranged for someone to deep clean the kitchen, but it's as if it's still in front of me. It's almost like I can pick up the Stanley knife she used.'

Nancy nodded and murmured an, 'I know love, I know.' She knew that those who found the suicide victims suffered from post-traumatic stress disorder, and she knew Barry would relive finding his child every time he walked into the room. She wondered if he'd consider moving, though some relatives preferred to stay in the same building, it brought them a feeling of being close to the deceased, that's why she never moved from her Highland village home, even though she spent a great deal of time travelling. When she was at home, she'd talk to her dead daughter, as if she were still with her. 'Where do you live, Barry?'

He was sobbing again but managed to give his address.

'Can you come to our meeting tonight?'

He grasped at this offer of help, 'I'd like that. I'll try.'

Nancy opened her eyes and was relieved to see that they'd shot through the tunnel. She looked at Mae, a lady she barely knew, who seemed to be listening to her call, though by appearance was flicking through her colourful magazine. Nancy didn't like to give out the venue times and places. One group had been infiltrated by a reporter writing a piece about suicide, and trust in the group had to be slowly rebuilt after his article appeared in a leading newspaper. 'I'll text you the directions Barry, and the time, will that be okay? I'm afraid that I have to get off the train soon.' As if confirming her account, the conductor announced the approaching destination over the public address system. 'Will you promise me you'll come tonight, it's only a few hours' notice, but I can help you Barry. The group can.'

'I'll try,' he said before breaking out into a heart-wrenching sob. He hung up before Nancy could say some well-meaning platitudes.

She looked down at her phone, placed it in her pocket and rose as she saw her station appear as the train finished braking. She looked for her Roland on the platform and was delighted to see him deep in conversation with an old lady. It pleased Nancy, for her overnight bag was heavy.

Mae rolled up her magazine, 'Well, this is me too. Perhaps we'll have that chat one day. It's amazing what you do,' she offered to Nancy.

Nancy, catching the eye of her son and waving for him to come onboard and get her bag, nodded in agreement with Mae. She turned back to her new pal and handed her a business card.

'I'll get the coffees in,' offered Oliver waving three chunky mugs with lids, 'the usual?' He reached across the reception desk and took out a tray.

Mitch and Nick nodded. Mitch was still grinning from ear to ear. Rachel had only forty minutes to spare for lunch, but they'd crammed in so much during this time, including an introduction to his mum and dad when they briefly interrupted the entranced couple and gave them two large camomile teas in reusable cups that they could take to their respective offices. His mother had insisted that Rachel come back for a free refill during her next break. That would be when her subtle interrogation would begin.

'Shall I get them?' offered Oliver, hoping to go via the fourth floor.

'No, these are on me this time.' Though Oliver always left extra money with Harriet or Jude so that Mitch was never out of pocket when taking a turn to fetch refreshments. 'I've my biscuits to collect.'

Mitch's and Nick's faces both looked solemn. They never knew what to say to Oliver about his group. Nick fiddled with his wedding ring, subconsciously thanking his lucky stars that his wife and child were well. He looked down at his hands, shocked at what he was doing, and hoped that his friend hadn't seen this unintentionally crass action. He needn't have worried as Oliver was already walking to the lift.

'We should eat something before the group, to keep our strength up,' Adam encouraged Corrina. 'I'll heat some soup and we can use up those rolls that your pals brought over.'

Corrina nodded, grateful that her chums had offered to take their children after school and having them for a sleepover with their children. They might talk with their friends. That left Adam and her to devote their time to gathering their strength for the support group. Neither knew what to expect. She knew it was bizarre, but she hated she was relishing eating her favourite lentil and bacon soup, knowing that Fraser would never have the joy of eating, or doing anything else again.

'You little devil!' joked Harriet as Oliver walked up to the till with three empty reusable mugs of various colours.

'Och, she was far too young to be company for me, Harriet. It's kind of you to make sure I have someone to talk with at lunchtimes, but I'm okay. Sometimes I enjoy being alone in busy places.'

She tilted her head as if to say, 'Really?' but made do with, 'It was sweet of you to play matchmaker with my boy, I've never seen him so enchanted.'

'He's still grinning from ear to ear. I don't think you'll be seeing much of him; I think his attention will be elsewhere.'

'It'll be worth it. I like to see the men in my life happy.' She gave Oliver another quizzical tilt of the head. Then she remembered his box, 'Just one minute.' She reached under the till and took out a golden-coloured cardboard box that had been secured with a neat thin red ribbon, tied in a decorative bow.

Seeing the package, Oliver offered, 'You must charge me for them this time.'

She gave a gentle, but insistent shake of her head, 'It's the least we can do, so don't make a fuss.'

Oliver thanked her and thought, 'If only you knew, what would you think of me then?'

Robyn walked confidently through her store, waving goodbye to each visible member of staff as she strode intently out of work and made her way cheerfully, as if walking on air, to the bus stop. She wasn't disappointed, Graham was there waiting for her. As she neared him, she put out her arm, and they effortlessly linked hands as they stood together awaiting their transport home.

Isobel inserted the plug into the socket, and the radio crackled into life. She familiarised herself with the buttons, and soon a cheerful jingle warbled out from the built-in speakers. It was the catchy tune that preceded and ended the local double-glazing firm's advert. It was a true earworm and most people in the city and shire could hum it and rattle off the name of the firm. It was clever marketing.

Yes, baby Lindsay would love to hear music and it was about time that Isobel heard her favourite songs once again. She may even e-mail requests to the DJ, like she used to do, asking for them to be played to coincide for when her Roy was coming home. By coincidence she was tuned into the drive time show and when the presenter came back on air, after the ads, she was pleased to hear that it was the same lady with the husky sounding voice that her Roy loved to have as company during his long drive home. She could tell baby Lindsay all about Roy's work, his cars down the decades, and all their favourite songs. They may even have a dance together, whilst she cradled her darling. She switched the kettle on for one last tea before she made her way to the group.

Judy paced restlessly around Monica's legs. Her babysitter was sat in the communal square, on the bench made from driftwood by one of the local artists. They were enjoying the last of the September sun, knowing that soon the harsh autumnal weather would be upon them. Monica sat back, listening to the squawking seagulls whilst the control room of a passing deep-sea trawler glided past over the rooflines ahead of her. The terraced houses hid the body of the ship, projecting this bizarre optical illusion. Monica never tired of this sight and waved cheerfully to the captain of this ship.

Suddenly Judy's ears pricked up, her snout twitched wildly, and then she ran towards the path. Monica, knowing that Judy smelt her mummy, wasn't concerned, and awaited the arrival of her pal patiently. The dog ran ten paces, ground to a halt, and then appeared to dance upon her back legs, throwing her front paws towards her mistress. A voice cried out, 'Mind my best nylons!'

It was Robyn's turn to dance, shuffling her stilettoed feet on the rough cobbles, trying to avoid her dog scratching her legs.

'Allow me,' offered Graham as he bent down and carried Judy under his arm, following Robyn as she walked up to her pal.

The two women looked on in wonder. Robyn broke the silence, 'She never lets men near her, except for Mathew with his ice-cream.'

Graham made a mental note to ask Robyn who Mathew was and to mansplain that dogs shouldn't have human ice-cream. 'She must sense that I love dogs, she looks just like my gran's dog and just as beautiful.' He tickled Judy gently on the ear.

Robyn turned to Monica, 'Thanks for looking after her. I'd best not keep you as I know you like to walk to the group.'

Monica grinned at her friend and gave a discrete nod to the man, 'Oh, I've plenty of time.'

Robyn took the hint, 'This is Graham, from the big house.'

Monica stretched out her hand formally and waited for Graham to put down Judy, on the bench so that the dog wouldn't go back to scratching Robyn on her legs. As they shook hands, she pointed to her cottage, 'I'm Monica. I rent the house next to Robyn. It's hers too.'

'Pleased to meet you Monica.' He thought her to have a wistfulness that robbed her attempt at cheerfulness and wondered why. He thought her to be painfully thin. He removed himself from their handshake, as if frightful that he would hurt this fragile woman, and turned back to Robyn, 'That's a sound investment, owning both homes. The market values around here have shown a steady growth over the years.'

'I'll tell you all about it later. Perhaps the three of us can have dinner together. I'll cook.'

'I'd like that,' accepted Graham.

Monica nodded her consent too; she knew her pal wouldn't be wearing her comfy pyjamas that night!

'Graham and I have the day off together tomorrow, so we're off for a run out in his car for afternoon tea.'

'That sounds delightful,' cheered Monica, pleased for her pal. She thought of the two-seater Porsche in the car park. 'I've work tomorrow, otherwise I'd have Judy for the day, but I'll let her out for her toilet as soon as I get home. If you are home late, I'll feed and walk her, it's no trouble.'

'It must be great, having your good pal living next door.' He saw both ladies nodding. They looked as thick as thieves. He hoped he wasn't intruding. 'We could take Judy with us. Robyn has been telling me all about her during our bus rides.' He sat down next to the dog and made a fuss of her, 'Do you have one of those special dog harnesses for the car?'

Robyn nodded, though she was confused about where Judy would sit in a two-seater. Then realised that she could sit on her lap, so long as they attached her to the harness, they wouldn't be breaking any laws. She'd hate for Graham to get in trouble with the police because of her.

'The place that I have in mind for us allows dogs in the restaurant area.' A look of incredulity crossed his face, 'Would you believe that they even bake special cakes for the dogs!'

The two women looked at each other and burst out laughing. Graham switched his gaze from one to the other in puzzled wonderment.

Oliver eased his car into the parallel space between two cars, by the row of houses, and gave his mirrors a last check before he shut the engine off with a turn of the key. As he did so, he took a note of the outside temperature that was displayed on his dashboard. It wasn't low enough to justify the cost of the church heating to the committee, but he made a mental note of the readings, just in case. The side mirrors flapped shut, and he exited the car and walked to the boot, opened it, and took out the carrier bag. He locked his car up and sauntered to the church hall, taking out the large key from his pocket. It pleased him that no one was waiting for him. He liked to open the doors at least thirty minutes before, though tonight it was a good hour earlier than needed.

He unlocked the glass door, closed it gently, almost reverently, and crossed the large lobby and switched on the lights. The nights were drawing in and he knew the gloomy hall needed the extra lighting. The committee could afford them that. He walked through to the kitchen area and placed his carrier bag on the worktop by a large metal urn connected directly to the wall's mains electricity. He unscrewed the top, looked inside, saw that the water level was low, and used the adjacent jug to fill water from the tap. It took three trips to fill the urn, and he then turned the thermostat switch that would produce steaming, boiling water in about one hour. Oliver then took out a much smaller key and opened the third unit from the urn. The others were all locked and had various labels such as Scouts, Brownies, and Sunday Club. His cupboard merely read Group. He opened the door and took out a tray of mugs and carried these to the sink. Though they had been carefully washed by him last month, he took the time to rinse them under the tap and dry them using a tea towel from his bag. It proudly displayed several castles from the National Trust for Scotland collection and had been bought by Emma on one of their visits, in-between miscarriages and before the stillbirth. It seemed apt that it should be used here.

Once dried, he returned the gleaming mugs to the tray and took out a jar of coffee, a small box of tea bags, a packet of sugar, a container of sweetener and Harriet's biscuits. These were placed upon the tray, almost like a vicar preparing the altar for communion, done in silence, slowly and carefully. He removed the red bow and placed the biscuits onto a plate. The vivid decoration didn't seem right. He put the box and ribbon back into the carrier bag. The drinks and sugars were all brand new, bought at his own expense, and were his contribution to the grieving mums and dads. He thought himself a fraud for being here. He'd not had the utter heartache of losing a child. He didn't seem to see his loss of a wife and several foetuses as an equal or even greater loss. He suddenly had a vision of his son who had been born perfectly formed, but fast asleep, never to awaken. No amount of cradling that day could revive him. He had held his tiny fingers, willing them to grip back.

An air bubble escaped from the urn, the gentle sound broke his reverie and he took out a small carton of milk from the bag and removed the lid and broke the seal, taking care to place this tiny scrap of rubbish back into the carrier bag. He folded the top of the bag and pushed it towards the tiled wall, double-checked the settings on the urn and then walked over to the heating panels. He hesitated for a moment, made his mind up, and turned the thermostat two degrees higher. He made a mental note to reduce it before they left. The grieving parents had enough on their plates without being cold. September nights in Scotland heralded the colder evenings to come.

Oliver then walked through to the meeting room and started rearranging the chairs into a circle around two low tables. He broke the church silence with an 'Ah,' and quickly returned to his carrier bag, took out several leaflets which detailed more about the bereavement charity and how it could help people further, and returned to the meeting room and placed these in a neat pile on one table. He scanned the room, counting out the chairs. He hoped they would be enough. He hated to see new members. It meant someone else had taken his or her life and left devastation behind.

87

The outer door gave a small bang as it was opened and closed, interrupting Oliver's counting. He walked back to the lobby and was pleased to see Nancy shrugging out of her jacket, 'You're fine and early tonight, no Roland?'

'Hello Oliver, no, I still can't convince him to come in and join our meeting. I know it would do him some good. He has come to the Edinburgh meeting though, we go by train and have a good natter, then he reads the newspapers whilst I have a nap.'

'That's good to hear, I'd like to meet him one day. He's coped so well after you lost Anthea.' A dark cloud overshadowed his narrowing of his eyes as he gently enquired, 'Are there new members coming tonight?'

Nancy sighed, 'I'm afraid so. Three that I know about. A couple who lost a son and a father who lost a daughter. He was in some state over the phone, I hope he's okay.' She shook her head slowly.

There would be enough chairs and mugs, Oliver knew people could only come here via a telephone call with Nancy, few knew of this meeting place, other than the charity HQ, not even doctors and counsellors knew of the location and times, not since that awful reporter.

'You'll be staying over at Roland's flat?'

'That's right, he's just had it decorated, you should see it, it's so lovely. He even had the decorator paint the entrance hall by his office, so that it looks more homely when you go through and up the stairs.'

'That sounds nice. I've often wondered, what does Roland do for a living?'

Nancy was about to answer, but a breathless lady who stepped through the church door interrupted the couple. 'I'm not late, am I?' She didn't give them a chance to answer, 'Or should that be Je ne suis pas en retard, je suis?' She looked from Oliver and then back to Nancy, rather satisfied with herself and boasted, 'I've been practicing all week!'

Nancy looked back in puzzlement, but Oliver thought he knew what the lady was expecting, 'Are you looking for French classes?'

'That's right, French conversation and dancing,' she shook a bag, 'I've baked some cakes.'

'You've come to the wrong church hall, I'm afraid. You probably want the Roman Catholic one further down the road, on the corner,' advised Oliver helpfully.

'Silly me, I'm always doing that. What's happening here, is it an interesting class?'

Oliver opened the door and pointed down the street, 'It's that way.'

'Oh, okay, thanks anyway. Perhaps if my French isn't good enough to understand the others, I can come back?'

'Peut etre,' he simply said, saw her puzzled look, smiled, and finished with an, 'Au revoir.'

She grinned and left Oliver with an 'A bientot monsieur!' and tootled down the road.

Oliver stepped back into the lobby, looked at Nancy, and they both burst out laughing.

'It's just as well that you speak French. I don't think she'd have found much joy in dancing here tonight,' joked Nancy, still giggling.

Oliver frowned, sighed, thought of the newly grieving parents, and simply said, 'No.' Then caught himself and continued with, 'We got the French contract.'

'That's brilliant news, I know that'll be an enormous boost to your company.'

Oliver nodded, they'd settled at three per cent, just like he thought they would.

A harried looking lady rushed past Monica, holding out a bag in front of her, like they contained delicate cargo. Their eyes briefly met, and each wondered where the other was going and what sort of life they led. Then Monica's attention was back to the gently gliding clouds that were settling down for the night in the glooming sky. She'd come the long way, to avoid the local park where she knew the children's laughter that she could hear carrying on this still night, came from. It was still too painful to see parents and children having fun; it was even more painful to watch a parent chastise their child: didn't they know that life was so precious and fragile and that they shouldn't waste a moment on the banality? She loved walking to the September group. The way the light slowly dissipated made her feel like she was being gently cocooned. She could hear a blackbird sing out as it glided down to rest within the shrubbery of an adjacent garden. Even the gentle hum of traffic sounded like it was gearing down for the peace of the evening. She gave a cheerful wave as she saw her pal, Isobel, walking from the other direction.

The two friends joined paths outside the church door and exchanged pleasantries and then Monica asked the question they were all eager to hear news about, for new life gave them all hope for the future, 'How is Lindsay?' She opened the door for her friend.

'Thank you,' Isobel acknowledged as she stepped into the lobby of the church hall. 'She's piling on the pounds. She's splendid company, she even had me singing lullabies yesterday, and today I looked out Roy's old radio to play to her.'

Monica did an obvious double-take, but recovered quickly as she followed her pal into the hall. 'That's wonderful, that's a good thing, isn't it?'

'Yes, I've lived with silence for too long, Lindsay is making me get on with loving living again.' She looked at Oliver and Nancy with guilt at what she was saying, 'And how has your month been?'

Oliver looked down at his feet, uncertainly.

Nancy took on the thread of the conversation, 'Busy. The other groups have seen a spate of new members, some, understandably, in quite a bit of distress. Though I had Roland helping me at the Edinburgh branch.'

Isobel began to say something, but as she opened her mouth to speak, a middle-aged couple walked through the door.

Barry sat at the table, one hand clasped his mobile phone, the other kept trying to dial Nancy's number. His index finger hovered over the screen like a kestrel riding a wind current, about to pounce on its prey below. He'd snatch back his right hand with each indecisive argument within his head. Then his mind relented, gave up its internal disagreement, and he slid the phone away from him and across the table, the place where his daughter had taken her life, and the place where he now sat, alone, always alone.

Adam gently closed the outside church hall door and turned briskly on his heels, like a parade guardsman performing an about turn. He looked around him, at the other members of the group. His eyes seemed wide to the others, like a rabbit caught in the headlights. He reached out and took Corrina's hand, seeking comfort in its weak grip. She was hesitant too.

Oliver, sensing their unease, broke away from the conversation between Isobel, Monica, and Nancy, and stepped over to the new couple. 'Hello, I'm Oliver, how was your journey here?'

Corrina stuck out her free hand for Oliver to shake, 'It was a pleasant walk. We only live a few streets away, though we've never been in this church. We used to go to the Church of Scotland Kirk, but not any longer, not since our son took his-' she cut off her sentence and sobbed.

Oliver broke off their handshake, unsure if he should offer a consoling cuddle to a stranger. However, he saw movement from his left and took a step over to Adam and placed his hand on his shoulder.

'Oh, come here love,' offered Monica as she stepped over to the crying woman and wrapped her arms around her and held her close. 'You are among friends here; we've all suffered a traumatic loss and can imagine what you are going through. We'll always be here for you. We've all stood where you are and broken down. Let the tears flow.' Not caring that her shoulder felt damp, she held Corrina close, as if willing her pain away.

Oliver gently took Adam by the hand, keeping his other hand on his shoulder, 'Let's all go through to the meeting room, we'll be more comfortable there. What's your name?'

'Adam,' he nodded to his wife, 'and my wife Corrina. We lost our son, Fraser, he was our eldest. It's hit us hard. Our GP recommended the group to us. Have you all lost a child?'

Oliver withdrew his hands and motioned for Adam to follow him. Isobel and Nancy were already walking through, deep in conversation, Nancy was handing Isobel something as they walked.

Monica continued to hug Corrina and make soothing noises, like a big sister comforting a younger sibling who had fallen over and grazed a knee. 'We'll go through when you are ready love, you let it all out.' She could feel Corrina tremble with each juddering outpouring of raw emotion.

Monica could see the pavement over Corrina's shoulder and the night had darkened. During their embrace, the automatic outside lights of the hall were periodically going on and off with each passing movement of pedestrians. Some were looking in as they passed,

93

shocked to see such a tight embrace by two women within the holy building. She didn't care.

A whispered voice gently muffled by Monica's jumper said, 'I'm okay now. It's hard, we have three other children, and I must be strong for them. I haven't been able to have a good cry.'

Monica, judging the moment to be right, broke off the embrace, walked over to the table and lifted a box of tissues. Oliver always had one box here and another in the meeting room. They were usually needed.

Corrina mouthed a thank you and pulled several tissues from the box, blew her nose with two and then wiped her eyes and cheeks with the other. She scrunched them into a damp ball and was grateful to Monica when she pointed out the bin below the table. 'I don't even know your name, I'm Corrina,' she offered.

'Monica. I never want to say I'm pleased to meet you to new people, because I pray no one needs to come here, but I am pleased that you've come, and I hope that you'll keep coming?' She nodded her head in encouragement.

'Thank you, Monica. That was comforting. Our doctor made us promise that we'll come to at least three meetings.'

'That sounds a sensible and caring GP.'

'Oh, she is,' nodded Corrina. 'She's been so good to our other children and Adam and I.'

'You are lucky.' She left it at that, not wanting to burden the grieving mum with the information that some of them had more challenging doctors whose idea of care was to tell them to get back to work as soon as possible and find something to do in their spare time to stop them dwelling on their loss. That didn't help at all. 'Are you ready to go into the meeting room, we usually sit in a circle and in about forty minutes Oliver makes the best tea and coffee in town and has some incredible biscuits.'

Corrina gave a short nervous laugh, 'That will please Adam, he loves biscuits.'

'That'll please Oliver too, he hates to see waste. His friend at the work café bakes them, especially for us.'

'That is kind. People have been so kind to my family, bringing us meals that just need reheating in the oven, looking after our other children, and even running the vacuum cleaner around the house.'

Monica thought of Robyn and how she literally picked her off the floor when she first lost Josephine and then her former husband, Josephine's father. 'Yes, you need your friends close at a time like this. Though they need to grieve too, it's their loss as well.' She looked to Corrina and could see that she was finished with this bout of crying. 'We take turns talking and you can say anything you like. But only if you feel up to it. I cried non-stop for my first two meetings, so you're doing so well. Shall we go in?'

Corrina nodded and followed Monica through the opened doorway, looked for Adam, and sat beside him, taking his hand as she sat down.

Monica gently closed the door. The sound of passing traffic subsided and silence fell upon the group. She walked to the spare seat by her new friend. Adam caught her eyes and mouthed a thank you.

'I'm Monica,' she whispered, reluctant to break the quietness of the room.

A motherly expression fell upon Nancy as she sat serenely straight and looked around her, almost like a reverend beholding her congregation from her pulpit. She waited a few seconds and then began her group meeting ritual. 'Hello everybody,' she let her eyes cast from Adam to Corrina, 'I'm Nancy, I'm the group co-ordinator. I lost my daughter to suicide.' With only a pause long enough to get a nod of acknowledgment from the new couple, she continued with, 'We might have another member come and join us this evening. Can I please remind everyone that what we say in here is private and not to be spoken about outside of this room? That way we can be honest with ourselves and others. You don't have to speak if you don't want to, but for the sake of Adam and Corrina, can the others please speak about their loss and who they are.' She nodded to Oliver, as if she were passing the heralded Olympic flame.

He took up the metaphorical baton, 'I'm Oliver. I've no children, well, sort of. My wife, Emma, took her own life soon after we had a stillborn child. A tiny baby boy. He was beautiful. She suffered four miscarriages prior to this and couldn't cope with the losses.' He stopped talking when he noticed Corrina reach for a tissue from the box on the table.

Monica reached over and rubbed Corrina's shoulder and then spoke softly, 'I'm Monica. My daughter, Josephine, took her life three years ago. Her girlfriend broke up with her and she couldn't cope. Then my husband, well we were divorced by then, took his life about two years later. I find the group comforting and I hope you both will too.' She stopped her rhythmic movements and withdrew her hand when she saw Adam doing the same on the other shoulder.

Isobel put her hand in her pocket, fingered the object given to her by Nancy, and debated to herself whether she should talk about it with the others. Seeing tears roll down Adam's face, she decided that now was not the time. 'I'm Isobel, my son's wife, Paula, took her life, she was mentally unwell for years, then my son, Aaron, took his life. They left behind an adolescent daughter, Wendy. I cared for her until she was old enough to lead her own life. I now care for her baby, Lindsay.'

Corrina looked puzzled as a beatific smile spread warmth across Isobel's face and her eyes appeared to dazzle.

'Wendy recently made me a great-grandmother and gorgeous Lindsay is bringing such joy into my life.' Her smile quickly disappeared as she remembered where she was and a more solemn expression reinforced what she further stated, 'I never thought that I'd be happy again. My husband died of cancer a year later. I totally stopped work and devoted my time to Wendy. She found love with Darren and they've a flat around the corner. I'd been so worried about her. She suffered from depression, not unsurprisingly, and needed some help when she went off the rails and got in trouble with the police. But she removed herself from that gang, changed schools, but left with no qualifications. But my Roy, my husband, left us well provided, even after the cost of funerals. Aren't they expensive!'

A collective nod spread around the room.

'But I'm waffling again!' She looked to the couple, 'Life has to go on. I reached the conclusion that neither Aaron nor Roy or Paula would want Wendy and I to be unhappy.'

Adam shook his head discretely to his wife, their earlier pre-arranged signal that either of them could not talk if they did this. He dabbed at his eyes with his fingers until Corrina passed a tissue his way.

Corrina nodded her head to him, 'We are going on for the sake of our other three children. But it's hard. Thank you for welcoming us to your group.'

'We all wish that you didn't need to be here, Corrina and Adam,' voiced Oliver on behalf of the group. 'It's a loss like no other. I can't explain it to my work friends, though they have been understanding, I don't think they quite get what we all go through. Especially when we go home and shut our doors.'

There were more nods of heads, and then the group's gazes settled back to Nancy.

'I find comfort in speaking to my daughter when I'm at home. I travel around the UK running other groups, but when I get home, I talk to her. It's as if she is in the room. My son, Roland, he's the same, though he never goes to the grave. Not since her funeral. He says that it is only her body there, that her spirit is free.'

'I used to believe in God and was a regular churchgoer, but I haven't been back since Fraser passed, just for the funeral,' confessed Corrina. 'I feel stupid for having had such firm beliefs, but now I hate God for taking him away,'

Nancy interrupted Corrina's flow with, 'We've all been there, but you will believe again, one day, and then you'll be ready to hear the voice of God, and your son again.'

Adam and Corrina looked up to Nancy, not quite believing her. They knew that they'd never again have faith. 'How could a loving God allow such a crime to have taken place and to cause so much pain to Fraser,' they both thought, but remained silent, not wanting to disagree with the group co-ordinator, not on their first night. They sat and listened to the group share their problems, emotions, and experiences.

Robyn, dressed in her skin-tight trousers, revealing blouse and best heels, tottered along the cobbled street, and knocked on the door of the big house. Graham answered immediately. As he opened the door, the sounds of Jazz wafted from speakers placed around the house. 'Oh well, no one's perfect!' she thought, knowing that is what her pal Monica would have said. She hoped that there weren't new people at the group tonight. Her pal was always low for a few days after.

Graham was barefooted, wearing jeans with frayed cotton at the hems and around the pockets, and sported a navy polo shirt with a jumping horse emblem surrounded by gold, red and black colours forming a shield on its breast. 'Robyn! Come away in, I'll pour you a drink.'

Robyn entered the light and airy vestibule, helped by the large chandelier which housed eight bright lightbulbs. There was a solitary table, despite the vast area.

'Come through to the lounge, wine okay?'

She nodded, still taking in her surroundings. This area was larger than her lounge. She followed him in awe as they entered a double-doored archway and into a cavernous lounge with several plush three-seater sofas, two deep recliners and stools, a large table, and the lushest carpet she'd ever seen. Paintings of trumpeters and saxophonists hung from the walls between several large speakers.

He saw her eyes loiter over the speakers, 'I do like to listen to my music wherever I go, that way I don't miss any of the tracks.'

Robyn didn't like to tell him that every Jazz track just sounded the same to her, a collective din, with each instrument played in a distinct style and a different tune to the rest of the band.

'Take a seat and I'll pour, red okay?'

She nodded, choosing the sofa that she thought they'd be most comfortable getting to know each other on.

'Did Monica get off okay? And where's Judy, I thought you'd have brought her with you?' He poured two half glasses of wine and placed them on the table beside the sofa and then sat down.

She was pleased to see that he sat next to her, just one seat away. 'Yes, she left in good time. Judy is tired from her walks with her aunty, so I've left her at home, fast asleep on the sofa.' She didn't like to add that she didn't want Judy getting between them tonight, not with this blouse and seductive perfume. It had taken her twenty minutes just

100

to put her make-up on. 'Monica likes to walk for hours, but poor Judy's small legs just can't take it, so she needs her alone time.'

'I did that, after my friend died, I walked for hours at a time, anything to take my mind off it. Goodness knows what Monica must be trying to cope with. That's why she is so thin, I guess?'

'She doesn't eat well either, I try to feed her up, but she just picks at her food. Would you believe she was a size twenty before Josephine passed? She's literally half the woman she was?'

'Should we invite her to afternoon tea tomorrow? I can add her to the booking?'

Robyn briefly entertained the idea, but remembered that it was group evening. Besides, how would she fit in to the two-seater Porsche? 'No, that's thoughtful, but she has a routine before and after group and it's best not to interrupt the pattern. If there are new people, she needs a day or two, depending on how many have attended, to herself. She closes all the blinds in her house and doesn't answer the door.'

'Oh! That can't be healthy.'

'No, that's what I first thought. I have a key to her house, I do for all my tenants, but I had never gone in before, not to any of those who have rented from me. But I was so worried for my friend's life. I inched the door open carefully and slowly and spotted her curled up on the sofa. I could see that she was breathing, and that there were no alcohol bottles or empty pill packets, so I left, but returned every few hours and did the same. She hadn't moved.'

'I don't know what to say, other than, poor woman. Thank heaven that she has you.' He wiggled along the sofa and placed a hand on hers as a show of support.

Robyn placed her other hand over theirs, all thoughts of seduction gone. She needed to tell him more about her pal. They sat there for another two hours, wine virtually untouched, and chatted about Monica and both of their lives.

Adam had his hand out, expecting a handshake, 'Thank you for the tea and biscuits Oliver, they were ever so tasty,'

Oliver accepted the farewell gesture, 'You are welcome, I'll let my friend Harriet know, she makes them specially. She says the lavender flavour helps to soothe the mind.' He withdrew his hand and reached into his pocket and took out his mobile. 'I send people a reminder of the next meeting date and time and any changes we have to make, or if we have someone from say an organisation come along and give a small talk. We had someone from Samaritans a few months back. I do this by e-mail. May I take yours and add you to the list?'

'No problem, that's thoughtful, thank you. We are under doctor's orders to attend at least two more meetings.'

'That's sound advice, I'm pleased that you'll come back, and we'll get to know you better.'

Adam was conscious that he'd not said much this evening, except to talk about biscuits. He looked sheepish and rattled off his e-mail address.

'Thanks.' Oliver put his phone back in his pocket. 'Let me get the outside door for you. It gets stiff and there's a knack to opening it.' He walked off to the lobby whilst Corrina said her goodbyes and joined her husband in leaving the building. Once they'd safely gone, Oliver quickly walked to find Monica, who was in the kitchen, drying the mugs and teaspoons.

She nodded to a plate with two biscuits on them, 'I'll wash the plate through before I go, but it seems a shame to throw those away.'

'I'll take them home, rather than waste them.' He rummaged in his carrier bag and took out the brightly coloured box. A piece of ribbon came out of the bag too. He looked startled, 'Sorry. Harriet always gives me a fancy recyclable box. I don't like to take it out when the others are around. It seems garish, given the circumstances.' He placed the biscuits into the box and quickly put it back in the carrier bag. He was about to pass the plate to Monica when their fingers delicately brushed as she was reaching for it. He laughed nervously, 'Sorry!'

Their eyes met and Monica was about to say something when Nancy walked in. 'Roland is waiting outside in his car, he wants me to meet one of his clients, for a quick drink in a bar, so I'll see you all next month. I think it went rather well. I hope the chap who didn't come phones me again. If not, I'll ring him in a few days and check that he's okay. See you.'

Monica and Oliver said their goodbyes to her. Oliver remembered about the heating switch and walked over and turned the thermostat down, happy knowing that the church committee wouldn't know that he'd been extravagant with their heating bill.

Monica quickly wiped dry the plate, not bothering to wash it. No one had eaten from it. She watched as Oliver placed the remaining tea bags, coffee, and sugar into his carrier bag. She knew that he'd always bring new ones. The same with the tissues and milk.

They were interrupted again, this time by Isobel. Her hand was rummaging in her pocket, like she'd lost something. An uncertain look was upon her face.

'Would you like to take the biscuits home, Isobel?'

'No, I'm fine, I really shouldn't be taking sugar, but I do like that one treat, every month. How's Harriet and her family?'

Oliver grinned, 'They are all fine. Mitch fell in love today!'

Isobel beamed back, 'His mum won't be seeing much of him then!'

Monica regarded Oliver. Words were dancing on her lips, but her tongue wouldn't let them perform. She remained tight-lipped for a few seconds, 'I'll be off then. See you both next month; keep safe and well.'

'I'll walk along with you, Monica,' offered Isobel, zipping up her jacket.

'Would you like a lift?' asked Oliver, directing the question to Monica. He knew Isobel was only around the block.

'No, I like the exercise, but thank you.' She lingered for a moment whilst Isobel waited in the doorway. She momentarily bowed her head, turned, and joined her pal, both soon deep in conversation.

Oliver checked the kitchen, locked away their mugs and plates, picked up his bag, returned to the meeting room, put back the table and chairs how they were before, picked up the box of tissues and switched off the lights to the meeting room. He stood in the darkened doorway, save for the light from the lobby, seeming to relish the silence. He'd wished that tonight he could have told them. After several minutes he closed the door, picked up the other box of tissues, turned out the lights, walked through the outside door and locked the hall door, grateful for the automatic outside lights. He slowly returned to his car, in no rush to get home. One o'clock seemed like a long time to come for him.

Bella and Irvine

The sun shone down on the granite buildings and appeared to give off a collective sparkle around the old fishing cottages. Robyn looked over to her friend's house and noted that the curtains were tightly shut, there would not even be the smallest of gaps to peer through. She knew that this heralded that there had been a newly bereaved mother or father, perhaps even several, and that she mustn't disturb her pal. Monica had given succour to the grieving, at the cost of her own mental health. Robyn had to trust her not to harm herself, but it didn't stop that gut-wrenching sinking feeling from hitting the base of her stomach. She wanted to hold her friend and offer support, but her pal just wanted to be alone with her thoughts. She turned and walked towards the car park with Judy trotting obediently by her side. The dog had been perfectly groomed and was sporting a pink hair tie that held together her longer hairs. Robyn wore a colour matching top and her hair was also tied carefully back; she expected the Porsche roof to be opened on this glorious September day. She would be punctual for the planned meeting in the communal car park if Judy didn't sniff every lamp post on the way.

The pair were soon safely past the row of recently urine marked lamp posts on which every male dog in the area had relieved themselves during their morning walks. Even Judy appeared eager to get in the Porsche this morning, for she'd not gone sniffing. Graham had insisted on an eleven-thirty departure to allow a sedate drive to the country location. She had hoped that he'd put his foot down on the accelerator so that she could experience the full might of the ferocious engine.

Owner and dog reached the car park on the allotted time and stood expectantly next to the Porsche. The almost midday sun beamed down on its highly shone metalwork and radiated its deep colours and soft contours. She stood in anticipation by the passenger door, Judy's special harness at the ready in her pocket.

Graham walked around the corner, whistling gayly. He broke into a beaming smile, as radiant as the yellow circle in the sky. He walked up to Robyn, kissed her fully on the mouth, the couple lingering in delight, until a jealous canine pawed at their legs. They broke off their loving greeting. 'Let me get the door for you.'

Robyn stepped back a pace, expecting Graham to unlock the car and help her in, but she was surprised to see him walk across to the other side of the car park, reach into his pocket, take out an actual key, rather than a fob, and unlock a dull, beige ancient car.

'Isn't he a beauty!' marvelled Graham as he pulled open the door. 'The trick with this side is to lift slightly as you open and close the door, the mechanisms don't align.'

Robyn was lost for words. Her lips were floundering, like a newly caught fish gasping for air. She looked from the car, over to the Porsche, and back again. She knew how game show contestants felt when they gambled at the end for the jackpot and failed.

Graham, oblivious to her shock, mistook her gasps for admiration. 'He belonged to my dear grandmother. The one with the

Yorkshire Terrier. They'd sit side by side and travel all over Scotland. She called the car Morris, and I've stuck to the name since. Once I could sit upright, I was soon joining her, and Sheba, her Yorkie, would sit on my lap. Sometimes we'd curl up in the back seats and have a nap during the longer trips. She was lovely, my grandmother, I miss her. She gifted me Morris in her will, and I've kept him since.' He nodded to the row of garages, 'He's normally kept in there, but it's a bit of a squeeze to get in and out, so I popped him out this morning. C'mon, don't be shy, sit yourself down and we'll get off.' He leaned forward and patted the passenger seat, almost like he was clapping a favoured dog.

'We could always walk along the promenade and get something local, you know, if you don't want to add mileage to Morris.'

'Don't you worry about that, Morris is where a lot of my money goes, well that and Jazz, I've a local mechanic who tunes him up for me every few months and keeps him ticking over. You know, I've never broken down in him. He's a sturdy old thing. The only thing is, there is no CD player, not even a tape deck, just a trusty old radio, so no Jazz, I'm afraid.'

She gave a nervous laugh to hide her discomfort, 'Thank goodness for small mercies,' she thought. She looked around at the bodywork, 'He's dull, the colour I mean.'

Graham looked around in disbelief, checking for specks of dirt in the gleaming surfaces, he'd spent a lot of elbow grease hours polishing Morris up. 'Oh, the colour,' he realised. 'Not at all, it's called dove grey. It was all the height of fashion when my grandmother was young.' He let go of the door handle and walked over to the front wheel, 'Just check out these tyres and hub caps. The contours and the contrasting white brightness. It complements the dove grey and the burgundy fold down roof balances the colour scheme with a hint of cheekiness, I'll soon have Morris's top down and the wind will flow through us, so keep your jacket on.'

She looked over jealously to the Porsche and sighed. She didn't want to crush his enthusiasm, so planted a false smile on her lips, leant forward, and kissed him, 'I can't wait. Shall we get set then?'

'That's the ticket!'

She sat down upon the passenger seat and gave a small startle as a spring dug into her bottom. Then she gave a louder cry of alarm as the seat dropped an inch. Judy yelped out in alarm and tried to jump from her lap.

'Sorry, he does that, original seats you see. The springs have yielded somewhat from all the years of me jumping around as a youngster.' He leaned forward and began unclipping the roof, walked to the driver's side and repeated the process, and then carefully, almost lovingly, folded the roof back in a concertina fashion and then he went back and carefully closed her door. He quickly took his seat and gave the steering wheel several pats. He looked across to her bashfully, 'Old habit, for luck, just letting the old boy know that he's to take care of us.'

Robyn pulled the zipper up on her jacket, reached into her pocket, and took out the car travel harness and connected Judy to it and threaded it through her seat belt. As she wrapped it around herself and clicked it into place; she refrained from making the sign of the cross in protection of their forthcoming journey.

'Of course, my grandmother always wore a headscarf, to protect her perm. You don't see many women wearing headscarves these days. Stores always had rows of them on display.' He gave a sigh at the happy memory. 'When we get home, I'll dig out my old photo albums and show you my grandmother. There are loads of photos of us on our adventures. She was never shy in asking a passer-by to snap a quick photo using her old Box Brownie. Now that was a camera.'

Robyn squirmed in her seat, finding an area that was spring free to rest her buttocks. She was glad that God had made her ample in that area, though she knew it was her love of chocolate and pizza that gave her natural padding. A smile of comfort passed over her as she reclined. 'It's surprisingly comfy when you yield to it.'

'British craftsmanship, you can't beat it.'

It surprised Robyn to find herself nod in agreement. She reached over and stroked Graham's left hand, lightly brushing the steering wheel. 'Thank you for sharing Morris with me, I just know that the four of us are going to have some glorious adventures, just like your dear grandmother, Sheba, Morris and you.'

Graham beamed brighter than any car headlamp as he used his free hand to start the engine.

The young man, in his early twenties, of broad build and with an unruly mop of hair, tiptoed across the room and sat by the forlorn young lady who was sitting on the windowsill, looking sadly out.

Irvine sat down next to his fiancée, reached for her hand, and took it in both of his. Her skin was cold, and she was painfully thin. Her long hair hadn't been brushed that day and was knotted and tangled. She wore yesterday's clothes and hadn't showered yet. She'd been too busy watching, hopefully, at the window, ignoring the well-intentioned neighbours and passing postal worker who waved cheerfully. 'Mum's made your favourite soup, I'll reheat it, whilst you shower?' He nodded his head in encouragement.

'Okay,' replied Bella in a monotone, 'You will come and get me if there is any news?'

'Of course, love, of course I will. But it's been three years. I don't think they are coming back.'

Bella bit her lip, tears formed in her eyes, giving the appearance of an early morning dew settling. 'I'll be as quick as I can.' She walked out of the room reluctantly and made her way to the bathroom, knowing that Irvine would have laid out a fresh towel and put a clean bathmat on the floor. He did so much for her, allowing her more time to watch from the window.

Irvine waited until she had left the room and he could hear the click of the shower pull cord switch on from the downstairs wet room. He then went to the kitchen and switched on the microwave and then the oven. The soup and heated rolls would be ready to eat upon her return. He knew it would be another day of watching her take just a few mouthfuls of each, before returning to the windowsill. He picked the leaflet from the table and read the information for the second time. He knew that this support group, if he could prise Bella from the window vigil, would help her acceptance and recovery. He pushed it to her side of the table, ready to be part of his explanation.

Robyn alternated between waving to pedestrians and fellow motorists and gently lifting Judy's left paw and giving her the action of a regal wave. She gave out a fresh peal of laughter as she saw more people's delighted reaction at the vintage car. 'You were so right; Morris is great fun!'

'I know, right!'

Neither cared that they were soon chugging along at thirty miles an hour down a country road, with a long tailback of frustrated motorists unable to overtake because of the steady stream of cars coming the other way.

Their respective hair was flowing gently in the wind and even Judy seemed to raise her head and enjoy the air flowing through her whiskers and beard. All three were caught up in the moment's enjoyment, and hadn't given their friend, Monica, a thought.

Monica was sitting in the lounge; the midday sun was trying to leach out from behind the closed curtains. She nursed a stale mug of coffee in her hand. There was a disc of cold milk floating on its surface. She looked up to the alcove, to the dust-ridden photo frame, laid on its front. 'It's so painful to see other parents suffer the way your dad and I hurt after you did what you did. The pain in their eyes, it's what we must have been like. I saw it in your dad's eyes, but he couldn't talk about you, or the pain you caused. Oh, Josephine, why couldn't you have told us, told me? We'd have helped you with your heartache. It would have healed. You were so young and beautiful. Someone else would have fallen in love with you. Their boy was only twenty-two. But I managed, I held her and comforted her, like I would have done for you. I should have told Nancy, Oliver, and Isobel, but I couldn't, not after seeing Corrina's distress.'

She put down her mug, pulled her feet up to the sofa, and curled back into a ball.

'I sent off for it because I thought you are ready to meet others in the same position as you. They can help you and offer you support,' explained Irvine.

'I know that I have to face reality,' whispered Bella reluctantly. 'They aren't coming back, are they?' She looked up to her fiancé with large pleading eyes, willing him to say, 'Yes, one day they would return.'

'No. They've been gone too long. They loved you and wouldn't leave you without a word. Will you go, please? I phoned the number on the leaflet and spoke to a sweet old lady called Nancy. Their next meeting is the first Thursday in October.'

She reluctantly nodded, 'Will you come with me, please?'

He reached across the table and took both of her hands. They were still cold, despite having been wrapped around the barely eaten hot bowl of soup. 'Of course. I'll drive you there, it's in the city, but will only take us forty minutes. I'll wait in the car.'

She looked up aghast, 'Don't make me go in on my own. I can't face strangers on my own.'

'Then I'll come in with you and I'll make sure that I sit beside you. I'll support you in any way I can.'

'Thank you, Irvine.' She rose, neglecting her roll and soup, and returned to the lounge window and sat down, eyes constantly moving from side to side.

Judy sniffed around, settled upon a favoured spot of grass by the car park, squatted, and relieved herself. Robyn looked back to Morris, taking in the sight of the car from a distance. She then checked that Judy had finished her pee and walked back to Graham. She ran her hand seductively over the bonnet of Morris as she walked. She neglected to see from his look of consternation that she was leaving smudge marks or fingerprints. 'You know,' she whispered into his ear, 'He's like you, he's got hidden depths, he looks quaint from a distance, you were so right about all the colours giving an overall appearance. He's so cute!' She playfully tapped his nose.

Graham wrapped his arms around her waist, pulling her closer. 'I knew you'd like him! I can't wait to get on a real road trip with you all.'

She snuggled up to him, with Judy squashed indignantly in the middle.

Over to their right was a picture postcard perfect cottage with a low thatched roof, a shingle pathway that led to a wooden archway draped in a creeping late-flowering plant and a low gate. They broke off their embrace and walked towards it, hand in hand like two carefree loved-up teenagers. Judy trotted proudly beside Robyn.

'Don't go straight in,' pointed Graham to his left, 'Let's go around the back.' He led the way, and the trio were rewarded with the sight of a lush green lawn which was interspaced with ornately carved wooden benches and chairs. Beyond the grass, now audible, was a gently flowing river, with crystal clear water. 'It comes off the hills and as it makes its way through all the natural rocks, it gets cleansed.'

'I've never seen such clear waters, what a lovely view.' She stood on tiptoe and kissed him on the cheek. 'If we keep our jackets on, I think it'll be warm enough to stay outside.'

Graham nodded to the modern-looking conservatory at the back of the cottage, 'All the glass absorbs the heat, so if you get cold, we can always warm up inside. In the winter they have some old-fashioned log burners to keep the building cosy. It's my favourite spot. We used to come here all the time.'

'With your grandmother?'

'No, it would have been a private home then. The new owners bought it, intending to run it as a restaurant.'

'Ah, with your ex-wife?' Robyn looked dejected. She thought it made the place less special.

'No, just me and Morris. When things got heated at home, I'd escape here. My wife never drove with me in Morris, she didn't like him, nor the expense I lavished on him. I always hoped to meet someone special and bring her here.' He looked deeply into her eyes, reached up, stroked her cheek, and kissed her. 'And now I have,' he said huskily.

Monica dried her tears with an already wet tissue, swung her legs out from the seat of the sofa, scrunched up and threw the tissue in the wastebasket by the table, then stood up and strode to the window with purpose and threw open the curtains. The sun beamed in, revealing tiny dust patterns in the air. She looked across to the neglected alcove, 'I have to go on, for the others.' She turned and walked to the front door, grabbing her coat, and wishing that she had a leash to unhook, and a dog to walk.

The waiter, dressed formally in black trousers, white shirt and tie, and a black waistcoat, with a folded clinically clean and starched apron completing the uniform, placed a bowl with several hand-baked biscuits and a portion of sliced steak, onto the floor beside an expectant Judy. Seeing her pink hair tie, he announced, 'Especially for madam!' Without a word to the couple sat on the bench. He turned and walked back to the conservatory.

Judy sniffed appreciatively at the dish, like a judge on MasterChef, and began devouring her meal.

'Dogs eat first here too!' exclaimed Robyn in delight, clapping her hands in glee. She saw the frown on Graham's face. 'Have you not tried the dog café along the beach?'

'No, it always looks so busy, and noisy.'

'I'll treat you one day soon. Mathew is such a lovely guy. He's the owner, he makes sure dogs eat first as well. Judy has ice-cream with Monica when I'm at work. It's their little secret.'

Graham nodded, though he was secretly thinking the world had gone mad. Though when he looked at Judy, he knew his grandmother would be looking down and approving.

Nancy hugged her son close, having to reach up to embrace him. Roland was a good foot taller than her, had a round, smiling face, bright green eyes like his mum, and short hair, combed straight down. It gave him a convivial look and spoke of kindness. 'You are doing such important work. Keep it up. I'm so proud of you, I'll see you next month, I'll stay overnight if I may?'

'Of course, mum, you know you don't need to ask, come and stay at any time. Now get on the train before the conductor shuts the door and tells you off again for opening it and jumping on last minute.'

Nancy looked up to the platform steps. Others were still rushing for the train, and the enormous clock on the wall revealed that they still had a few minutes. 'Will you come to the meeting with me in October?'

Roland looked to his feet and gave an awkward shuffle, 'It's not quite the time for me to come, maybe in a month or two.'

Nancy nodded, she knew he knew best, 'Love you!' She leaned up and kissed him on the cheek.

'I love you too mum, let me know when you get home safely. I'll disappear now, I've an appointment to keep.'

'Okay, son.' She reluctantly picked up her bag, boarded the train, sat down at an empty table with four seats and looked out of the window to wave at Graham. He'd gone, keen to get back to work. However, she saw a fellow passenger and newly found friend Mae run down the platform and step into her coach. As she came through the sliding doors, Nancy waved to her and as Mae neared her, she said, 'There's a spare seat here, Mae.' It dismayed her when Mae ignored her, looked straight ahead, and made for the next carriage.

Several weeks lapsed and the members of the group watched patiently as each day passed and then September gave way to October and the colder nights shrouded the city and surrounding shire.

Bella and Irvine sat in their car outside the church hall, watched as a lone figure slowly reversed his car into the space in front, then took out a bulging carrier bag from the boot, and ambled to the dark building. An outside light sprang to life to reveal the man, about fifteen years older than them, feeling in his trousers and then jacket pocket for some keys. He unlocked the glass door, entered, and then went around switching lights on and feeling along radiators. He took his carrier bag from doorway to doorway.

Irvine broke the silence, 'I think that's the right building. We are quite early, but that's okay. I know you were getting restless and needed to be out of the house. Shall we go in?'

Bella pulled her arms tighter around her, tucking them under her armpits. She drew her knees up towards herself, heels dug into the edge of the car seat. She was replicating the posture she adopted when looking out of the lounge window. She remained silent.

'That's okay, love, we'll wait a while longer. We'll go in when you are ready.'

Gregor

The former bank building at the corner of the street retained a counter feature when it had closed and was immediately refurbished by the new owners. A bolder, longer counter, arced along the principal room, served a different client group and currency. It was now an upmarket bar, sparkling gold dazzled along the optics shelving and carefully placed lights shone on this row of enticing bottles. The spirits drew the eyes of most customers, as did the row of local draft ales and lagers, interspersed with fizzy sugary drinks with easy to dispense nozzles. Gregor ignored the latter and pointed to the golden-brown liquid on the shelving behind the barman. To reinforce his choice, his shaky hand waggled the small, empty glass next to his half-drunk pint of lager. He then put it down and gave the two signs with his fingers.

The barman, having no other customers, obliged straightaway, and in silence. He hadn't been able to draw a simple conversation from this man, despite his best efforts. His customer only spoke minimal orders to him. He'd arrived already smelling of stale booze, looked like he hadn't shaved for several days, needed to run a comb through his hair, and had been agitated from the moment he arrived. He'd also dropped his money during each transaction, partly because of his haste, but probably mostly due to his shaking hands. The barman had seen many customers with the shakes, caused by withdrawal of alcohol and perversely from drinking too much. He'd learned all about the DTs on his recent course, and this man had the delirium tremens badly. But he wasn't here to judge, just to serve. He took the empty glass, turned around, and filled it to the required double measure, turned back, and rattled off the price.

Gregor peeled off a ten-pound note from a small wad of money in his trouser pocket and tried to place it in the barman's hand. It fluttered from his grasp as he lost his grip during another tremor of his hands. It fell on one of the drip trays. He then put the other notes in his pocket, reached for his pint, and drained it dry. He looked up at the clock, 'Another one with the change.'

The barman merely nodded in acknowledgement, took up the damp note and larger empty glass, and got busy whilst his customer drained the whisky in two swift gulps.

Monica walked through the church hall outer door and was pleased to see Oliver; he was opening the oblong cardboard strip off a fresh box of tissues. She watched as he thoughtfully pulled out a tissue so that it stuck halfway, ready to be plucked by a tearful group member. 'Let's hope we don't need them.'

Oliver nodded, 'Is it selfish to wish that it were only us regulars who came each month?'

She shook her head, 'If only we could pick up our newspapers and not read about someone found dead in no suspicious circumstances. You just know that someone may have taken their own life. Did you hear about the suicide who jumped in the harbour with weights in her pocket?'

Oliver nodded solemnly, 'Poor soul.'

Monica nodded, 'I wish people could be helped. How's your month been?'

'Just the same, how about you?'

'The same too. My friend is head-over-heels in love with a man and his car.'

'Who, Robyn?'

'That's right, he's a lovely chap. Graham. We've all had dinner and drinks together a few times. But I felt a gooseberry.'

'Robyn won't mind, from what you've told me about her, she seems a great friend. Is it a sports car he has?'

Monica laughed, 'An ancient Morris Minor!'

Oliver looked puzzled, 'Okay,' he drawled as a mental image formed, 'I can't see the attraction myself. Does he like Judy and, more importantly, does she like him?'

'It's like they were made for each other. His grandmother had a Yorkie too, so he's always making a fuss of her. I miss her when they all go off together.'

'Do you never feel like meeting someone new, you know, romantically?'

Monica looked straight at him as she contemplated his question, 'Maybe, one day, how do you feel about meeting someone new?'

He was saved from answering when the outer door opened, and a young woman and man walked in. The man led, with the woman almost walking right behind him. She was clasping his hand. The man gave a nervous cough and then asked, 'Is this the right place for the support group?' He looked to Monica, 'Are you Nancy?'

'No, but she'll be along in a minute. Come away in from the doorway, I'm Monica and this is Oliver.

Both men nodded as a greeting, Bella looked down at the floor. 'I'm Irvine and this is my fiancée Bella.'

A pitiful greeting, barely audible, even in the lobby's silence, was given as she then took a step forward with Irvine, all the while gripping his hand. She then looked down at the floor again. Another person walking through the door saved her discomfort.

'Hello everybody,' smiled Isobel, until she saw the young couple. She stopped herself in time as she was about to extol her news about her great-granddaughter. She made a mental note to save that conversation until the teas and biscuits heralded a subtle change in the group, when they'd pair off into groups and talk about their personal lives. She turned to the couple, 'I'm Isobel.'

'Hello Isobel, I'm Irvine and we're here for Bella, my fiancée.'

She nodded to each in turn, 'Hello Irvine, hello Bella. I lost my son and my daughter-in-law to suicide. Shall we go through to the meeting room? It'll be warmer. I'll get you settled.' She pointed and then led the way.

Oliver watched them go, forgetting about their earlier conversation thread. Once they were through to the main meeting room he turned back to Monica, 'As it's me here first each month, do you think I should text or phone Nancy on the day of the meeting and ask her if we are to expect new members?'

She nodded her head vigorously, 'It would save any embarrassment and awkwardness, especially for the new members. Then we can say a more welcoming hello. First impressions are so important. Have you heard any more about being deputies?'

'No. You?'

'Nothing. Nancy says she put a reminder to the charity three months ago. You'd think we'd have been put forward for the training course by now.'

Oliver nodded his agreement, 'I'll ask her again tonight.'

'Thanks, so how's Mitch?'

'He's still love-struck. There must be something in the air. She is a lovely lass, though. Harriet has baked us some delicious-looking biscuits again. She still won't take any money from me.'

'I must come and try that café with you sometime?'

Oliver nodded absently, 'The food is cracking. Who knew that vegan food could be so tasty?'

Monica waited for an invitation, but it wasn't forthcoming. 'I could walk over on my day off, one day, and meet you?'

Oliver stifled a yawn, 'Sorry, late night, what did you say?'

A momentary look of sadness crossed Monica's face. She reached up to Oliver's jumper and brushed down his chest. 'You've some crumbs.'

Oliver looked down just as the outer door opened wide and a man staggered in, 'Is this the meeting, for suicide survivors?' he slurred.

Monica instinctively took a step back; she could smell alcohol on the man's breath. It smelt worse than a brewery.

'Welcome, I'm Oliver and this is Monica.'

'I'm Gregor, the lady said to come. My son took his life, it was my fault.'

Monica stepped closer to Gregor, now understanding why he'd needed a bit of Dutch courage in getting here. 'I'm sorry to hear that Gregor, but you mustn't blame yourself. You've done the right thing, coming here. We meet through there,' she pointed to the double doorway. 'But perhaps I can make you a coffee first? With a biscuit or two?'

'No, I've drunk enough today.'

Monica agreed, though she knew it hadn't been the most appropriate liquid. He must have been at the bar for several hours after his work. She was startled to hear his next words, as if he had read her mind.

'When I finish work, I'm a plumber, I go straight to the pub, I had a few before coming, sorry.'

'There's no need to apologise Gregor, you are amongst friends here. We all cope in our own ways, but alcohol isn't always the answer. Mind you, I need a glass or two myself, most nights.' She led him to the kitchen as she talked.

'He told me he was going to do it, you see.'

'Oh.'

'He had mental health problems. He had been diagnosed with a personality disorder years ago. He was always threatening to take his

125

life. For years he'd say it. But I was so tired that night and left him to go to bed.'

Oliver's head snapped in Gregor's direction as he said this, a look of consternation on his face. He couldn't follow the thread of their talking as they entered the kitchen. Then his attention was directed to the outer door opening and Corrina and Adam entering. 'Hello, it's great to see you both return. How has your month been?'

'Hello Oliver,' replied Corrina as Adam helped her out of her thick coat. 'It's all been a bit of a blur, really. Our doctor has diagnosed us as having clinical depression and the tablets she has us on make us dopey.'

Oliver nodded, 'There is nothing wrong with getting help from your doctor. It's a catastrophic loss you've suffered. I'm pleased to hear that you have a sensible GP.'

'That and knowing what happened to our lad,' agreed Adam as he hung the jackets up.

Oliver waited for the conversation to flow; the couple hadn't revealed in the last meeting why their son had taken his own life.

They walked over to the meeting room, 'We're through here again?' pointed Corrina.

'That's right, I'll just be here if you want me, I like to greet any newcomers and make them welcome. I've had the heating on for a while, so it should be cosy.' He watched them disappear through the double doorway.

Monica deftly picked up a mug and spooned coffee into it and hoped that Oliver had switched the thermostat on the water heater early enough. 'But you weren't to know, not if he said it before and didn't do it.' She hoped she was saying this soothingly enough.

'But it only took this once for him to succeed, and now my boy isn't here, and it's my fault.' He sat down on the seat by the small table, head in his hands, crying.

Monica made the coffee, allowing him to have a cry, being wary of offering immediate comfort because of his alcohol intake. She decided he needed an arm around him and put the coffee and a plate with two biscuits down on the table and put an arm on his shoulder. 'There, there, you let it all out.'

He sobbed for a few more minutes, then sat straight, wiped his tears with the hem of his sweater's sleeve and patted Monica's hand. 'Thank you, Monica. Sorry, I'm drunk.'

She nodded.

'I'll drink this and eat these; they'll sober me up.'

She nodded some more. 'Don't you worry. We've all come here in a state. You should have seen me when my Josephine took her life, I was a nervous wreck for a good year. My good friend picked me off the ground so many times or laid down with me and held me whilst I cried for hours. But don't drink as much, or not at all, before the next meeting?'

He nodded meekly, reached for the coffee, and started sipping, despite it being hot. He then took a biscuit, munched, and looked up in delight, 'Nice biscuits!'

'Let me tell you about the kindness of others when they know you've lost a child.' She kept him listening whilst he sobered up.

'Will you come in tonight, Roland? They'd love to see you and learn all about you.' Nancy looked across the car eagerly to her son.

He shook his head, 'The timings aren't quite aligned. Perhaps next month mum. Though I think the Edinburgh branch meeting went well, I'll come with you to those. I made some new contacts there and I feel the group valued my input.'

'Okay, son,' she sighed. 'You know best.' She leant in and kissed him on the cheek.

'I'll come and wait at the usual time, but don't rush, you take as long as the others need you for.'

'Thank you, Roland. We've at least three new members. It's so sad, isn't it?'

'Yes, but they have your expertise to help and guide them. From what you've said about Oliver, Monica, Isobel, and the others, you've helped them immensely. All those hours on the phone and all the meetings you attend up and down the country. You deserve a medal. No! An honour from the Queen herself!'

Nancy sat up straight in her chair, her shoulders back and chest proud at the thought, 'Imagine that!'

'Off you go mum, or you'll be late.'

'See you later.' She left the car and walked up to the hall, all the while thinking about being knighted by her Monarch.

But these happy thoughts soon dissipated as she entered the lobby and only saw Oliver. The group always met in here first. 'Only us two?'

'No, there is Gregor in the kitchen with Monica. He's had a few drinks.'

She shook her head in disapproval.

'We couldn't turn him away. He's lost a son.'

She nodded slowly, 'I've had a few phone calls with him. I'm glad that I convinced him to come. I didn't know he had a drink problem.'

'Monica will have made him a coffee and given him some biscuits. There is a young couple, Bella, and Irvine, in the hall with Isobel. She took them through to get them settled. Then they were joined by Adam and Corrina, from last month.'

'That's about us then; unless any of the others who have been before turn up.' She was thinking of the ones who come for one meeting and didn't return. She always hoped that these lost souls would return to her flock. 'Shall we go through too?' She didn't wait for a reply as she was eager to meet Bella. She walked straight through and introduced herself to the young couple sat by Isobel.

'I'll just refill your coffee, and then we'll go through to the meeting Gregor, if you feel up to it?'

He nodded meekly, 'I have had no dinner, so I've been drinking on an empty stomach.'

129

'That's never a good idea,' she replied softly. 'You make sure and have a few more biscuits in the break, they'll only go to waste if you don't. If you are anything like me, the coffee will go straight through you.' She pointed past the kitchen door. 'The bathroom is to the right. If I see you get up and go, I'll let the others know you are okay and just taking a comfort break. It'll save Oliver following you out; in case he thinks we upset you. Now, only talk in the group if you feel comfortable.'

'I'm really sorry about this, what must you think of me.'

She patted him on his shoulder as she walked over to the water urn, 'I think you're incredibly brave coming here and I hope you'll come back. No one will judge you, we all come with baggage.' She thought about her own secret, one she hoped to share one day. She quickly made another coffee and noted his shaking hands. 'I'll carry this through, you just follow me.'

He obediently went through to the meeting hall with his new friend.

'You were miles away?' suggested Graham as he reached for his stereo remote control. He turned down the music, 'Penny for them?'

Robyn broke from her reverie, 'It's Monica's group tonight. I just worry about her and what it's doing to her emotionally.'

'Let's hope that there aren't many over-wrought families. I can't imagine how she finds the strength to get out of bed each day and put one foot in front of the other. And then help others. She's a remarkable lady.'

'Yes. We are both lucky to have her as a friend.'

He sidled up closer, taking a second to remove an indignant Judy from her comfy blanket in the middle of the sofa. He placed her on his lap, gave Robyn a one arm embrace, whilst pacifying Judy with several strokes. He was inwardly proud of his multitasking.

Monica placed the coffee mug on the table nearest to where Gregor sat. 'Sorry we are late folks, this is Gregor.'

There was a collective, 'Hello Gregor,' as Monica sat between him and Bella.

She turned to the new couple. 'I'm Monica.'

Bella gave an almost imperceptible nod of her head whilst Irvine introduced them to Monica.

Nancy looked on in disapproval, 'Shall we start then?'

She waited for the group to settle down and fix their eyes on her.

'My name is Nancy,' she offered, looking to Gregor, Bella, and Irvine. 'Welcome to the group. Please be assured that whatever you say here is confidential and that you can speak about anything. I lost my daughter to suicide, six years ago. I have a son, Roland, who I hope will come to the group one day.'

There were nods of approval from Monica and Oliver, though a shadow of doubt spread across Isobel's frown as it creased in thought.

Nancy continued, 'Shall we go around the group and introduce ourselves?' She nodded to Oliver.

Oliver told the group about himself and then looked across to Isobel. She did the same and looked at Adam and Corrina. Adam spoke this time of his love for his son, other children, and his wife, and then looked to Monica. She too told the new group members about Josephine and her ex-husband and then finished with, 'Only speak if you feel up to it,' and looked to Gregor and then Bella with a kind smile.

Gregor, still full of Dutch courage from the bar, replied, 'I'd like to speak, I've no one else, we lost contact with my son's mother years ago. She broke off all contact with him, I think that was a lot of his problems. He developed a personality disorder and when he stopped taking his pills, against medical advice, he had what they called intrusive thoughts that they thought he'd act out on. Only he never did until that one time when I was too tired to care.' He broke off and took a few breaths, not wanting to cry in public.

'You are doing so well, Gregor,' encouraged Monica. 'What was your son's name? We like to say our lost one's names, it helps with keeping their memory alive.'

Gregor looked across to Nancy. He hadn't recalled her giving her daughter's name. All the others had named their child and wife. 'Martin,' he managed to say.

'It's a tiring job, looking after someone who is suicidal twenty-four-hours a day, without a break,' voiced Oliver in a low voice. 'You mustn't blame yourself.'

'But I do. That's why I drink, to blot out the memory of our last night together and him storming off. He had such an anger issue.'

Nancy tutted as he said this and muttered something incoherent under her breath, then offered her opinion, 'It's not right. You shouldn't be drinking. You won't find the answer at the bottom of a glass. It won't do you any good at all.'

Adam, Corrina, Monica, Oliver, and Isobel collectively looked shocked as Nancy was saying this, all not quite believing her chastising manner to this fragile father. Monica recovered first and spoke over Nancy, 'Would you like to keep talking Gregor?'

He looked to Nancy with anger apparent in his eyes. He shook his head.

Monica looked to Nancy, challenge in her eyes, and then turned quickly to Gregor, 'That's okay Gregor, thanks for sharing with us.' She handed him his coffee, hoping that his shaking hands, which looked worse, wouldn't cause him to scald himself. She turned to Bella and Irvine, 'Welcome to you both. Would you like to talk about who you lost?'

Bella pulled her sweater sleeves down, causing her fingers and thumbs to delve within the fraying fabric. She forced her knees to her chest again and almost toppled her chair over. Fortunately, Irvine could see it tilt back from the corner of his eyes and wrapped his arm around her in a protective embrace. She leaned into him, looked down at the floor and whispered, 'My brother Paul was killed in a road traffic accident, we found out later that it was a drunk driver, the one who worked in the undertaker who cared for him, though we didn't know this at the time.' She paused for breath, keeping her gaze to the carpet, so missed the puzzled look from Monica.

'Oh, that's awful love, but I think you've come to the wrong support group,' offered Monica as delicately as she could.

Bella looked up, 'Sorry, you were in the other room when I spoke to the others, you see my parents disappeared the next day. I left them, after an argument, at the undertakers. I haven't seen them since. I look and look, but they never come home. The police think they'll never come home, they think that they've driven their car somewhere and ended their lives. Police divers have checked the local harbours and below cliffs. There have been no sightings of them, nor of their car. The undertakers, not that we trust them now, they've no log of them coming in and when the police asked to check their CCTV, it had been broken and wasn't recording that day. It's like they've vanished off the face of the earth. But I just know they won't have left me on my own, they just wouldn't.'

Irvine pulled her closer to him to show that she wasn't on her own. He was about to say something when a short, stout, elderly man of about sixty burst into the room shouting.

'I found her, I found my girl, oh what a state she was in.' He sat down in the spare seat next to Nancy, 'What am I supposed to do without my daughter. There was so much blood, I can see it now. Every time I close my eyes, that's all I see.'

Bella leapt to her feet and backed away from the broken man. A look of shock was on her face. Irvine followed her and gently took her hand.

Oliver was on his feet too. He walked over to the stranger and placed both hands on his shoulders and crouched next to him, waiting for him to make eye contact. He'd never seen such a visceral look of grief before, 'Take a few breaths mate, you are nice and safe now. That's it, in and out slowly. What's your name?'

Nancy tutted her disapproval and then interrupted with, 'You must be Barry. You said you'd come last month but didn't. You've not been answering your phone.'

Adam and Corrina looked aghast again at Nancy. It was almost like she'd taken her filter off this evening. Corrina remembered how she felt last month when this woman interrupted her and talked over her, in rather a patronising way.

Oliver stood up, glanced to her in disgust, then turned back to the distressed man, 'Come with me, we'll go into the other room and you can tell me about your daughter.' He kept one hand on his shoulder, to ensure he stood up. Once the stranger was on his feet and following him, he began talking in a soft, low voice, 'My name is Oliver. You are amongst friends now, but I think you frightened young Bella, it's her first meeting as well. I lost my wife and several children. I'll tell you some more in the other room, and then you can tell me your name and all about your girl. I'm sorry that you lost her.'

Monica looked on approvingly as she watched Oliver tactfully and delicately remove Barry for the benefit of Bella. She turned to offer her support to the young couple and was relieved to see Isobel consoling the young girl. She turned to Gregor, ignoring Nancy, 'Please come back into the kitchen with me Gregor. It seems a right time to make everyone a coffee or tea. You can have another biscuit or two whilst I fill the pots. Normally Oliver does this, but I know he won't mind me doing it this month.'

Gregor nodded, picked up his mug, drained it in one gulp, and strode past Nancy and followed his new best friend. Adam and Corrina trailed them to the lobby, not wanting to be alone with Nancy.

Nancy watched them go, giving another tut or two as they passed her. More mutterings followed as she looked from them and then to the trio on the other side of the room, far from the circle of empty chairs. She had never had such a disruptive meeting. She was now shaking her head in disbelief.

Barry looked around him, seeing the rows of hooks, empty, save for one solitary jacket hanging up. He was only now taking in his surroundings. He hadn't realised that he was in the church's cloakroom. It had that old clothing smell, like in a charity shop. He'd spent the last five minutes doing a breathing exercise, mimicking the man sat across from him. Two solitary chairs were all the furniture in this room. They had been set up by Oliver to foresee such a need. He'd followed his softly spoken instructions. 'I feel much calmer, thank you. I'm so sorry about that.'

Oliver shook his head, 'There is no need at all to apologise. You truly are amongst friends here. I'll take you through in a minute and introduce you to the others. You look much calmer. It's a simple breathing exercise taught to me by a mindfulness expert. You can also visualise a favourite place when doing it, or birdsong, or a peaceful stream. If ever you get a chance to do a relaxation course, I'd highly recommend it. You'll learn some self-hypnosis techniques. Some people find apps on their mobiles help. I'm sorry about this room, we aren't allowed to use the other rooms, just the main hall. Is your name Barry and what was your daughter's name?' he gently probed.

'Yes, I'm Barry, I just couldn't face answering the phone. I know it must have annoyed Nancy. My daughter's name is, sorry, was, Kimberley, we called her Kim. I don't know how I'm supposed to go on, I don't know how I've made it this far, without my daughter. She's all I had. My wife and I divorced years ago. Children aren't supposed to die before an old man like me.' He leant forward, cupped his head, and cried.

'You'll find a way,' replied Oliver reflectively, thinking of his life without Emma. He waited for Barry to compose himself. 'It's an adage, but taking one day at a time is true. You will build a new life, a new normal, which isn't normal, if you see what I mean. It'll be a struggle, perhaps for months, even years, but you can go on. Please keep coming here, and before you go home, I'd like you to take the leaflets and cards from the table in the hall. They have other bereavement charities and phone helplines who will help you through the tough times. Do you feel ready to go back through?'

Barry nodded, still close to tears, not trusting his voice.

Oliver looked at him in doubt, 'We'll give it a few minutes.'

Monica slid open the kitchen hatch, revealing the main hall. She could see Nancy sat, arms folded, watching the trio in the corner. None had returned to the circle of chairs. She couldn't see Adam and

Corrina. She patted the wooden shelf, 'If you could please put the tray here Gregor, we'll get it from the main meeting place.'

Gregor silently carried the tray of drinks and biscuits. He had felt better for having another one of those biscuits and a fresh cup of coffee. He looked in disgust at Nancy, through the gap, 'I'm just going to the bathroom.'

'I'll meet you in the hall then?'

Gregor didn't reply as he walked to the doorway.

'Wait for me,' pleaded Corrina as she tried to match pace with her husband. He'd walked straight out of the building and was making his way home.

He stopped, turned back, and waited for her to come alongside him, 'Sorry. But that woman, she's so rude. I think I may have said something I'd have regretted. You know what my temper can be like, especially now. We need to be surrounded by caring people. She interrupted and talked over you last time, and now the way she reacted to that poor man. You saw how distressed he was.'

'I know, but the others seem nice and caring. Look at what they did, they took everyone who was upset out of a stressful situation and I bet that Oliver, Monica and Isobel are consoling them.'

'But what about us?'

'We have each other,' she simply stated.

He reached for her hand, acknowledging her reasoning. She always knew how to end an argument or disagreement. She always made him see sense.

'Let's go back,' she pleaded.

'Give me one good reason?'

She shivered, 'I've left my jacket.'

Monica loitered outside the gentleman's toilet, listening intently. She was relieved to see Oliver come out of the adjacent doorway, alongside Barry. 'I think Gregor is in there, could you please check that he is okay, Oliver?'

'Sure.' He nodded to Barry, 'This is Barry.' He left the couple and entered the bathroom.

'I'm Monica. I lost my daughter, Josephine, to suicide. I found her in a similar way.'

'It's awful, there's no other word, is there?'

'No, Barry, I'm afraid not. But I hope that we'll get to know each other better in the coming months?'

'Yes. Oliver has been so kind. He's taught me a breathing exercise to do when my mind spirals out of control.'

'That's good. He's a thoughtful man who has been through much too.'

The door opened and only Oliver stepped out. 'The cubicles are all empty, he's not in there.'

Monica looked startled, 'Oh!'

Adam shrugged off his jacket, he'd kept his on in the hall, and hadn't realised how cold this October night was until he saw the small puffs of air coming from his wife's mouth each time she had spoken.

He wrapped it around his wife, 'We'll give it another try, for each other's sake, and for our other children. But don't expect me to talk to that woman, not until I've calmed down. He put his arm around her, and they walked back to the church hall. He wasn't surprised when he saw the door open and Gregor go storming off towards the bar on the corner by the looks of it. Adam followed his progress from afar as he walked back to the hall with Corrina.

Isobel was pleased to see the fear in Bella's eyes reduce as she talked to her and Irvine calmly, telling them more about the group and how they would find it helpful. 'I'm afraid that sometimes we get other parents, siblings or children who come and over-share. They don't mean to say anything disturbing, it's just that, as you know, emotions are all over the place and sometimes people don't have another outlet. They see here as a haven. I hope you'll stay and talk more. We are good listeners.'

Bella looked at Irvine; uncertainty was in her eyes.

Recognising the look, he offered, 'I think you should. You've made significant progress. I know how much stress you were under, coming here. But it's great that you've recognised that your parents have taken their own lives. I don't know if we'll ever find them. You know that my dad and I have scoured the coast, but you can't sit at the lounge window all day. It was good to see you leave it the other day and go to see Dotty in her house.'

Bella bit her lip, 'They aren't coming back, are they?'

'No, darling, no, they are not.' He gently continued with a firm, 'You have to face up to that, I'm afraid.'

Bella nodded, in slow, steady movements, as if hearing and accepting the truth.

'And you have our support,' said Isobel, feeling like she was disturbing an intimate moment of realisation.

'Thank you, Isobel,' sighed Bella, bowing to the inevitability of it all. 'I miss my brother, mum and dad.'

'I wish I could take your pain away,' murmured Irvine helplessly.

Isobel placed her hand on his shoulder, 'Come back to the circle. When you are ready. You are both doing so well. Oliver will have ensured that Barry is calmer.'

Irvine nodded, then cuddled Bella tight as Isobel walked over to the ring of almost empty seats. She sat down at the one opposite Nancy, face defiant.

Monica opened the church hall outer door, just as Adam and Corrina returned. She took a step outside and looked down both sides of the street.

Adam, seeing her, mistook her actions to be seeking them, 'Sorry, we needed some fresh air.' He spied Barry through the door and lowered his voice, 'It got rather heated. Is he okay?'

'Yes, but we are missing Gregor.'

'I'm afraid that we saw him leave as we were walking back. We saw him go into the pub. Shall I get him?'

Monica shook her head, 'I think he's best left alone. I know we should help him, but drunk people can be so unpredictable, and I think the charity would rather not have had him in the building. I know other charities have a strict no drug and no drinking policy. I can see why. Come away in.'

Corrina took hold of the door, barring Adam from entering. She waited for Monica to turn back from looking forlornly at the pub building. 'Is she always like this? She seemed a lovely lady on the phone. Nancy, I mean?'

'She's the group co-ordinator and has to run it, though Oliver and I have asked to be deputies so that we can take turn chairing meetings and answering the local helpline phone. Bear with her, you'll find the group usually supportive.'

Corrina looked dubious, frown lines creased her forehead, as if disagreeing. She looked to Adam, 'Let's get in out of the cold.'

Monica followed them through the doorway, 'I'll bring the drinks to you, I left them on the hatch shelf.'

Oliver too followed them, first ensuring that Barry was making his way to the meeting room. He seemed more settled. He'd make sure he had one of Harriet's special biscuits.

The meeting progressed, with the small groups coming back together for the sharing of drinks and biscuits, then went back into their cliques, with Monica staying with Barry and Oliver. Nancy went largely ignored, except when she announced she had to leave on time.

'Roland is waiting for me. I mustn't keep him. I hope he'll come along next month and talk about his sister. See you all next month.'

Adam and Corrina looked down at their feet whilst Barry looked away. Bella and Irvine gave a casual flick of their heads in reticence.

'I'll lock up,' volunteered Oliver and turned back to Monica, hoping to catch her and offer her a lift.

'I'll be going too,' answered Isobel. 'I want to have an early night, I've baby Lindsay to look after tomorrow. Do you want to walk home together, Monica?'

'Yes, that would be lovely, we can have a catch up on the way.' She ignored Nancy and hadn't even noticed her walk away. She turned to Bella, Irvine, and Barry, wishing them as good a month as they could have and expressing her wish to see them next month. 'Bye Oliver.'

Oliver wished he could chat with her on her own, but he sensed Barry needed him, and he also needed to get Bella's e-mail address before she disappeared. 'Bye Monica, I'll be fine and early in opening up next month.' He hoped she understood his meaning and then returned to chatting to Barry with some reluctance as Isobel and Monica also left the meeting.

Adam and Corrina waved the two women away and then caught the eye of the others and gave them a brief wave, then made their way to the cloakroom for Corrina's jacket. They then discretely left for home, ignoring the stares of a young man sat in a car with Nancy. Neither couple waved to the other.

Bella and Irvine had sat patiently in the meeting room whilst Oliver and Barry were deep in conversation. After a few minutes they sidled up to Oliver, not wanting to interrupt the chatting men. During a pause in their conversation, Irvine interjected patiently with, 'We'll be off. Thank you for the drinks and biscuits, Oliver. It was nice to see you, Barry.'

Oliver stood up and took out his mobile phone, 'May I please take your e-mail address, Bella? I like to send a reminder of the date and time of the next meeting.'

Bella nodded meekly, not quite trusting being near Barry. She gave Oliver her e-mail, not taking her eyes off Barry.

'I'm sorry, Bella,' murmured Barry in a deliberately low voice, not wanting to scare the young lady again. 'You are about the same age as my Kim.' He began weeping again.

Bella surprised Irvine by taking several quick steps towards Barry and then wrapping her arms around him. Apart from his parents and himself, she'd not allowed anyone to embrace her since her parents disappeared. Irvine couldn't help a momentary smile, and then remembering where he was, he replaced it with a solemn look. 'Would you like my e-mail too, Oliver?'

'That would be great, it's your loss as well. They were part of your family. You are a welcome part of our group.'

Irvine nodded, 'Paul was to be my best man. We put the wedding on hold, hoping that Bella's parents would return. They were lovely people; you couldn't have met a nicer couple.' He watched on proudly as Bella comforted the old man. He spelt out his e-mail address.

Oliver tapped away on his phone and as he slipped it back into his pocket, he glanced around for Monica and his shoulders seemed to sag as he saw she was long gone. He'd hoped that she'd have accepted his lift home. She had a long walk home after seeing Isobel to her door. He always expected to see her return to the hall, changing her mind and walking back from Isobel's house. He nodded to Bella and in a barely audible voice, not wanting to interrupt the flow of comforting words she spoke, 'Her parents would be proud of her Irvine.'

'Yes, they would.'

Cherie, Andrew, and Shaun

Andrew looked to his mother, Cherie, with deep worry etched on his face. She hadn't eaten for eight days, had barely drunk. Just a few sips of soup and tea. She'd lost weight, a startling amount, since his sister, Fiona, had taken her life at Dundee University five weeks ago. The police had released her property last week, and that's when Cherie had found Fiona's course notebooks and sketch pads. His mother had immediately stopped eating and talking, like a switch had gone off in her brain.

Fiona had been studying graphic art and was hoping to become a full-time comic book artist. The family had thought that she'd embraced the student life and was happily on an exciting career path. She'd already had one comic strip published, and the editor wanted her to contribute another in the series. The family were proud, especially her father, Shaun, who'd continued his love of comics into adult life. He doted on his children and had bought them all sorts of magazines and graphic novels over the years.

The family had opened the first of the boxes, carefully packed by the University and police. Cherie had taken out a hoodie and t-shirt, held them close to her chest, as if cuddling her dead child. She breathed in the longed-for smell of her daughter, and took to wearing the clothes, insisting that they weren't to be washed. And then they opened the notebooks and sketch pads.

They expected to see more wizards and dragons, a continuation of the story arc, instead they found intricately drawn self-portraits of their daughter in a range of poses and deadly postures. Cherie only saw those in which her daughter was hanging, laid in bed with empty bottles of vodka and packets of pills and of being run over by an articulated lorry. Shaun had snatched the sketch pad from her and went into another room to flick through the other pages. His wailing pierced the household.

A numbed Cherie then unpacked her daughter's University lecture notes. She skimmed through the early lecture transcripts and then found the last six pages. She had started to rock as she read them; and hadn't stopped her nervous swaying since. She'd read, and re-read, that a group of drunk students had raped her beloved daughter during freshers' week. Her drink had been spiked, and she'd been taken back to the student accommodation, to her room, and had woken up to being violently penetrated whilst others looked on, cheering, and yelling. The remaining pages expressed her disgust with herself, how she couldn't bear to tell her family, and how she didn't want to tell the police.

Consequent meetings between Shaun and the police and University staff revealed they hadn't known; that there had been no suicide notes and that neither party had been aware of the contents of the notebook.

Andrew, aged eighteen, and due to start University next year, to study journalism, had phoned in long-term sick from his temporary job in the take-away. Since then, he'd become the reluctant carer for his mum. Dad just couldn't get away from his job in the energy sector and was currently overseas. He had the maximum two weeks off, even though Fiona was nineteen, and he wasn't strictly entitled to the time off. His employer thought this was understanding enough. Shaun had reluctantly gone back to work as they needed the money to pay their hefty mortgage.

Cherie was rocking again, not as fast as usual, more slow, rhythmic back-and-forth motions. She was sat at the kitchen dining table; Fiona's books were spread out in front of her. She was clutching her daughter's favourite pyjama top. She fretted at the cloth, transferring it from hand to hand, taking the occasional deep inhalation whilst holding it to her nose. She hummed a nursery rhyme that Andrew recognised from a long-forgotten childhood. She'd sing it to him and his sister whenever they grazed a knee and needed comforting. Now it seemed like she was humming it to pacify herself. Only it wasn't working.

Andrew didn't want to phone his dad and disturb him whilst he was in Norway. He had enough on his plate. He'd been fighting to get some sort of justice for his girl. The police investigation seemed to get nowhere.

He toyed with the leaflet, given to him on another visit to the doctor with his mother. This time was to get a short course of sleeping pills to top up the diazepam he'd given to her for her nerves. Andrew hadn't slept well since his father left for his business trip. He now knew what sort of pressure Shaun had been under. He mustn't have slept either, having to keep his wife safe from harm. She'd also threatened suicide as the grief of losing her daughter in such a way preyed on her mind day and night. Andrew had locked away any pills and sharp objects on the advice of the GP.

He decided, crossed to the kitchen door, and quietly pushed it back, enough so that his mum wouldn't hear him and get distressed, but with sufficient space to see her. She was still rocking in a world of her own. A world of pain. He rang the number.

'Hello,' came a terse voice.

'Sorry to bother you, my doctor gave me your number. Is this the support group?'

The voice softened, 'Yes, it is, sorry, I'm in the garden, there are so many dropped leaves, I've been putting off this job, I've been so busy up and down the country. You know how it is.'

Andrew replied, 'Yes,' but hadn't a clue, he'd never helped in the garden.

'I'll go indoors now. I'll talk and walk. Who have you lost?'

'My sister, Fiona.'

'Bless you dear, my son Roland lost his sister too. He'll be coming along to the meetings soon. You'll like him. He has a special way about him. Your mum and dad must miss their daughter terribly.'

'Yes, that's why I'm ringing, mum isn't coping too well, can I please bring her to your meetings?'

'Of course, dear, my Roland and I can soon help you both. Bring your father too.'

'It'll just be me and mum to begin with. Dad has to work overseas.'

'That must be hard. I find employers are either supportive, or just don't seem to care that a loved one has passed over. Your mum is so lucky to have you looking after her.'

'I've given up work. It was only a stopgap until I go to Uni. Though after what happened to my sister, I don't think I will.'

'Oh, but you must,' insisted Nancy, 'My Roland thought he couldn't pursue his new career after losing his sister, but now he does it in memory of her, to keep her in his thoughts.'

'I hadn't really seen it that way,' he looked back to his mum, not convinced.

'We meet on the first Thursday of the month, so that's this week, can your mum manage that?'

'I'll make sure we can.'

'That's good, I am pleased.' She gave Andrew directions to the church hall.

'We can get the bus there. I'll check when the last bus home is, so we might have to leave early. I'm afraid that I don't drive, and mum is in no fit state to be getting behind the wheel.'

'That sounds sensible. How is she?'

'She isn't eating now, she's getting so thin, and she's not sleeping. The doctor gave her a week's supply of sleeping pills. I had to argue with him for them. Mum is a nurse. So he gave her a lecture about addiction and how she should know this. But her mind is not thinking straight. Not after reading the notebook, that's all she does now, reads each page over and over.'

'Notebook?' probed Nancy carefully.

Andrew looked at his mother. The rocking had grown and was now at a furious pace, she'd flicked through to the last page with Fiona's handwriting. 'I'd better go Nancy, see you in a few days.'

Nancy was about to wish him well, but the phone went dead. She returned to her garden, making sure that she had her phone in her pocket. There were so many to help, and so few hours in the day.

'They never see each other outside of the group, never go out for drinks or meals?' questioned Graham as he walked arm in arm with Robyn. Judy was trotting by his side; she'd gone to her daddy today when Robyn had shouted walkies.

They were walking along the beach promenade, back from the golden sands. Both were wrapped up in puffer style jackets, jade coloured for her and boring black for him, their fleece lined hats were of the same style and navy colour. Their jeans almost matched - a dark shade of denim. 'No, never. I guess it's not what you celebrate with an office style party.' She thought about her staff Christmas party next month. She couldn't wait to share Graham with her other pals.

'I guess not,' he clucked his tongue to Judy. She was sniffing at a deposit left on the pavement by a thoughtless dog owner. 'Good girl!' he encouraged as she left it and came back to heel. 'Though wouldn't they form a friendship? She's been going there for a few years now.'

'She speaks about them to me, but she doesn't seem to want to get too close to them, not to anyone really. She's not a hugely sociable person since losing Josephine and then her husband to suicide. She doesn't have anyone to her cottage, just me.'

'And me! I've loved our nights together. She's a lovely person. I wish she could see that. She needs to let people in and become more trusting. Has there been no one else since her husband?'

'No, they split up a few months after Josephine died, then formally divorced. She couldn't make the marriage work.'

'That's so sad. I'd love to see her happy. I've only known her for a few months, but I can see what an extraordinary person she is. She's so strong, going on after losing Josephine. I find it strange that she doesn't have photos of her daughter around her home. Just that one lying face down.'

Robyn thought back to Graham's second visit to Monica's cottage and how she had to hiss harshly for him not to pick it up when he was absently looking amongst the alcove whilst Monica fetched snacks. 'The others are in a box in the spare room. I took that one out. It was in such a delightful frame, and Josephine looked so beautiful. Monica finds it too painful to see who she is missing. She turned the frame down the day I put it out, and it's stayed down. I can't imagine what goes through her mind now. I hope one day she'll find peace.'

Judy gave a tiny series of barks, almost in agreement, though she was really warding off a nearby crow that was picking at a discarded chip tray. She was making the most of what would be her last walk of the day. She would be under strict curfew on this bonfire night so that fireworks wouldn't startle her. Graham had bought her a state-of-the-art sonic diffuser that let off a relaxing lavender scent and played special noises that only dogs could hear. The manufacturers said it would help nervous and reactive dogs to keep calm.

'Let's get ourselves back in the warmth,' declared Graham, sensing he needed to change the subject.

Robyn leaned up and quickly kissed him, 'I can think of a great way to get warm!'

Oliver stifled another yawn as he went from room to room in the church hall, turning up individual radiators and depositing boxes of tissues and leaflets. He'd come an hour early, hoping that Monica may have heard and remembered his subtle hint from last month's meeting and would soon join him. He wanted to be open with her, to tell her something he'd kept hidden from the group. It had been preying on his mind, almost to the point of distraction. He hoped she would understand and forgive him.

The firework zoomed far into the blackened sky, burst enthusiastically amongst the clouds, and dazzled the spectators with an eruption of green, red, and white lights. A quick succession of similar rockets joined this intrepid missile and lit the skyline like a nocturnal military firefight. An assortment of bangers accompanied them, and some households had lit their Catherine wheels, which were busy gayly whirling around front gardens whilst families cheered, and youngsters waved their lit sparklers that danced and frolicked like caught fairies on a tight rein.

All this was lost on Monica as she walked towards the group. She almost found the sound of joyful children overwhelming and tried hard to block the sounds out. She reached up and pulled her woollen hat further down over her ears to screen out the cheering. She made a mental note to wear earbuds next November and listen to some soothing music. Though the fifth of November only fell on the first Thursday of the month occasionally, and she wondered if she'd still need to go to group in seven years, eight if you took in the leap year. She rarely looked beyond the week these days. All hope for a bright future had vanished the day her daughter took her own life. All her dreams had been wrapped up in her. She hoped that she'd still be friends with Isobel and Oliver; she needed them; they gave her stability. Her thoughts drifted to Adam and Corrina, and then to poor Barry. She prayed they would find some sort of peace, though she didn't consider herself the best role model for that. She hoped to get to know Bella and Irvine better; they seemed a loving couple. She chided herself as she realised that she'd neglected to think of Nancy. Though her inner dialogue was now ruminating on what on earth was Nancy thinking last month? Her words were not at all helpful to Gregor. Monica doubted he'd return. By coincidence, she was passing the bar he'd returned to. She peeked through the pub windows. The building was empty, except for a solitary barman, stood forlornly at the inside of the door she now passed. He was trying to see the fireworks. His customers must all be out enjoying the many displays held around the city. She had watched the throng of cars and pedestrians make their way down to the beach where the Council held their annual display. She'd heard the loudspeakers warbling out the local radio station, and street food smells had tried to entice her stomach as she hurried past earlier.

She reached the street of the church hall and was pleased to see that the lights were on. The group had held their regular meeting because it would have proved difficult to secure the building on another night as it was so booked up in advance with various clubs and organisations. They all agreed that they wouldn't be out celebrating and that fireworks had no appeal to them, not anymore, not now that their days and nights had been darkened by the suicide of a loved one.

Oliver saw her coming as soon as the outside light sprang on, trying to act in competition to the visual light feast up in the air. He opened the door and gave her his warmest, most welcoming smile. 'Hiya Monica, some light show.' He nodded up in the air.

'Yes,' she offered, though her expression looked grim. 'It doesn't have the same appeal as it used to, mind you, Josephine used to enjoy going to the beach display.' Her eyes seemed to come alive and gave off a sparkle at the memory, 'Her face would be sticky from the toffee apples her dad always relented and bought her.' Her eyes dimmed again as she realised her loss once more. 'Do you enjoy them?'

'No. It seems wrong to enjoy such trivial things. Though I can see the attraction. Mitch and Rachel are off to the beach display. You probably passed them without realising. They are walking down. Mitch took his mum and dad last year, in his car. It took him thirty minutes to just get out of the car park. He said he'd never do that again, he's quicker walking.'

'They are young, it won't take them long.' She leaned forward instinctively and brushed the front of his jumper. 'Sorry. I couldn't help but see the crumbs. You really should look in the mirror before you come!' she joked, more to cover her embarrassment at touching him so naturally and without invite.

'I'm glad that you put me right. About that, I wonder if you'd mind-' he hesitated and was almost relieved when a young man poked his head around the doorway.

He was of medium height and build, wearing a grey-woollen type jacket that went down to just above the knees. A bright red scarf was wrapped around his neck several times. 'I've left mum outside. Is this the right place for the support group?'

'Yes, please bring her in, I'm Monica.'

'Oh, hi, Monica, I'm Andrew, I'll just be a minute.' He spun and went back along the pavement. Seconds later he led a smaller built lady with a gaunt, ashen face by the hand. She was taking small, almost controlled steps towards the door.

Monica opened the door, spotted Nancy, and a younger man in the car outside, waved to her, and then snapped her attention back to the young man and his mum. 'Come away in love, it's so cold, isn't it?'

A frown crossed the woman's face, like she was fretful, then she turned to her son, an uneasy expression so apparent. She remained silent.

Her son spoke up, addressing Oliver and Monica, 'Mum won't speak, I hope that's all right?'

'Of course, most of us spoke little for the first meeting or two,' Monica gave a nervous laugh. 'Now you can't shut us up!'

Andrew didn't return the laughter. 'It's not that. Mum hasn't spoken a word, not since, well, not since finding out what happened to my sister.'

Oliver stepped forward, 'That's okay. The shock can do that. You're safe and amongst friends here. I'm Oliver. Would it help if you saw the room where we meet first?'

'Thank you, Oliver. I'm, Andrew, and mum's called Cherie. My dad, Shaun, might come next month, he's had to go away on a business trip. He couldn't get out of it; he needs the job to keep us all going.'

'Come through Cherie and Andrew.' Oliver pointed to the doorways to his left before he started walking, 'That's the bathrooms if you need them.' He walked through to the meeting room, turned back, and was surprised to find himself alone. He walked back to the doorway.

Andrew had one arm supporting his mother's back, and the other was holding her hand. He seemed to support her body weight, mindful that she wouldn't fall over. He looked just like a nurse walking an elderly patient. Cherie was taking one step at a time, slowly making their way through the doorway.

Oliver stepped back, counted out the chairs and mentally thought out which two would be best for them. He didn't want them to be too near Nancy's favourite chair, not after her performance last month. He pointed to the two chairs which faced the doorway. 'I think you'll be comfy in these two, it's less of a draft and nearest to the radiator.'

'Thank you, Oliver,' said Andrew, not relinquishing his grip or attention to his mother. He waited until she was in front of the chair and slowly turned her around, then undid her jacket zipper and helped her out of her coat. 'Sit yourself down, mum.'

She obeyed and looked around the room, then settled her vision on the carpet in-between her feet, and started a slow, but rhythmic rock.

Andrew hooked her jacket over the back of her chair, unwound the scarf from his neck, shrugged off his jacket and placed it on the back of his chair. As he sat, he whispered discretely, 'Mum, I need you to stop that, just while we are here. I don't want you distracting anyone.'

She immediately ceased, then turned ever so slowly to him, cupped his face in her hands and murmured, 'My beautiful boy.'

Andrew first looked dumbfounded and then gave a wry smile at hearing his mum speak for the first time in weeks.

Oliver, feeling intrusive, made his way quietly back to Monica.

'Are you sure that you won't come in Roland, it would be nice for me if you were there. Last month's meeting didn't go very well,' implored Nancy.

'Next month, definitely next month, mum. It feels the right time. Besides, you don't want to spring me on your group, we'll learn from the Edinburgh meeting and maybe you can tell everyone who attends tonight that I'll be there in December.'

'Good. That's settled then. I've something planned for our pre-Christmas meeting. I did it last year in the Newcastle meeting and people seemed to find comfort from it, especially the parents.'

'I remember you telling me about it. Yes, December will be good for me too.' He rubbed his hands in nervous anticipation and to bring some warmth back to them. 'I'll be here waiting as normal, but don't rush back. You were over early last month.'

'Okay. I'm sure this meeting will go much better. That man should not have been drinking before a meeting, it was a disgrace.' She kissed her son on the cheek and exited the car, leaving Roland to think about the special meeting next month.

'What was it you were saying, Oliver? Before Andrew stepped in?' asked Monica as he walked back to her.

He was about to answer when their attention was again distracted by Nancy entering the lobby and then another gust of cold air followed the opening of the door and Isobel stepped through, followed by Adam and Corrina. The group exchanged greetings, though Adam and Corrina were tentative in asking Nancy how she was.

Bella and Irvine were next in, closely followed by Barry, who burst into tears as he closed the door. Bella drew him into a cuddle, much to the approval of Monica who gave them a hesitant smile, 'How have you been Irvine?'

'So, so Monica. Bella doesn't sit by the window so much now, so that's a good sign, and she's eating better. Coming here has been a turning point.'

'That's so good to hear,' she considered Bella's thinness and couldn't help but contrast it to her own sparse figure.

'There should be a mum and son joining us tonight, though he put the phone down on me,' interrupted Nancy indignantly.

Oliver nodded, 'They are already here, I settled them in the hall. About that. As I'm always here first, perhaps I should get to know who's coming. That way I can greet them by name. It would save them feeling awkward.'

Monica joined in this conversation thread with, 'That makes great sense, and has there been any news about our training days to be deputies?'

Nancy made a fuss of taking off her jacket and checking something in her bag. She turned to Bella and Barry, making sure that he had stopped crying, 'Shall we all go through?' She didn't wait for a reply and walked off.

Monica and Oliver looked at each other in puzzlement, Oliver's mouth was agape, as if he were about to say something to the retreating figure.

Monica placed her hand gently on his shoulder, 'We'll ask her over coffees, and maybe you can have time to ask me your question?'

'I'd like that,' he watched as the others followed Nancy. He preferred to go in last, not wanting to take a preferred seat. He wanted the group to be as comfortable as possible, but when he walked through the doorway, it worried him to see Nancy sat next to Cherie. He hoped she wouldn't upset this new member too. His thoughts turned to his e-mail list. It was full of names of people who had come for just one night and never returned. They all had one thing in common, Nancy had upset them. Monica had chosen the seat by Andrew, which pleased Oliver; Andrew needed the support of a steady member.

Nancy watched like a mother hen as her brood settled upon seats, and then she took control of her group by greeting them all with a nod and explaining to Cherie and Andrew how it worked and about confidentially. Then she appeared to brighten up, 'My Roland will come next month.' She looked across to Barry, Bella, and Irvine, reminding them, 'That's my son, he lost his sister.'

'What was your daughter's name? I couldn't catch it last month?' asked Irvine innocently. He remembered someone saying that they liked to call the deceased by their names, to keep their memories alive.

Nancy either didn't hear him, or ignored him, 'That Gregor was so disruptive. We have a strict no drinking policy. It should have been adhered to.' She looked through Cherie and to Andrew, almost accusingly, 'And no drugs.'

Andrew missed her look; he was too busy worrying over his mum and trying to stop her rocking again. He had hold of her delicate hands over her knees.

'Let's introduce ourselves for the benefit of the group. I'm Nancy, I lost my daughter. I was at her grave again today, though my Roland has still not gone, not since the funeral. She's buried in our peaceful village. I find solace there, but my Roland says that her spirit isn't there, so there's no point in going. I'm the group co-ordinator. I run several groups up and down the country. Would you like to speak next Cherie?' She swivelled expectantly in her seat.

Cherie appeared not to have heard Nancy. Her head was bowed low to her chest and a brief silence fell upon the group.

Andrew spoke up instead, 'Mum lost my sister Fiona. She was a student at Dundee University.'

He was about to continue but Nancy interceded with, 'I run a support group there too.'

Andrew didn't see the disapproving looks the other members of the group gave Nancy. Nor did he see Monica's shaking head. He continued with, 'Something bad happened to her.' He stopped talking when he noticed his mum rock again and he leant over and softly whispered platitudes in her ear. Then he continued with, 'Mum can't speak sometimes. She hasn't spoken many words since. Well-' he left the sentence unfinished and looked around the group.

'You are doing so well,' encouraged Oliver. 'It's good that you've come here together. Would you like to go on?'

Andrew nodded and was about to speak up, but Barry blurted out, 'I just can't get the sight out of my head, finding her like that.' He burst out sobbing uncontrollably. Bella rose from her seat and cradled him. It looked almost like a daughter comforting her father to the others, who gave them a minute or two to let the tears flow.

Oliver reached over the table and plucked up a few tissues from the box and stretched over and gave them to Bella. She gathered them in a ball and delicately dabbed at Barry's eyes.

Monica caught the eye of Andrew, 'Only go on if you want, we find it best to let each other have a good cry.'

Corrina nodded in agreement, 'I had a good weep the first time I came here, and I was so grateful to Monica for allowing me to sob on her shoulder.'

Monica broke the ice with, 'And I got ever so wet!'

All gave a little titter, other than Cherie and Andrew. Their solemn expression soon spread around the room.

Bella took the wet tissues from Barry, walked over to the waste bin, and allowed them to drop in. She went back to the group, looked to Barry, was given a nod of thanks and then turned her attention to Andrew, 'We must be the same age Andrew. I'm Bella and this is my fiancé, Irvine. I lost a sibling too, my brother, though that was to a road traffic accident, and then my parents, well, I've thought long and hard since the last meeting, I have to recognise that they took their lives too. But their bodies have never been found. My first meeting was hard. I don't think I spoke a word.' She could see Adam nodding and thought he was agreeing with her, not realising he was bowing his head up and down because he'd never spoken a word on his first meeting. 'I hope you'll keep coming back so we can get to know you better. Your mum is lucky having you to care for her.' Irvine patted her hand in encouragement.

The others in the group introduced themselves and spoke about their lost love, and then a natural silence filled the meeting room. Oliver broke it with, 'You can speak about anything here. Sometimes we talk about all the good things that have happened to us lately, or about how we are feeling, or what's on our minds.'

'I have depression now,' stated Adam. 'We had some tablets from our doctor for the first few weeks, to help us sleep. But now she thinks I'm clinically depressed. Is that normal after a suicide?'

'Well, we've all been there,' sighed Nancy. 'Tablets aren't always the answer.'

Monica gave her a withering look, then looked to Adam kindly, 'It's a new normal, but abnormal to others. I've been on anti-depressants after Josephine took her life. They saved me. My mood got so low. They helped. You keep following your doctor's advice.' She looked sternly at Nancy, then back to Adam, 'Corrina spoke about your doctor last time, and you've a great GP there, so follow what she says to you.'

'I get a better sleep after taking them, otherwise I'm up and down like a yoyo, always wondering what if?'

'They are such intrusive thoughts, but not always helpful,' revealed Oliver. 'It's best to be kind to yourself. Acknowledge the what if's, but always remind yourself that it wasn't your fault,' he broke off and remained thoughtfully silent.

164

'I found going to Cruse Counselling helped,' offered Isobel. 'I had a lovely lady who had taken their advanced grief course. She turned my thinking around. It's another great bereavement charity. You must wait six months to get on the waiting list to see a counsellor, and I saw her after my husband, Roy, died. But we spoke a lot about my son, Aaron, and daughter-in-law, Paula, who I lost to suicide.' She looked to Cherie, trying to catch her eye, 'And of course my friends here helped.' She hoped this newcomer was hearing this.

Nancy looked around, making sure that everyone was listening, 'Before we break for coffee and tea, I'd like to tell you about my pre-Christmas plans. I know that it's a tough time of the year for most. I'm spending it with Roland this year. I've booked the church minister to come along and give a small talk, and I hope no one minds, she'll offer prayers for our loved ones. I know that faith isn't something we all have, but since we rent their hall, I thought it only polite to ask her, rather than have, say, a humanist, for example. Would everyone please bring in a picture of who they have lost. I thought we could put the photos on a table, light a candle and offer a prayer, or stay silent with your own thoughts when the minister prays. How does that sound?'

Oliver was surprised, but admired Nancy for her thoughtfulness. She seemed back on form. 'That sounds lovely. I don't pray or go to church, but I'll bring a photo of Emma.'

There were murmurs of agreement across the group apart from Monica, 'Sorry, I need the bathroom, I had a large coffee before I came out. I'll be back in a minute.' She rose and quickly left the room.

Oliver discretely watched her; it worried him she'd become upset. He rose to his feet, 'I'll get the teas and coffees. Harriet has been experimenting with a new recipe for her biscuits, I've to let her know what you all think of them.' He left the room and got busy in the kitchen, keeping an eye on the doorway.

He was midway pouring boiling water into a coffee pot when he spied the bathroom door open and shouted through, 'Are you all right, Monica?'

She walked towards him, 'Yes, I think it's the cold weather.'

'I thought maybe you got upset?'

'Oh no, nothing like that.'

'That's good. I like to think that we can tell each other anything.'

'I do too. You were about to ask me something earlier.'

Oliver made himself busy with loading the trays, buying himself some thinking time. Resolved, he turned to face her, 'Can I give you a lift home?'

'That's kind, but I know it's out of your way.' She looked at him with a frown on her face, 'Are you all right?'

'It's this time of year, you know?'

'Yes. It's the anniversary coming up, isn't it?'

He slowly nodded his head, 'Emma's family still doesn't speak to me. It makes each anniversary of her suicide hard.'

'And you? How are you feeling about it?'

'I'd like to move on. I'll always love her, but it's lonely, on my own. Especially after work.'

166

'I know what you mean. We lost our spouses at about the same time, didn't we? Robyn waggles her phone at me from time to time, asking if it's time I went on Grinder.' A look of astonishment crossed her face as she saw him burst out laughing.

'We are two dinosaurs. It's called Tinder.'

'Oh. What's Grinder then?'

He explained to her, and then it was her turn to laugh, surprising Isobel as she walked innocently in, about to offer Oliver some help.

Roland had the engine idling over to keep the car heaters going. He didn't want his mum catching cold, otherwise she wouldn't be able to keep up her important work. He watched the church hall doorway open and close and deposit first a solitary lone, plump figure, an elderly man who walked with a slight stoop. He thought that this must be Barry. He recited in his head what he knew about him, from what his mother had told him. Then a middle-aged couple went in the opposite direction, and he guessed correctly that this must be Adam and Corrina. Mum had spoken about them too. Then a much younger couple got in the car in front and soon sped off. He assumed that this was Bella and Irvine. Soon after a young man came out holding a frail-looking woman by the hand, with the other supporting her back. Roland made a mental note to ask his mother about them before he came to the next meeting. He was looking forward to telling everyone about himself.

'Are you sure that I can't tempt you with a lift home,' offered Oliver hopefully.

Monica turned from him to Isobel reluctantly, 'We'll walk home as usual, it gives us a chance to catch up. I'll see you next month, though. I've never seen a photo of Emma; it'll be good to see her.'

'Likewise, with Josephine, see you,' but Monica had already gone, walking through the door with Isobel swiftly behind her. Nancy briskly followed them. The silence of the empty building enveloped him, making him feel desperately lonelier. He looked at his watch. One o'clock seemed an eternity away.

Roland

Baby Lindsay burst from under Isobel's recliner, her favourite hiding place since learning to crawl two weeks ago. Her great-grandmother saw a flash of green and red from her new seasonal romper suit, whizz across her carpet and make for the half-bare artificial Christmas tree. Her giggling slowed her down and gave away her position to her mother, Wendy.

Isobel joined in with her own delightful chuckling, taking pleasure in seeing her granddaughter, Wendy, and great-granddaughter, chasing each other around her room.

Light-hearted children's Christmas songs were singing away on Wendy's phone, on the top of the large cabinet, out of the reach of Lindsay.

'I'm going to get you!' teased Wendy, as she scooped her arms down to Lindsay and playfully missed her by inches, making crab pincher like movements with her fingers.

Lindsay crawled deeper within the base of the tree. She reached up only to find they had moved the baubles further up, well out of reach.

'Ha, ha! We are far too clever for you. Your grandfather Aaron used to do the same thing. When we moved the decorations up higher, he'd shake the tree. We thought it would fall on him, so we were treeless that year. Christmas was still fun.'

Wendy turned to her grandmother, 'It's nice to hear you talk about my dad, I can't believe that you've been without music for all these years. I just didn't realise. I always wore my headphones. I didn't even notice the radio go up in the loft.'

'You were busy being a teenager, you coped so admirably when you lost your parents and then your grandpappy. You didn't need to be worrying about me, and I'm glad you didn't. You've done me proud; Lindsay is so adorable.' She bent over and toyed with her hands under the tree, trying to reach the child. 'Santa will leave presents under the tree for you soon, oh yes he will!'

'Thanks for having Christmas lunch at ours this year, I know you'd have preferred us all to come to you.'

'Don't be daft. You've your new home now. Besides, I get to play with Lindsay, without the mess to clear up. And no cooking! That will be a treat.'

'Promise me you'll stay the night if you feel lonely. You can have our bed and we'll sleep in the lounge.'

'Och. I'm only around the corner. Besides, I'll have Call the Midwife to watch when I get home. You'll all be shattered by then.'

She pointed to the top of the other cabinet, the one containing miniature houses, in the style of elves buildings, 'I like that you've put up another photo of my mum and dad and another of grandpappy, it's good to see them all looking so happy.'

'It's for my group tonight. I needed ones I could carry.' She nodded to the portrait on the wall, 'That's too big and heavy. We are having a special service by the minister and lighting candles. It'll be the first time that I've seen my friends lost loved ones.'

'That sounds lovely.'

'You've always been welcome to come.'

'I know, but I think it's best kept just for you. I have my Darren now, even if he stinks of fish!'

Isobel winked to Lindsay, who was poking her head out from under the tree. She then clamped a finger and thumb over her nose and sang, 'Stinky daddy, stinky daddy! When he comes home from work!'

The trio burst into laughter just as a well-known cartoon character finished his song.

Monica was standing looking at her lounge alcove, hands crossed behind her back, like a private on parade, and stood at ease. 'I'm supposed to take you with me tonight, but I just can't.' She looked at the back of the photo frame, a thick layer of dust coated it. 'I'm sorry.' She turned and paced around the lounge, not settling. The room was barren of any Christmas decorations. The few cards that she'd received remained in their envelopes in the kitchen, tucked behind the bread bin. Though it was only the first week of December, her pal next door had already put flashing lights in the window and a real fir tree reached up to the ceiling and tickled the paintwork. She'd helped take delivery of it when Graham and Robyn were at work. Graham had arranged for it to come when Robyn was away, paying extra for the staff to come with it in their van. He didn't want dropped needles in Morris. He then came home early from work and had decorated the house with a reluctant Monica as a fun surprise. Monica had tried to enter the spirit of the season, but it was still weeks away to the big day, a date she seldom found joy over.

She walked through to the kitchen, intent on another cup of coffee, but found herself unable to even perform this simple task. She ignored the kettle. She needed a proper caffeine hit. She looked at the clock. If she left now, she might just see him there. She walked out of her cottage, pausing at the coat rack to grab the clothing needed to keep herself warm for a brisk walk into town. She hoped it was the right building she was heading towards.

Oliver waved a twenty-pound note towards Harriet, 'Please take payment for the biscuits this month, Harriet,' he implored.

She shook her head, 'I will for your lunch though, just move over to Jude, he's on the till today.' She carefully took out two golden cardboard boxes with a bright red ribbon on top. 'I've made extra, for the minister, I know how much clergy like their grub. They are cinnamon flavour. I won't tell you where to sit today, I've put you down as a lost cause.'

Oliver gave her a wry look, 'Thanks for stopping sending people my way, I really do just like to eat and watch the world go by. I've a conference call I need to head back for, so I shan't be down here long. Thanks for the biscuits, the group really looks forward to seeing what you've baked for them. I'll see you tomorrow.'

'I look forward to it.'

172

Monica strode purposely away from her beloved beach and into town, not stopping to chat with any of the dogs and their owners today. She zipped her jacket up an extra inch, almost until it hid her neck. The North-East winds were biting today. Her arms swung like pendulums in a race against the clock.

Barry sat at his kitchen table, sobbing uncontrollably, wiping fruitlessly at the cascade of tears with a damp piece of kitchen roll. His favourite photo of his daughter was laid on the bare wooden surface. She was dressed in her school blazer, a prefect badge proudly worn, her tie loosened at the collar and worn at a jaunty angle. He didn't think he had the strength to go to the group tonight. He didn't think he'd survive a Christmas without her. His free hand trembled as it reached for the first of the packets of tablets.

Shaun unlocked his front door and heaved his suitcase and briefcase into the lobby. The sound of passing traffic eased to a gentle hum as he closed the door. He stood by his coat rack listening for any sounds in the house. All he could hear was the relaxing, steady tick of the grandfather clock by his side. He'd always come and stood here in times of stress. He found listening to the clockwork mechanism soothing. Months ago he would have shouted his homecoming, years ago he would have waited for the thudding of running children's feet eager in anticipation of a present from his business travels, usually some chocolate from the airport, but now he knew he'd face gloom, perhaps for the rest of his married life. He couldn't tell her of his genuine feelings, of the savings he'd squirrelled away to pay for a flat of his own. He couldn't leave her, not now. He walked through to the lounge where his son sat patiently with his blank-faced mother.

Gregor tried to open the new tap packaging, but his shaking caused it to slip and fall to the floor. He ignored it. He was in a half-finished kitchen. The owner had been putting pressure on him to finish his part of the job by the end of the week. He wanted to move his new girlfriend in by Christmas and move out of the family home. Gregor hadn't cared. All he could think about was clocking off time. He looked around him. The carpenter had gone off to the depot for a replacement part, leaving Gregor alone. He reached into his low pocket by his thigh and took out a hip flask. It was a gift from his son. He ignored the engraving, unscrewed it, and took a long, hard, swallow. The whisky burnt the back of his throat, caused a scorching sensation down to his belly, and warmed him up. It brought little cheer and barely satisfied his intense craving, but it would get him through the rest of the afternoon.

A serious look was planted on Corrina's face as she sat by Adam in the doctor's room. 'I think you should increase his dose ever so slightly, doctor.'

'Och, there's no need doctor,' argued Adam belligerently. 'I get a few hours' sleep.' He patted his growing girth, 'And I'm eating plenty. For the first few weeks after losing Fraser I couldn't face food, now it's all I think about.'

'It's a common side-effect of the tablets, I'm afraid,' warned Dr Munro. 'Especially at night.'

Adam turned to his wife, 'That's when I get the munchies. It's just a few biscuits.'

Corrina looked at him doubtfully, one eyebrow shot up higher than the other. 'More like half a packet.'

'Please try to watch your weight, you'll see the benefits later in life,' reasoned the doctor.

Adam tilted his head quickly from side to side. He wanted to argue what would be the point. He didn't want to make old bones, not with Fraser having had such a brief life. It didn't seem fair. But he held his tongue, he really didn't want even more pills prescribed, no tablets could take away his heartache.

'Your prescription will be ready to collect from the pharmacy, and I'd like to see you next week, I know this will be a tough time for you both. Monday if possible, I've study leave for the rest of the week. You are both doing ever so well.'

Adam nodded reluctantly and rose, 'Thank you, doctor.'

Corrina wished her a pleasant weekend and followed her husband to the receptionist's desk. She hoped they'd be home soon; they had a meal to prepare for their children before the group.

'It's all changed since you were last here,' enthused Irvine. He squirmed in his car seat as he delved into his trouser pocket and then handed her his mobile phone. 'I'll walk you through it, then I'd suggest you download the app when we get home.' His stomach rumbled in anticipation of their late lunch at his favourite fast-food restaurant. Since Bella ate so little, it hadn't seemed fair to take her here. Besides, she'd always kept her window vigil. But since the group, she seemed to spend less time there, and today she'd only sat for an hour and then suggested they treat themselves.

'I'll just have a kid's meal, the chicken nuggets and fries, but don't go large. Maybe even a strawberry, no, a banana milkshake. One of their small ones.'

'Great!' enthused Irvine. 'I'll have their new triple cheeseburger, I saw an advert on the telly last night, it looks amazing.' He swivelled further around in his seat so that he could gaze directly to her, 'I've missed coming here, with you.'

She stroked down his face, lingering with her gentle caress, 'I am getting so much better. My appetite is slowly coming back. That's a good sign, isn't it?' She bit her lower lip anxiously.

'Yes, it is. My old Bella is coming back to me. I love you.'

'And I love you.' She leant across and kissed him, then brought her attention back to the phone. 'Let's get ordering. I think I can see how it works.'

'They even have table service now. When we get in, we go straight to a table, sit, and put the number in the app. It's brilliant!'

She let out a loud laugh that echoed joyfully around the confines of the car, 'You've given yourself away sunshine, you've been coming here on your way home from work.'

His face reddened. 'Sorry. It's just that you've not been eating, and the soup mum makes for us just doesn't fill me up, even with the rolls. Don't tell her.'

Bella winked, 'Your secret is safe with me. Let's order, I'm getting hungry now that I can see all the things you can order.' She squinted at the screen and didn't see the huge grin and sparkling eyes of her fiancé.

Monica scanned the forecourt of the café, glancing to each table as disappointment spread across her face. She visibly sagged. She walked up to the counter, taking hesitant steps.

'All right, love, what can I get you?'

Monica looked up to the kindly eyes and her face lit up, 'You must be Harriet. I've heard so much about you, Jude and Mitch.'

'All good I hope.'

'Yes. You make the special biscuits.'

Harriet nodded towards the till, 'They are over there. Would you like a drink with them?'

'Sorry, I mean for our group.'

'Ah, I see. Yes.' She looked to Monica, taking her in for the first time. She lowered her voice, 'It's the least I can do. You are all so very brave.'

Disappointment showed in Monica's eyes, 'You don't know who I am?'

'No. Oliver rarely talks about the group. He's an incredible man. He's my Mitch's boss, he's so thoughtful.'

'We have a strict confidentiality policy, that'll be why. I'm Monica.'

'It's nice to meet you, Monica.'

'And you.' She looked around. 'I was hoping to join Oliver for lunch.'

'He was in earlier. Most of our customers have had their lunches now. You should come again. I hate seeing him sitting all alone.'

A sad expression fell upon Monica, and the astute Harriet saw this.

'I can call him, ask him to come down. My Mitch is on their reception desk. But Oliver was in early for his lunch and took the biscuits. That usually signals he won't come back. He said he had an important conference call.'

'Not to worry. He wasn't expecting me. I thought I'd surprise him.'

Harriet took off her apron. 'Please stay, have a late lunch with me. It's my break time. A sandwich and green tea? On the house.'

Monica shook her head, 'I've heard that you make the best coffee in town. Make mine black.'

Harriet grinned, 'Coming right up.' She pointed to Oliver's favourite table. 'You get comfortable and I'll join you straight away. Then you can tell me all about yourself.'

'If we leave in thirty minutes, we can do a bit of late-night Christmas shopping in the city, I'd like to choose our gifts to your parents this year,' suggested Bella.

Irvine, lying flat out on the sofa, content from having a full stomach, looked up from his magazine, mouth agape, 'That would be great. I never know what to get them.' He sat up, recovered from the shock, and rattled off several shopping centre's names.

'I think we should try all three, your mum and dad deserve something special, and you can have dessert at one of their cafes, before driving to group. I've looked out my favourite photo of Paul and my parents.' She slid it across the table.

Irvine leaned forward, regarded it, and nodded, 'I miss them terribly too. I'll always look after you and love you.'

'I know. I love you too. Now put your feet back up, I've the vacuuming to do.'

His mouth dropped even further.

Roland spread the intricate and colourful deck of cards in front of him, turning them over thoughtfully and slowly. His touch lingered on the last as he placed it back down on the green tablecloth. He tapped it with his forefinger, deliberating. A tranquil expression flowed over him, making him feel aglow. He nodded to himself, content with what had been dealt. An alarm on his wristwatch buzzed, breaking his concentration. He stood, looked back at the table, nodded again, and then left his flat and walked towards his car. He was off to pick his mother from the train station. He'd then treat her to a carvery meal at the local restaurant, then join her for the group.

Harriet had been nattering to Monica about all sorts of trivia whilst she ate her sandwiches. She'd stayed off any heavy topics, talking about the other businesses in the building, her favourite customers and how much she loved catering for them. She sensed an extreme sadness in her new friend and hesitated over asking about her loss.

After an hour had passed, Jude had come across and introduced himself whilst providing a fresh pot of green tea for his wife and another black coffee for Monica. She'd declared it the best she'd ever had, and he left them beaming away like a proud new parent.

'Sometimes I never know what to say to Oliver. I know about the losses he's had, but he seems so lonely. He's always yawning, and Mitch helps him with his appearance before important meetings. I don't think he takes proper care of himself. I'm always trying to feed him up. I send Mitch up with all sorts and my son says he always eats well here, but I don't think he cooks for himself. I worry about him at weekends.'

'We don't meet outside of group. Today was a spur-of-the-moment thing. I don't know why.'

'Is it the time of year? It must be difficult for you all.'

'Yes, but it's something else. I can't explain it, I just have a bad feeling, you know the sort, that starts in your tummy.'

Harriet couldn't help but look at where Monica was pointing to herself. She thought she was abnormally thin. She judged, correctly, that coffee was her main diet. 'I think so, but God forbid, I've had nothing bad happen to my family. I hate seeing Oliver sitting by himself. I used to send over any single people to him. I'd tell them that all the tables were reserved, but that they were to join Oliver. Most obeyed, that's how my Mitch met his new girlfriend. Oliver played matchmaker.'

'That's so sweet. Though I hate to think of Oliver being lonely. He struck me as coping with his losses. He's the anchor of our group. Making sure the meeting room is warm and laid out properly. He even puts tissues in every area we use.'

'I imagine they need them.'

'Yes, I've cried so many times, and I'm not alone there.'

'You're all incredibly brave.'

'I don't feel like it sometimes, I'd rather face the wall and curl up some days.'

'Oliver and your friends must be a great support and comfort?'

'Yes, and I have a great pal who lives next door. But I don't know if Oliver has anyone?'

'Mitch thinks he hasn't. Nick, his deputy, is efficient at his job, but Mitch doesn't think they socialise at all outside of office hours.'

'Losing his wife and the stillbirth hit him hard. He found her, you know.'

'I thought as much. The poor man. What can we do?'

Monica looked up towards the lift and then the row of office company names on the panel next to it. She wondered about going across and reading which was Oliver's. 'I'll try to have a chat with him this evening.' She looked up to the gigantic clock on the wall, 'Good Lord! I didn't realise the time. I've kept you from your work and need

181

to get ready for group, though I could probably walk from here.' She thought to the neglected photo in the alcove, 'I don't need to go home for anything.' She rose to her feet, 'It was so nice to meet you, Harriet, and thank you for the coffee.'

'It's been a pleasure, Monica. I hope you'll come back for lunch one day soon?'

Monica looked to the lift doors expectantly, 'I will.'

Bella ran her fingers idly over the perfume counter and picked up random bottles, gave them a sniff, put them down and then finally allowed one to be sprayed upon her delicate neck and slender wrists. She rubbed them together and took a sharp inhalation. She nodded away, picked up a shiny box with a full bottle and popped it in her basket. Irvine followed her to the display with face creams that claimed to remove wrinkles and marvelled at the transformation that came over Bella today. It was almost like a switch had been flicked in her head. He was overcome with a sudden rush of emotion as he dreamed about their future life together.

Roland lifted Nancy's small suitcase with a playful groan, as if it was a heavy weight. 'We'll get you warmed up soon, mum. You'd think that ScotRail could get the heating on their trains to work nowadays.'

'Thanks, son. They are old trains. But it was a cold journey. I'll soon get warm in the meeting hall. Thanks for coming along tonight. You'll do well at our group.'

'Yes, I know I will. We'll be there in an hour. We'll get you warmed up at the restaurant and prepare ourselves. We can have a quick chat about the members.'

Nancy walked over to the passenger seat and sat down, eager to get to the group.

Oliver shivered as he entered the church hall building. He went straight to the boiler and turned on the heating. Then he went from room to room, turning up each radiator to its maximum, then leaving extra boxes of tissues on tables. In the main meeting room, he left several scattered about the tables. It would be a challenging time for many. He always found this time of year doubly difficult, with the anniversary of Emma's death and Christmas.

He dragged two of the taller tables together, just outside the circle of chairs. Then he went back to the lobby, reached into his bag, and took out a mahogany framed photo. He looked at it longingly. It was of his two lost loves, Emma cradling their perfectly formed, but dead child. He looked fast asleep, swathed in blankets, still pink from the womb. Their midwife had taken the photo, Oliver had been too distressed to pose or to use his camera phone. Emma had fallen into some sort of catatonic trance, with only eyes for her child. Her expression was one of utter grief mixed with sheer love for her stillborn child. She had remained cradling it for hours, only allowing another midwife to take her away once she could be convinced, ever so gently, that he was indeed dead. Oliver had never felt so impotent in all his life.

He failed to hear the outside door open and close quietly. He was too busy caressing the glass of the photo, as if he were stroking Emma's hair.

'She was so beautiful,' whispered Monica, now by Oliver's side.

Oliver removed his hand, as if scalded, he stuttered, 'Oh, hi Monica, how are you? I didn't hear you come in.'

'I'm so sorry to have intruded Oliver, but I've been walking around town for what seems like hours, and it's getting really cold.'

'Come away into the meeting room, I've boosted the heating. I was about to put my photo on the table. Are you all right? Why have you been walking for so long?' He looked quizzically at her empty hands, wondering where her photo of Josephine was.

'I'm restless today. I don't know why. It's like a dread feeling.'

He nodded. 'It sounds bizarre, but I've been feeling odd today too. I just thought it was my anxiety. I haven't been doing my meditation exercises as often as I should.' He lifted the frame higher. 'Do you think it's because of the time of year, or because we are sharing our photos tonight?'

'I guess so.' She nodded to the photo, 'He looks like he's fast asleep. He was so handsome.'

Oliver sighed, 'He was perfect looking, that's what made it so hard.'

Monica took Oliver's free hand, gently, like two lovers. She spoke softly, 'What was his name?'

'The hospital padre came and blessed him, I guess it was like a Christening. I can't really remember his words. It brought little comfort, but we named him, Finn. After his grandfather, Emma's father, Findlay. We had him cremated, Emma didn't like the idea of him being in the cold ground. We had his ashes in an angel urn. When I received Emma's ashes, I scattered them at the same time. I like to think they are together, somewhere. I don't have any religious beliefs.'

'Me neither, but I think that it's sweet of the church minister to say a few words tonight.'

'I'll put Finn and Emma on the table.' He kept hold of Monica's hand, finding comfort from it as they walked through. He only let go when they reached the table, and he needed his hand to steady the photo frame. He took a step back, as if admiring his family, then looked to Monica expectantly.

She looked back at him with puzzlement, then it dawned on her and she looked down at her feet. 'I've been trying to chat to you about this for months. I think you'll understand. Nancy isn't the best listener, and I didn't want to burst Isobel's joyful bubble, nor bother the new people with my troubles.' She looked back up.

'You know you can always chat to me. I've a good listening ear.'

'I know. It's selfish of me, but we keep getting interrupted. Can I see you outside of the group?'

He nodded eagerly, 'That would be lovely. Why don't you put Josephine's photo next to Finn and Emma, then we can have a chat?'

'That's what I need to confess to, I haven't looked at Josephine since the undertakers.'

Oliver creased his brow in confusion.

'I mean her photos. Daft, isn't it?' She looked pleadingly into his eyes.

'No. I get it, and only members of our group can say that. Others wouldn't understand. Is it too painful to see her?'

'Yes. See, I knew you'd understand. We've come to know each other so well over the years.'

'I think of you and Isobel as my best friends. I hope the others in the group will become our chums.'

'I think they already are. I hope they won't think it cruel of me not to bring Josephine along. It doesn't mean that I don't love her.'

'I know what a loving mother you were. I bet you were a brilliant wife too.'

'I tried with my husband, but we grew apart. His behaviour changed. I guess I did as well. I'm so glad that I had Robyn. She's been brilliant, letting me move in next door. Checking in on me all the time.'

'I've heard you talk about her in the group. She's a great pal to have.'

'She really is. I hope you'll meet her one day.'

'I'd like that.'

'What about you? Have you someone to look out for you?'

'I have my friends at work. Mitch straightens my tie and Harriet bakes our biscuits. I wish you'd try one. They smell so tasty.' He lowered his voice conspiratorially, 'I sneaked one out of the box earlier and had a good nibble. They are cinnamon flavoured. Yummy!'

Monica was about to confess that she'd met Harriet and had a good chinwag, when the lobby door opened and in bustled Nancy and Roland. They came straight into the meeting room.

'Oh, no, this won't do at all. Help me move these tables to the other side of the room, Roland,' ordered Nancy as she rushed past Oliver and Monica and grabbed an edge.

Roland, ignoring the duo, strode to the other side of the table and lifted his side. Emma's photo wobbled precariously.

Oliver grabbed it, took Monica by the shoulder, and walked out of the way with her. 'Let's leave them to it,' he murmured under his breath. 'Can you help me in the kitchen, please?'

'Yes. I think that would be a good idea. We can introduce ourselves to Roland once Nancy has the room how she wants it.'

Barry was hunched up in his padded jacket as he trudged to the meeting hall, as if in protection against the chilly night. He had a carrier bag clasped tightly to his chest, as if it contained his utmost treasure. He saw Isobel coming from the side road and met her as the pavements crossed. 'Hello Isobel, I've got my daughter with me.' He stretched out the bag, as if she could see through the plastic.

'I look forward to seeing her. I bet she was beautiful. I've bought my Aaron and his wife. I've also tucked in a photo of my Roy. I miss all three of them. They'd have loved to see baby Lindsay. Well, not so much a baby, as a crawling menace now.'

Her joke was lost on the man. He was too wrapped up in his own thoughts to acknowledge it. 'I found her you know.' His

187

shoulders heaved as tears fell from his eyes. He clutched the bag tighter to his chest, drawing little comfort from its content's square edges.

Isobel slotted her arm through his and put her shoulder next to him as they walked to the group in silence together, broken by the sobs of an inconsolable man.

'Do you think they've finished?' whispered Monica, looking through the gap in the closed hatchway.

'I feel like a naughty schoolboy!' declared Oliver.

'Me too! Well, I mean, a schoolgirl.' Their eyes met, and each made the other burst out laughing, such were their gleeful expressions. They tried to curtail their merriment, given the solemn occasion about to occur, but this caused them to giggle and snort more.

Oliver walked over to one of the kitchen units and took a few tissues and blew his nose, then took the box over to Monica. 'I haven't had such a laugh for a long time. She was cross with us. I hope she hasn't heard us.'

Monica plucked two from the box and dabbed her eyes, 'Who cares. It's nice to see you having fun.'

'Me too. You look so much younger when you laugh. It takes years off you.'

She gave him a playful thud on the chest, 'Just how old do you think I am?'

He looked at her seriously for just a moment, then creased up again.

She joined him in carefree hilarity, not worrying how loud they now were.

Roland stopped dragging the chair and glanced over to the hatchway, a scowl etched on his face. He looked over at his mother. She hadn't seemed to hear it, or chose to ignore the laughter. She was too engrossed in laying out a plush tablecloth, straightening it out with the flat of her hands, and then positioning candles at each end and in the middle. She put a box of matches on the table, then appeared to have a think, and then slipped them into her pocket. He knew she wanted to be the one to light them. He'd learned over the years to allow his mother to have control. The trick was to allow her to think that she was in control.

Bella appeared to skip along the pavement. She was so light on her feet as she trotted along, almost appearing to be dragging Irvine. He was finding it difficult to keep up the pace with her, he'd a full stomach after eating several doughnuts from his favourite café and they were sitting heavy on his stomach. Though he was already wondering what sort of biscuits they'd have over teas and coffees tonight.

Gregor's hands shook as he tried to lift the pint glass with amber liquid to his lips. An empty whisky tumbler sat idly by it. He steadied his trembling hands by placing them flat on the bar top, then used both hands to lift the glass, like an inexperienced toddler. He took a long drink, draining the contents. He turned around, looked to the glass door of the bar, seeming to stare along the road, then turned back to the counter and caught the eye of the barman and signalled for a refill for both glasses.

Adam and Corrina exited their car as Shaun, Andrew, and Cherie neared the church hall door. They exchanged pleasantries as they made their way into the building and joined Bella, Irvine, Barry, and Isobel in the lobby. All were looking through to the kitchen where muffled giggles could be heard. It seemed incongruous, given the intense grief some of them were experiencing. The men shrugged their shoulders and Isobel declared, 'It's nice to hear them having fun, it's a lovely sound.'

The outer door opened, and a red-cheeked woman walked in. She had a small rucksack bouncing on her back with each movement. 'It's so cold tonight, I wish I'd worn my scarf.' She thudded her hands together in emphasis and the cosseted fingers gave a dull thump in the padded gloves. 'Hello everyone, I'm Shelagh, the church minister.' She held out her hand, about to say individual greetings, but Nancy interrupted her. She seemed to run towards her.

'Glad you could make it Shelagh, come on through, Roland and I have set the room up.'

Shelagh followed Nancy through to the meeting room, shrugging off her rucksack as she went. She then unzipped her jacket to reveal a striped patterned jumper, a hand-knitted gift from a grateful parishioner. Her blouse high collar revealed her white ministerial uniform.

Monica and Oliver came sheepishly out of the kitchen and greeted their friends. After a few minutes Oliver looked at his watch and announced, 'Let's go through.' He took a step back and allowed the families to enter first, led by Monica.

Monica gave a slight gasp as she entered the meeting room. The lights had been turned off; the tables were draped with deep green cloths and there were several thick, white candles on them. They were lit and cast shadows around the room. Roland and Nancy stood at either end of the conjoined tables. The scene reminded Monica of a religious ceremony, or like a sacrificial altar in a ham seventies horror movie. She was taken aback, recovered quickly as her eyes adjusted to the dim setting, and then walked straight to a seat and got comfortable.

'Please put your photos on the table,' ordered Nancy tersely.

Shelagh frowned at the formality and made a mental note to introduce a bit of individuality to her brief sermon. She hoped the group would share the names of those they lost to suicide. She watched as people placed a mixture of photo frames and prints on the table, almost reverentially. She noticed Monica hadn't moved, so she walked over to her chair and sat by her. 'Hello, I'm Shelagh, the minister.'

Monica instinctively held out her hand and was about to introduce herself, but she was interrupted.

191

Nancy had moved away from her post at the table and had sat down at the chair nearest to the photos. She patted the seat next to her, 'Come and sit here Shelagh, the group will see the photos and watch you give your talk.'

The minister acknowledged Nancy with a slight dip of her head, then turned back to Monica, 'Thank you for allowing me to come to your special group. What's your name, love?'

'Monica. I lost my daughter, Josephine.'

'That's such a loss.' She looked to the table, 'Sometimes it's hard to look at their faces, knowing we'll never see them again.'

'Yes,' croaked Monica, near to tears at the intimacy and kindness she was shown.

'Josephine is such a beautiful name. How old was she when she was taken from you?'

'She was only eighteen.'

Shelagh sighed, 'Such a tender age. I'll have a chat with you later if I may? Nancy is keen to start. She's had a long day of travelling.'

'Thank you, minister.'

Shelagh reached out and took Monica's left hand and held it lightly in both of hers. She sensed the others had finished putting their photos on the table, and then she withdrew and took her seat next to Nancy. Roland was sitting by his mother's left side.

Oliver carefully put his photo between that laid down by Cherie, Shaun, and Andrew and that of Barry's. Both showed girls in their school blazers and tie. He turned and was pleased to see that the chair by Monica was vacant. As he sat, he caught the eye of Bella and he couldn't help giving her a broad smile. She looked so well. Her pale complexion had given way to a more colourful pallor, with a hint of make-up, her hair had a great sheen, appearing to glow in the subdued lighting. She was sat up straight and attentive to Irvine and Barry, who had taken to sitting by her side, like he had in the last meeting. In contrast, Barry looked unkempt, hadn't shaven for what looked like days. His head sagged to his chest, and he appeared to be crying silently. Oliver knew he'd have to check in on him before he left. The first Christmas without a loved one was always the hardest.

Nancy clapped her hands twice, like a teacher to an unruly class, to get the attention of the group. Then she spoke in staccatos, 'Welcome, Shelagh, to our group. I'll ask everyone to introduce themselves.' She pointed to Roland, 'This is my son, Roland,' she proudly stated, before dropping the bombshell, 'He'll be taking over the group in the New Year.' She nodded to Cherie.

Cherie remained silent. Her hands were clasped together and hung loosely in her lap. She looked down at them, appearing not to have heard, despite Nancy's intense stare.

Nancy's look to the fragile woman was so concentrated that she missed the open mouths of Isobel, Oliver, and Monica. The trio glanced from one to the other, not quite believing what was just said.

Monica recovered first and tried to catch the eye of Nancy, 'When you say taking over, what do you mean, as co-ordinator. Only Oliver and I should have been deputies by now.'

Nancy ignored her and instead spoke to Shaun, 'Perhaps you can introduce your family to Shelagh and who you've all lost.'

Shaun looked around the group. His eyes lingered on Monica, hoping she'd repeat her question. After a few seconds he hesitantly spoke to Shelagh and then remained silent whilst the circle introduced themselves to the minister. Some pointed to the photo of their loved one as they spoke his or her name.

When it was Monica's turn, she looked at Roland, and then Nancy as she talked about Josephine and her girlfriend and then began describing how much the group had helped her, then finished with, 'Oliver, Isobel and I have been coming here the longest, apart from Nancy, of course. But we've never seen Roland before. Is he even qualified to run the group?'

'He is,' flustered Nancy. 'He lost his sister to suicide. He knows the pain of suicide.'

'Though I like to think her spirit is still with me,' countered Roland. With almost a theatrical flourish he whipped out a small Polaroid from his shirt pocket, 'This is Anthea, she's at peace now.' He looked around him and was pleased to see Shelagh nodding in agreement. He walked over to the table and placed the photo against one of the burning candles. He paused for a moment, looking at his sister, almost seeming to give a prayer, then he bowed his head and turned. 'I hope to get to know you all better after Shelagh's service.'

The group looked at him in expectation, wondering if he'd finished his performance.

Oliver looked at Monica; his eyebrows shot up quizzically, like Spock's in Star Trek. He hoped he conveyed his worry to her.

Shelagh began her brief talk, praying that it brought some comfort to the bereaved, though her thoughts were wondering what she was caught in the middle of and when she could make her earliest excuses to leave.

Robyn

The music shook the speakers and rebounded around the function room, blaring in competition against the hum of chatter and excited voices. A glass was dropped and smashed to the floor, and a loud, collective cheer went up. A waitress scurried off in embarrassment to fetch a broom and dustpan. Several people were already on the dance floor, a meal having been eaten, and the drinks were now flowing.

Robyn was towing a reluctant Graham along, going from each table, introducing him, and proudly watching as all her pals made a fuss of him. Several gave her a wink and whispered naughty words in her ear.

Graham watched coyly as she threw her head back and laughed hysterically. He gave cautious glances to the dance floor with some trepidation. He hoped he wouldn't have to dance. The DJ wasn't even playing any Jazz tonight, just a succession of crummy Christmas songs heard throughout shops up and down the country. He hoped Judy wouldn't sulk when they got home, probably in the small hours. He'd give her a favourite biscuit when he tucked her in. He felt his arm yanked, and he looked in fear as Robyn beckoned him seductively with a curl of her free index finger. She was leading him to the dance floor, they'd reached the last table and now the inevitable was happening. He gave a nervous gulp, shrugged his shoulders, and gyrated his hips and swayed his legs. A fresh burst of raucous laughter amongst the women broke out.

Oliver was the first to thank Shelagh for her kind words of comfort. He briefly watched as the others thanked her, and then he slipped off to fill the tea and coffee pot. He hoped Shelagh would stay and join them for refreshments so that he could truthfully tell Harriet that the minister thought his biscuits were divine.

He was engrossed in filling the pots and hadn't realised that Isobel and Monica had followed him to the kitchen.

'Did either of you know about Roland taking over?' asked Isobel.

Monica shook her head, 'I've been asking Nancy if Oliver and I could train as a deputy. The charity runs a two-day course to prepare us. But she's never answered my questioning.'

Oliver replaced the lid on the full teapot, 'It came as a shocker to me too, I've never seen the bloke before, until tonight.'

Isobel shrugged her shoulders, 'What should we do?'

Oliver put the teapot down onto the tray and walked to open the hatch, 'Let's see what the night brings.'

Graham took another deep gulp of the strange concoction that was handed to him. He'd never seen a shot glass plunged into a taller glass before. The resultant colour reminded him of witch's brew. He looked around at the women yelling, 'Shot, shot, shot!' to him and refrained from making a quip about Macbeth. He bowed to the inevitable, swallowed it in one gulp, grimaced at the taste, then stuck out his tongue as the fiery liquid hit his stomach and belched out fire. Soon he wasn't worrying about Judy and was back on the dance floor, dragging a cackling Robyn along with him to the beat of another loud Christmas rock song.

'I can cure you of your depression, Adam,' declared Roland as he sidled up to him as Oliver, Isobel and Monica walked back into the room.

'How did you know I had depression?' quizzed a puzzled-looking Adam.

'I can see the sadness in your eyes,' offered Roland.

'I am under the doctor for it. I'm taking tablets though. She assures me I'll be my old self soon. Though I doubt it.'

'You don't need them. Stop taking them. I can help instead.'

Adam looked at the strange expression that came over Roland, like he was summoning something. 'How?'

'I have an office in the city, above one of the shops. I use past life regression therapy. The answer is in your past.'

Oliver almost dropped the tray he carried from the hatchway.

Adam was about to say something, but Roland ignored his incredulous expression.

'You should come to see me. I keep normal office hours, but I also work in the evening. I know you miss Fraser terribly. I can help with that too.' He smoothly handed Adam a business card and then was off to speak to someone else.

Adam looked at the card, did a double-take, then looked from Roland and back to the card.

Corrina walked back to him now that she'd had a chat with Shelagh. 'You okay, love?'

Adam's hands trembled with rage as he handed her the card without a word. He just couldn't get a sentence together.

Her jaw dropped as she read the front and then saw the images on the back.

Isobel looked over her shoulder, a quick glance told her all she needed to know, it was the same business card that she received from Nancy all those months ago. She turned back to warn Monica, but Shelagh was now chatting to her. She shadowed Roland and hovered beside his conversations. He was now chatting to Barry.

'Her spirit is all around you, she hasn't left your side. She loves you!' declared Roland.

'You can really see her. My Kimberley?' Barry looked over his shoulder with hope, tears now long-gone. 'My Kim, back with me!'

'Yes, she is beautiful.' Roland looked by Barry's shoulder, a calm expression upon his round face.

'I can't see her,' moaned Barry. 'I so want to see her. I want to hear her voice, just for one last time. I'd do anything, give you anything, please. I blame myself.' He sobbed again.

'She says you mustn't.'

'How could you!' hissed Bella as she hugged Barry, forcing him to his feet and making him take a few steps away from Roland. 'Can't you see how fragile he is? How all of us are?' She turned Barry around and took him to the refreshments table.

Roland calmy walked over to Cherie. She was alone whilst her son and husband were fetching drinks. He sat down beside her and took her hand, 'You can hear her voice again, through me.'

Cherie slowly turned towards him and mouthed some words, though no sound escaped her throat.

'But not yet,' teased Roland. 'I did a tarot reading today, and the timing isn't quite right for you.' He looked up and saw the two men about to turn from the table. 'I'll chat to you again, after Christmas.' He left her as she rocked again, a low humming sound was just audible above the sound of conversations around the room.

Oliver watched him go. He was lost for words.

Monica nudged him, 'What should we do?'

'I don't know. I just don't know,' He watched as Isobel continued to tail Roland, who was now making for his mother. Nancy was beaming away, maternally with great pride.

Graham thrust his left leg out whilst frantically clutching at Robyn's waist. He shuffled furiously to keep up and time his in and outs of various limbs to the tempo dictated by the laughing DJ. A strange pair of slender hands were squeezing his midriff and now and again, as the group snaked its way around the function room, they slipped down and felt his bottom. They were deliciously warm, but every five feet, he felt a hard smack on his left buttock. After several laps, the record finished and the conga line dissolved, giving Graham a chance to look behind him. A tall man overshadowed him, blew him a kiss, and tipped him a cheeky wink. Graham went bright red as the women broke into a fresh set of filthy laughing and wolf whistling at his expense. He stretched forward and up, grasped the man's cheeks, and kissed him full on the mouth.

Nancy switched the room lights back on and then tapped a teaspoon furiously against her mug and waited for silence to fall upon the meeting room. She glowered at Monica, Oliver, and Isobel, until the trio abandoned their talking. 'Please thank Shelagh for such a lovely sermon. She's going now. She says she's been called out to one of her parishioners.' She gave a clap of her hands and showed with nods of her head that the others were to do the same.

The group joined in and there were several, 'thank you,' and 'comforting service,' words spoken.

'It's so touching that you allowed me to join your group. My church is always open for you.' Shelagh looked nervously from Roland to Nancy, 'You can always chat to me about anything. I'm just sorry that I can't stay longer. Bye for now.' She left the room, not bothering to put on her jacket or rucksack. She had them hung loosely by her side as she quickly left the building.

Adam muttered something to Corrina, and she walked over to Cherie, crouched, and murmured to her. Then she walked over to Barry and gave him a cuddle and then hugged Shaun, Andrew, Bella, and Irvine.

Whilst his wife was saying her goodbyes, Adam walked over to Isobel, Oliver, and Monica. His eyes roved between them, 'Thank you for making us so welcome to your group and for the refreshments every month. You've been a great comfort to Corrina and I.' He glared back at Roland and Nancy, 'But we won't be coming back.' He turned swiftly, strode to his wife, nodded, and they left for home.

Nancy blew out the candles and was busy rolling up her tablecloths, not caring about how clumsily she lifted photos out of the way. She placed her belongings into her bag and pointed to it when she caught the eye of her son. She addressed the hall, not looking at anyone in particular, 'We'll be off too, have a lovely Christmas. I'll probably only come to a few meetings next year until Roland finds his feet.' She didn't wait for a reply, she simply made her way to the lobby.

Roland obediently lifted the bag, walked to the table, retrieved Anthea's photo, placed it gently in his breast pocket, then reached to the back of his chair and put on his jacket. 'I'll see you all in the New Year. I'm really looking forward to helping you all. I have a special set of skills.' He followed his mother away from the dumbstruck group.

They remained silent until the outer door banged shut and each was looking to the other for answers as to what just happened that night. The sobbing from Barry broke the hush of the building.

Bella helped him into his jacket and turned to Oliver, 'Irvine and I will take him home safely and see him settled. I don't know what to say. We'll see you next month, I think.' She bit her lip nervously and looked to the lobby with trepidation.

Irvine followed them out, Bella was saying low comforting words to a distressed-looking Barry. Irvine took the last biscuit from the plate as he passed the refreshments table.

Shaun was helping Cherie into her jacket, with the help of their son. 'I don't think my family needs this in our lives. It isn't proper. But I wish you all as good a Christmas as you can.' He walked slowly out of the room with his wife taking ginger steps. Her husband supported her fragile weight.

Andrew delicately took the photo of his sister from the table, waited until his parents had left the room, and shrugged to the trio left behind. 'I can't believe that just happened. I don't know what that lunatic said to my mum, but it's set her back.' He sighed in desperation, 'She's so fragile.' He didn't wait for a reply and left.

Oliver looked to his two friends. His shoulder seemed to sag and then his legs felt suddenly weak and he slumped back into his chair.

'We can't let that monster loose on our friends. He'll do untold damage,' avowed Monica with sudden fire in her eyes.

'I'm so sorry,' wept Isobel. She confessed, 'I just didn't know what to do.'

Oliver and Monica looked at her with confusion and concern etched on their furrowed brows.

Isobel dipped into her back pocket and produced one of Roland's business cards. 'Nancy gave me this a few months ago. I should have said something, but I didn't know what to do.'

Oliver took it gingerly from her, read both sides to himself, and then turned it back over with astonishment. 'He's calling himself a psychic medium and tarot card reader.'

'No way,' Monica shook her head vehemently. 'No way are we letting that monster loose on our group.'

Oliver handed the card back to Isobel, 'But what can we do? He's the new co-ordinator.'

Isobel took it reluctantly back and stared at it as if it were on fire. She was relieved when Monica took it from her.

'May I keep this please Isobel?'

She nodded furiously and relinquished her hold of it. 'Can you imagine if he were talking to my Wendy soon after losing her parents, he'd have had her believing all sorts of lies about her mum and dad. You know how much she misses them, and her grandpappy. That man would have claimed to have messages from them. She was so delicate, still is. We have to do something.'

Monica looked at the clock, 'I'm in no hurry to get home. Oliver, I will have that lift home tonight. But first, I'll make us a fresh pot of coffee, then we can sit back down and work out what to do. Let's go in the kitchen and tidy up whilst its brewing.' She smiled to Isobel, 'We want to hear all about Lindsay first, we can do with some cheer.'

Isobel's eyes lit up and appeared to twinkle as she described the crawling menace to her chums.

Robyn leaned across the bar, pressed her mouth into the barman's ear and shouted, 'This is for the next two rounds of drinks please.' She slipped him several fifty-pound notes and then a solitary twenty-pound note, 'And that's for you.' She gave him a cheeky wink, 'For putting up with us all!'

He grinned, 'It's my pleasure.' He slipped the note discretely into his waistcoat pocket and then counted the rest into the till and got out his notepad and pen, before taking the first order from a surprised man who was told to put away his wallet.

News soon spread, and a happy queue was forming at the bar.

Robyn tottered over to each waitress and waiter, walking gingerly on her tallest ever heels. 'This is for you. Thanks for looking after us all. Sorry if we got rowdy. We only let our hair down once a year!' She put a folded twenty-pound note into each of their hesitant hands and was rewarded with beaming smiles and dazzling teeth.

'That's decided,' agreed Oliver. 'We'll each telephone the charity and talk about Roland next week, after we've slept on it over the weekend. We'll give them the facts and leave them to make any tough decisions.'

Monica nodded her consent, 'I'm going to ask about why we were never given the deputy training. It should be one of us who takes over as co-ordinator, not some moron who believes he can speak to the dead.' She shook her head, 'You really couldn't make this up. If I read it in a novel, I'd be shouting, "really," to the author.'

'I think he needs to be seen at the psychiatric hospital. I know that he's grieving, and grief does strange things to our minds, but what the actual f---!' Isobel took a sip of her tea, not seeing the merriment spread across her friends' faces. They'd never heard her swear before.

Robyn grasped Graham by his cheeks and was gently shaking his head, like she was ruffling the ears of her favourite pet dog. 'I love you, so I do.' She repeated the words as she tousled him from side to side.

'I think you are a little drunk.'

'I am!' She lifted him to his feet, 'Let's dance!' She ran to the dance floor, dragging her prized possession with her.

Oliver stifled another yawn and tried to disguise it with his hand. 'Sorry, late night.'

'We should really lock up,' prompted Isobel. She was thinking of her early start babysitting.

Oliver looked up at the wall clock, 'It is rather late, I hadn't realised the time. Though I'm in no rush, I don't go to sleep until around two o'clock.'

Isobel looked at him with doubt, 'Why do you stay up so late. Haven't you work at nine?'

Oliver looked sheepishly at the floor, then to his two friends, 'I know it's not rational. But I stay up until after the time I found Emma. It's almost as if I expect her to come out of our closed off lounge.'

'Closed off lounge?' prompted Monica in surprise. 'Do you mean from when the police finished with it. Surely you can go in now, after all these years.'

'It's true what you said Isobel, grief makes us all do strange things,' replied Oliver, fudging around the question.

Monica asked gently, 'So you've never been into the lounge, after the police took Emma's body away?'

Oliver shook his head slowly. A look of embarrassment crept upon him.

Monica looked closely at her friend, realisation dawning on her. The stain on his shirt front was another tell-tale sign she had overlooked. 'Would it help if we came with you, went in together?'

Oliver looked up keenly, 'I'd like that. I've often wanted to ask you both, or one of you.'

'I'll do that for you Oliver, of course I will,' murmured Monica softly.

Isobel regarded them both. She suddenly felt like she was disturbing an intimate moment between the couple. 'I'll just rinse through our mugs.' She rose and returned to the kitchen with their tray.

Roland heaved the suitcase onto the single bed and then plumped up the top pillow by the pine headboard. He switched on the ornate lamp with pictures of tarot cards hand-painted along its glass shade. A skeleton appeared to be dancing on the one that faced towards the bed.

His mother had followed him into the spare room of his flat and was busy unzipping her case. 'I think that went well. I'm sure the families found some comfort in our service tonight.' She pulled out the local newspaper and handed them to Roland, 'Here you are, son. There are three new obituaries, you get busy reading them, and then you can contact the relatives.'

'Thank you, mum. I can help those poor bereaved souls too. Yes. Your tablecloths and candles gave it all a sacred effect. It was lovely and intimate. I can't wait to start work with them all next month. I've planted a few seeds in their minds tonight. I performed the most powerful tarot reading this afternoon. I'll be helping Cherie and Barry first. I've left the deck undisturbed in the lounge table for you to check over.'

'Good boy,' murmured his mother. 'Your sister would be so proud of you.'

Roland, ramrod straight and clasping his hands in a steeple in front of his stomach, like an altar boy, gave a cherubic-like smile.

Oliver parked alongside Isobel's front gate. He gave the area a once over, taking in the expensive-looking cars parked in driveways, the lack of wheelie-bins scattered haphazardly on pavements, and the well-manicured lawns, lit proudly by subdued lighting that threw their beams across the grass to light the way for any passing hedgehog. This was one of the posh ends of the city. He was pleased for his pal. If only her husband had lived longer to enjoy it. Though he knew that Isobel, and her Roy, would rather that Aaron had the extra life.

Isobel broke into his reverie, 'Thanks for the lift home, Oliver. I could have walked.'

'It's no bother at all. We weren't about to let you walk home on your own this late at night. Especially after the shock we've all had.'

Monica, sat in the front passenger seat, like the second half of an established couple, confirmed this analogy with, 'No, we weren't.

Now don't you be fretting about that man. We are doing the right thing.'

'Definitely,' affirmed Isobel. 'I hope there will be another group, so I'll see you all next month.' She thought about baby Lindsay and her granddaughter, 'I'm really looking forward to Christmas for the first time in years. I'll tell you all about it. Please try and enjoy it in your own way. Bye for now.' She sidled out of the car as the duo bade her a 'Good Christmas.'

Oliver watched whilst she fumbled in her handbag for her keys, unlocked her door, turned, and gave a cheery wave and entered her house. He was about to give her a merry toot of his horn, but then the dashboard clock reminded him it was almost midnight. He wouldn't be that man who woke the neighbourhood by blasting a noise when he'd just said a verbal goodbye. He drove off to the junction. 'Are you still living down near the harbour?'

'That's right, next door to Robyn. We really don't know enough about each other, outside of the group, do we? I don't even know where you live or have your phone number.'

'No, other than we know how kind each other is. We see that from the comfort we give to others during group. Let's exchange numbers before we say goodnight.'

She reached over and lightly brushed his hand as he changed gears, 'Would you like me to come to your house and help you enter your lounge?'

Oliver thought for a few seconds as he drove past an empty park. Its Victorian era style lights lit up the walkway between tall, magnificent oak trees. It looked temptingly serene, and he was almost enticed to park up his car and take Monica for a midnight stroll. 'I don't think I can cope with seeing it for the first time at around the same time that Emma took her life.'

'I'm so sorry Oliver, what was I thinking!' blushed Monica.

'You were being kind, that's what you were thinking. I'm not tired, though. I don't seem to need much sleep these days. I get a deep sleep for about four hours, then I have to get up, otherwise I can feel the walls closing in and my mind races away.'

'Yes, I know that feeling only too well. Adam at the group has the right answer. He tells me that his anti-depressants knock him out for a solid seven hours.'

'He's doing all right. I hope he and Corrina come back to group. I thought I'd use the e-mails and drop everyone a line or two, maybe some words of comfort before Christmas.'

'That's a great idea, Oliver. If you aren't in a rush to go home, would you like to go somewhere to talk? I have a little secret of my own. I figured you might have seen tonight what I didn't do.'

'Yes. I haven't had the chance to talk to you on your own. But I think everywhere will be closed now, certainly the pubs and cafes will be. I doubt any restaurant will still be open.'

Monica spied the bright yellow neon sign high in the sky as they passed the Edwardian built hotel which dominated the corner of two streets. Many of its bay windows were alight with guests bedding down for the night. She pointed to her left, 'How about there, they serve great coffee.'

Oliver duly obliged by indicating.

Graham slipped the taxi driver an additional ten-pound note and thanked him for their lift home and wished him a good shift. He closed the door and turned in time to see Robyn, standing on one foot, trying to unhook her shoes. She was swaying from side to side, not from her awkward position, but from too much alcohol. He couldn't help but laugh as he went over and offered her his shoulder to lean on.

'Thanks,' she slurred. 'No way am I trying to walk on these heels on our cobbles.'

'I think the neighbours will thank you too. But best we keep our voices low, otherwise old Jeanie will be out chasing us with her brush!'

Robyn sniggered, 'That's if she isn't out riding it! The old witch!'

Graham tutted, 'Don't be cruel now, she's from a long line of fishing family. It's nice that one descendant is still living in the community. She tells some interesting stories.'

'Sorry, I don't mean it, really. I love a good gossip with her.' Robyn tapped her nose several times, 'That's how I got to know more about you, sweetie!'

'Ah. Now the truth is coming out. Maybe I should get you drunk more often and chat away with you.'

She hugged him tighter, 'We won't be chatting much when we get home!' She gave a filthy laugh as she draped her hands around his shoulders and snuggled into his neck as they tottered home.

Graham wondered what Judy would think of them when she saw the state of her mother.

'How do you do it? I've never seen someone drink so much coffee, especially at this time of night,' marvelled Oliver as he tucked into a limp, squashed burger that oozed ketchup as he bit down.

'I don't have much of an appetite these days,' Monica confessed. 'It keeps me awake, then I don't have the nightmares.'

'You too? Sometimes I wake up crying for Emma. The dreams can be most bizarre. Are you eating enough though?' He looked at her gaunt face, her high cheekbones apparent under taut, pale skin. She appeared so tired, her eyes almost seemed to sink into her skull and her face was a worrying deep shade of grey.

'Probably not. Robyn tries to feed me up.'

'Harriet, at the work café, does the same for me.'

Monica was about to say how lovely she was, but she didn't want to reveal that she'd been at his place of work earlier. 'Do you eat well at the weekends; when the café is closed?'

'No. Cooking for one just makes my loneliness so much more painful. I just eat crisps and snacks, a bit of fruit as well. Or a pre-packaged sandwich from the local shops.'

'That's not good for you. I'm going to insist that I cook for you at weekends. You can come to mine, we'll invite Isobel. You can e-mail her and invite her.'

Oliver put down his burger and wiped sauce and grease from his face, 'That would be lovely. This weekend?' he asked eagerly.

212

'How about from next weekend, it'll give me a chance to tidy the house?'

'It's a date!' he declared enthusiastically. He saw the look of surprise on her face, then muttered a faint, 'Sorry.'

'Don't be daft, it'll be lovely. Maybe you can bring a bottle of wine?'

'I don't really drink wine, but I love that fizzy grape juice. It's like wine. If you close your eyes.'

'That'll be lovely. I drink too much anyway. Robyn is a bad influence.'

'I'd like to meet her. She sounds interesting.'

'She has her work Christmas do tonight. I bet she's having a whale of a time. She's taking her bloke, Graham, along to meet her pals. They'll eat him alive!'

'It sounds fun. I think we need more of that in our lives.' He looked serious again, 'You wanted to tell me something. I think I can guess. I couldn't see a photo of Josephine tonight at group.'

'No, you didn't. It's my secret, I guess. I can't explain it, but I just can't bring myself to look at photos of her.'

'Like me and not going in my lounge. I can understand your reasons, I think. It's perfectly rational, you've had a tremendous loss and find it too upsetting to see her. Don't be ashamed or think of it as a secret.'

'Yes, that's exactly it. Robyn was so kind and helped me move out of my old home. I put a lot in storage, including the old photo albums and camera memory cards with Josephine's pictures on them.

But Robyn saved my favourite photo. It used to sit in a beautiful frame on my bedside cabinet.'

'That was kind of her. You can look at that one?'

'No. Please don't think me a wicked person, but it's on a shelf, lying face down. I can't even bring myself to dust it, let alone see the other side.'

Oliver quickly wiped his hands on his trousers and then reached across the table, took the paper cup from her, placed it to one side, and gently took her hands. 'If I can go in the lounge with you, perhaps you can turn over the frame. Dust it off and look at Josephine once more? I can be there with you.'

She relished the warmth of his hands on this December morning and was disappointed when he took them away. 'I'd like that. Will you take me home now, Oliver? You can come in and help me.'

'Of course, let me tidy this away,' he looked at his half-eaten burger. 'I miss Harriet's cooking when I'm not at work. I bet you are a skilled cook.'

He was rewarded with a resplendent smile and glimmering eyes that told him all he needed to know.

The key was aimed at the lock but missed and scratched the tarnish before it was withdrawn. Robyn stuck out her tongue in concentration, narrowed her eyes, and thrust it towards the door for the fourth time. It failed to dock.

'Here, let me use mine. Yours doesn't seem to work tonight!' Graham gave a subdued giggle and cast a quick, fretful glance towards

Jeanie's bungalow cottage. He had success in his first attempt, and he opened the door. Light from the open lounge door and the lobby lit their way and there, sitting disapprovingly, was Judy. Her small tail failed to wag. Her nose was furiously sniffing the air, as if smelling the alcohol fumes coming from her parents.

'Hello darling!' garbled Robyn as she stepped in and stooped over her canine chum. She stretched out her hands, ready to scoop her up for an embrace.

Judy gave another cautious sniff or three, turned on her heels, and ran to her basket in the kitchen.

'I'll get you some water,' offered Graham.

Robyn wasn't sure if he was talking to her or the dog.

'On the left is our car park. You don't need a permit, there are no students or businesses near here, not like in the main part of the city. Just take any space you like,' explained Monica.

'I haven't been down here for years. It's a lovely area.'

'It's nice and peaceful. That's why I'm reluctant to leave. Robyn wouldn't take full rent from me for years. I was naughty and transferred a lump sum into her account and insisted she keep it. I know she was struggling with both mortgages.'

'Friends like her are rare.'

'I know. Besides, what am I going to do with all my money from the sale of my house?'

'I received a huge pay out from Emma's insurance. It was supposed to be our nest egg when she reached sixty. It would have paid her an annuity, had she lived.' He sighed, 'It doesn't seem right that I benefit from her death. It's just sitting in the bank.'

'You should talk to Graham. He'll help you invest it wisely.'

'Perhaps. Should we go and see Josephine?'

'It is getting late, are you sure?'

Oliver nodded, 'I wouldn't go to bed if I went straight home. I wouldn't be able to sleep, knowing that I could have helped you.'

'Okay. Let's go before I change my mind.'

They exited the car, both trying to close their doors as quietly as possible. Oliver locked the car and stood there for a moment, as if taking in the fresh sea air, 'It's so still down here, away from the bustle of the city. I love the gentle sound of the ocean; I can just make it out.'

They walked in companionable silence, each lost in their own thoughts. Monica reached a darkened doorway and swiped her hand in the air, like a Jedi Master casting a spell on an Empire Stormtrooper. 'It's on a motion sensor, but the settings are high,' she explained.

'What a lovely place to live.' He stood patiently behind her, waiting to be asked in.

Monica turned around suddenly. They were face to face with noses almost touching. She could feel his hot breath on her. The warmth radiated enticingly from his skin. She instinctively leaned forward and kissed him, a lingering kiss with the softest of touches. She broke away when she felt no pressure from his lips. She looked expectantly at his surprised face in the night's silence. His mouth was agape, and she could see the white, cold air escape and mingle with hers in a lover's dance.

He was in utter shock and remained rooted to the spot and the only word to escape his open mouth was, 'Oh!'

Retreat

'I'm so sorry,' whispered Monica. She turned swiftly, went into her house, and closed the door on Oliver.

He was about to say something, but she was too quick for him. The intimate kiss which he could still feel on his lips had momentarily stunned him. He reached up his hand, intent on knocking softly on the door, but movement at her window caught his eye. She had furiously snapped her curtains closed. He turned to walk reluctantly back to his car. As he ambled off, the door next to Monica's opened. Oliver was passing it after several paces and a woman poked her head out.

'Is she okay? I'm Robyn. Who are you?'

'Hello Robyn, I'm Oliver,' he replied with confusion and doubt spreading across his face. 'I think she's all right. I wanted to make sure she got safely home.' He neglected to tell her about the kiss. 'We've had quite the eventful meeting.'

'At your group?'

'Yes, I'm afraid so. Will you please check on her, I don't like to see her upset?' He looked back to Monica's door, half expecting her to come out.

Robyn stepped out of her doorway and looked to her friend's window. She saw the closed curtains. 'Ah, I'm afraid that she won't answer the door, even to me, if the curtains are closed. It's usually a bad sign.'

This wasn't the reassurance that he wanted to hear. 'I'll be off to bed then. I'll contact her in the morning.'

'Goodnight, Oliver. It was nice of you to bring her home. It was lovely to meet you. Perhaps I'll see you again?'

He cast his eyes over to the darkened window, 'I hope so, Robyn.' He walked away, a solitary figure disappearing into the night.

'I'm glad that I didn't bring you tonight, Josephine. That wicked man would have used you to spin a tale of deceit. Hearing the voices of the dead indeed. He deals out Tarot cards, you know. But enough about him. I don't want him to sully you. He doesn't deserve it. And no way will I allow him to break up group, nor to lead it. Shame on him, and on Nancy. The charlatans. It's unforgiveable. What were they thinking?' Her hand hovered by the photo frame. 'You'd have loved Oliver. He's such a kind man.' She looked back to the locked door. 'I've scared him off though. I've been so stupid. Who am I kidding? He's a few years younger than me. Why would he be interested in me?' Tears fell from her face as she banged her fists against her head. The pain seemed to silence her morose thoughts, and soon she had recovered from her negative emotions. She stood silently at the alcove for several minutes, head bowed, as if in contemplative prayer.

She thought she heard voices coming from outside. She assumed it was Robyn and Graham coming home. She hoped that they'd had a pleasant night out.

After a few minutes she walked into her kitchen, opened the cabinet door under the sink, and withdrew a duster and polish. She returned to the neglected alcove, and she spoke to her daughter again, 'I must take you with me, it's part of the criteria. The paperwork I received had it in bold capitals. Oliver was kind enough to come and help, but I scared him away. I seem to scare everyone I love away. Look at you and your father.' She sighed, 'I hope you are together, somewhere. You both deserve that. I wouldn't want either of you to be alone, not like me.' She banged her hands against her thighs, the metal polish can dug into her muscles and smarted. 'I have to do this. I have to,' she repeated with determination.

She closed her eyes tightly, screwing up her face, like a child about to take some awful tasting purgative medicine, she let go of the can; the carpet absorbed its impact and stopped it rolling far. She reached out with shaking hands and grasped the photo frame, then with her other hand, she rubbed furiously away at the cobwebs and years of dust. She failed to see the small spider scurry up her arm and fall to the floor. She turned the frame over and repeated the dusting. Then she opened her eyes. A deep wail escaped her lips, and she fell to the floor, not caring that her knees impacted on the can. Tears flowed desperately down, wetting the carpet. She blinked furiously, desperate to see the photo of Josephine. A rage of impotence flowed through her and ate at her marrow as she cried out, 'You were so beautiful.'

Robyn slunk down the adjoining wall. The paintwork here was darker, with greasy smudge stains. They fitted perfectly around the outline of her body. She drew her knees up to her arms, as if hugging them, and leant her head against the plasterwork. It was the nearest she could be to her friend. Tears fell from her eyes and were caught by a hand that reached out with a tissue.

Graham then sat beside her and placed a box of tissues on the floor by their feet. He remained silent as he held her tight.

Four legs padded through from the kitchen and Judy snuggled up between them. Her ears pricked up, and she tilted her head to the side, as if hearing through the wall. She gave a low growl of despair for her pal.

Oliver hung his jacket over the bannister, gave the lounge door one last desperate look, and slunk off up the stairs. His shoulders sagged forward and his head almost to his chest as he took one reluctant step after another, like a naughty toddler sent to his bedroom.

The seagulls squawked awake as dawn cracked open, spreading its narrow beams of light across the working harbour. The harbour master's office was fully lit as they communicated with awaiting cargo ships at anchor across the wide beach. A large trawler was already negotiating the narrow inlet where several eager lorries were awaiting their treasures to take to the nearby fish market, hoping to secure the best prices for the weary trawlermen.

This was all lost to Monica as she carried her small suitcase across the cobbles, not wanting to drag it by the wheels in case it woke one of the neighbours. It surprised her to see Robyn's lights on at this time of the morning, especially after such a hard night's partying. She crept quietly past her friend's house as she knew what a light sleeper Judy was. She soon found herself at the car park where a lone man sat in a taxi. She made for its boot.

The alarm on Oliver's phone buzzed by his ear. He reached across to his bedside cabinet and switched it off. He hadn't slept well, barely at all. Thoughts of Monica were whizzing through his head. He'd enjoyed the kiss. It was so unexpectedly welcome. He sat bolt upright, grabbed his phone, and then realised that he didn't have her phone number. The group never communicated outside of the church meeting rooms. Just a few words of greetings or goodbyes on the pavement. They'd neglected to exchange numbers.

He padded through to the bathroom and emptied his bladder. As he was washing his hands, he realised he had her e-mail address. That would have to do. He quickly dried his hands, forgoing his morning shower and shave. He returned to his bed and began composing a sentence. He stopped tapping away. But what could he say? His index finger hovered over the screen. He looked at the time at the top of the screen. It was probably too early to disturb her. But Harriet would be preparing breakfasts for the early workers. Her porridge was legendary. Oliver had never tried it. He always grabbed a coffee and croissant to go. She was so keen to play matchmaker over the last year. He knew she wouldn't mind asking Jude to take over her tasks whilst she helped him compose the right words.

Oliver nodded, slipped on yesterday's clothes, grabbed his wallet, phone and keys, and ran out of the room.

Monica slipped the man a twenty-pound note, 'Thanks for taking me here so promptly, please keep the change.'

The taxi driver changed his sullen expression to one of glee. This last fare had made the long night's driving worthwhile. None of his other customers tipped so well. 'Let me get your case. It looked heavy.' He switched off his engine and used his key fob to open the boot. It was wide open by the time they got there. 'Have a safe trip.'

'Thank you. Enjoy your sleep, you've earned it.'

'Thank you.' He whistled as he returned to his cab, he'd park up and treat himself to a greasy breakfast, the one with the jumbo sausage.

'She was in here, yesterday, looking for you,' confided Harriet. 'She looked so upset when I said that you'd gone back to work.'

'I had that important conference call,' murmured Oliver.

'That's what I told her. But we had a good chat. She seems lovely, maybe a bit lost. But that's understandable. And she kissed you?'

'Yes. I didn't see it coming. I thought she was only wanting to be my friend. I didn't kiss her back. I wish I had. I've grown to love her over the months and years of group.'

'Then that is what you should say,' encouraged Harriet wisely. 'To start with.'

Oliver grinned at her, 'See, I knew you'd know what to say.'

Harriet looked him up and down, 'Let me get you some porridge, and when you go to your office, make sure you change into that spare shirt you keep in your locker just in case she comes here again.' She wrinkled her nose, 'A bit of deodorant or aftershave wouldn't go amiss. Ask my Mitch, he'll have some in that man bag of his. He's always spraying it on before he meets his girl.'

Oliver nodded absently; he was too engrossed in composing an e-mail.

Graham rose from the floor, careful not to disturb Robyn. He'd brought their duvet and pillows from their bed at about three in the morning. He had wrapped it around Robyn, carefully lifting her head when she'd fallen into a deep sleep. Her plush carpet made for a nice mattress and he'd left Judy curled asleep in her mother's arms. He'd kept vigil. The crying and screaming coming from next door had abated an hour later and there was just silence. He hoped their friend was all right.

Robyn yawned and stretched out. 'Sorry, I must have dropped off.' She looked in surprise at the pillow, doing a double-take when her arms felt duvet and stopped her from extending her limbs. 'You are thoughtful.' Then she remembered why she was here, on the floor. She sat up, wakening a grumpy Judy as she fell from her arms. The dog scrambled for the front door.

224

'I'll let her out for a pee,' offered Graham.

'I think she wants her auntie. Last night was the worst I've ever heard from Monica. I thought the wailing would never stop.' She put her hands to her head, 'Ouch!'

Graham couldn't help a laugh, 'Serves you right. You were guzzling away the booze last night.'

'I'll feel better after a few glasses of water. But first I think we should check on Monica.'

'Are you sure? I thought she likes to be left alone.'

'Usually. But Oliver said something occurred last night. I don't care if she's cross with me. I can't leave her anymore.' She walked into the kitchen and picked up a set of keys and returned, making for the front door, 'I'll use the spare set and poke my head through.'

'I'll come with you. I've been worried about her too. It suddenly went quiet an hour ago.'

They left their house with Judy trotting obediently between them.

Robyn put the key in the lock, having a better aim than last night. She cracked the door open and peeked in. Then she opened it wider and thrust her head through the gap. She could see through to Monica's lounge. Her friend was not on her sofa or armchairs. 'I think she may have gone to bed. Can you please wait here with Judy? I just want to go through and check on her. I'll tiptoe in.' She gave her, 'Wait there,' hand signal to her dog.

Judy sat, her tail gave a tentative wag on the cobbles as she watched her mistress extend her arm and hovered her palm, face

225

down, fingers stretched, and then walked through the door and out of sight. It relieved her to see her come back in a few seconds, though she sensed that her mummy was unhappy.

An alarmed look was clear on Robyn's face as she returned to Graham and Judy. She gave one last look inside the hallway, as if double-checking. 'She's not there.'

The bus pulled out of the busy station and swung right, affording Monica the view of a magnificent Victorian three-storey brick building with high arched windows. Colourful banners furled slightly in the breeze, advertising the performances of the seasonal pantomime. She thought of Josephine and how much she loved this theatre and shouting out various catchphrases. She wondered if the dames still threw sweets out to the audience, directing them to the children. Health and Safety probably stopped this tradition.

She was pleased to have a seat by herself and she allowed her thoughts to drift away and she soon thought of the retreat in Perth and what it would be like. She hoped to find compassion, empathy, and perhaps some meaning to take home with her. From what she'd read on their website, and in the pamphlets, she knew she wouldn't be alone. It was shocking, the number of mums and dads who waded through life without their child.

She reached into her pocket and withdrew her phone. It had been digging into her hip. Monica idly looked at the screen, fiddled with her settings and logged into the free Wi-Fi of the bus. She looked through her e-mails. Most were work related, but there was one from

226

Oliver. Her heart fluttered, like a pair of dove's wings were gently caressing her core. It's subject simply said 'Kiss.'

She steadied her trembling hand by clasping the other firmly on the phone and then tapped open the message. A broad grin spread over her face as she read through the message. Then her phone battery went flat.

Harriet was in reception, talking to Mitch, making sure that he had helped tidy up the appearance of his boss.

Oliver walked out of his office, saw her, and sauntered up to Mitch's desk.

'Has she replied yet?' she quickly asked, eager for news.

'No. It's been a few hours now. I think I've really upset her.'

Mitch looked up from his computer screen with concern, he'd never seen his boss so upset. Well, not since the weeks and months after his wife had taken her own life. 'Nick and I can manage, why don't you go off early for the weekend.'

Harriet nodded her agreement. 'Go home, have a shave and shower, buy some flowers, and then go to her.'

Oliver contemplated this, shook his head and sucked air through his teeth, 'No. I wouldn't want to make a fool of myself. I wouldn't want to bother her.'

Harriet took him by the shoulders, looked deeply into his eyes, and reminded him, 'She kissed you.'

Oliver beamed, 'She did, didn't she! I'll just finish what I was working on, then I'll go to her.'

Mitch shook his head, 'No. I'll finish what you started. You grab your coat. It's about time that you put yourself and your own needs first, for once.'

'Thank you. Both of you. I wish I'd kissed her back. I really do.' He strode off with purpose.

Monica put her phone to her lips and gave it a brief kiss. She'd read the important parts of her e-mail before the screen went dead. If only she'd thought to bring a charger. She rarely used her phone. She didn't know what made her check her e-mails. Boredom? A sixth sense? Hope? Whatever it was, she was glad that she had. She headed towards the retreat with expectation and love in her heart.

'Why didn't you tell me mum? I hate the thought of you worrying all these months. What a thing to do!'

Isobel looked sheepishly at her granddaughter, 'I know. I feel like I've let the group down.'

Wendy spoke with vigour, 'You've not let anyone down. You shouldn't have been put in that position. I've half a mind to go over to his so-called office and put a brick through his window, the scheming so and so. There must have been pound signs in his eyes when he saw you all.'

Lindsay looked up from under the Christmas tree, checking in on her mummy. She sounded strange. She crawled over to her and was rewarded with being picked up and cuddled.

'Oliver and Monica said so, but I wondered if they were just being polite.'

'No, they talk sense, not like that nut job. It's crazy, thinking that you can hear the dead.' She looked up to the portrait of her parents, 'We know they don't speak, not to anyone.'

'It's the others I feel for, especially Barry, he lives on his own. He would do anything to hear from his daughter again.'

Wendy looked hard at her mum, 'You are going to phone the charity, aren't you?' She stared until she got a reply.

'I think I'll leave that to Monica and Oliver. They should have been deputies by now. I don't want to be the one to rock the boat.' She rang her hands over and over in worry, 'I don't want to upset Nancy. She's been running the group for years.'

'If you won't phone them, then I will. Nancy put you in the position in the first place, so don't you give her another thought.'

'But she knows where I live and has my phone number. She'll probably have given it to Roland. I don't want him coming here.'

'Promise me that if either of them does, then you'll phone the police. You can block their number on your mobile. You don't have your landline installed anymore, so that's not a problem. You don't have to answer the door. My Darren done good, installing that video camera.'

Isobel leaned in and tickling Lindsay under her chin, 'Who's got a clever daddy. Making sure great-grandma is safe,' she cooed, though her expression looked dark with worry.

229

The heavy tumbler was put into the sink and the whisky bottle was stored into the back of the cupboard, alongside bottles of cooking oil and sherry. Barry then scooped up the various packets and bottles of pills, ranging from ibuprofen, paracetamol, and his stock of prescribed heart tablets from his doctor. He put these back into the kitchen drawer. He returned to the table and sat down, facing the photo frame of his beloved daughter. 'I don't need to take an overdose, sweetheart. I wanted to be with you. But Roland has promised me we can chat. I can't wait.' He kissed his fingers and then placed his hand gently to the lips in the photograph. 'I love you, darling. We'll speak soon.' He walked out of his house with a spring in his step as he went to buy a newspaper, the first since his bereavement.

'I will not sit at the window anymore, Irvine,' declared Bella. 'That man last night has made me see sense. Thanks for phoning in sick. I just didn't want to be alone.'

'I'd do anything for you,' avowed Irvine, taking her hand.

'I know that they've gone. I must face up to the fact that Paul really was in that coffin and that I must trust the professionalism of the undertakers and that his body wasn't fit to view. My parents must have been beside themselves with grief, and whilst their minds were unbalanced, they must have killed themselves.'

'Yes, my love, I think that's the right way to see things.' He patted her hand with his free hand and then clasped hers tight.

'Perhaps one day their bodies will be found, and I can bury them next to Paul. They would have wanted to be together.'

'I hope so, Bella.'

'It's taken a maniac to make me see sense. I hope he doesn't bother Barry and the others.'

'We should never have been exposed to that freak,' seethed Irvine, taking away his hands and then clenching and unclenching them under the table so that Bella couldn't see his rage.

'No, but he acted as the catalyst that broke my trance at the window.'

'You probably needed all those months to quietly contemplate and accept your loss.'

'Yes, that's a good way of seeing it. I'm not sure that I want to go back to group, but I will for the sake of Barry, and to keep that lunatic away from him.' She stood up and walked to the coffee table, picked up a magazine, returned to Irvine with a shy look upon her face. Then she put down the publication and wrapped her arms around him. 'Turn to page fifty-two,' she huskily whispered into his ear. She gave it a seductive nibble for good measure.

He picked up the bridal magazine with a glint in his eye, turned the pages to the required fold, and a broad smile spread upon him. He saw a handsome groom in a kilt, waistcoat, and black jacket with tails.

'I'm not going to show you what I'm going to wear, but my dream is to see you at the altar wearing something like this.'

He stood up, turned, and swept her up in a loving embrace. 'I can't wait to see how beautiful you'll look in your dress.'

'I'm afraid that I need to take more than today off,' reasoned Shaun into his phone. He waited a few seconds whilst his boss vented down the line. He thought to his nest egg; the money would come in handy now. 'That's not my problem, I have to put my wife's needs first. She needs me to look after her.' He looked across the room, Cherie was sat in her armchair, staring blankly at the switched off television. She was slowly moving forward and back whilst seated, her spine not quite contacting the rear of her chair. Shaun hung up, not caring that he may have lost his job. He'd send the personnel office a letter confirming the reasons for needing to go long-term sick.

The front door opened and closed, allowing a brief flurry of winter air to swirl around the silent house. Andrew, sweaty from running in the park, poked his head around the doorway to the lounge, 'All right if I have a shower dad? Does mum need me?'

Shaun ruefully shook his head as he thought back to the phone call. He'd just lost the best job of his life. He sighed, 'No son, you take your time. I've left my job. I'll look after mum now. You've done a brilliant job, but we both want you to concentrate on your education and do us proud.'

Andrew stepped into the room and squatted by his mother, 'I will, I promise.' He turned to his father, 'Can we afford for you to be off work? Will we lose the house?'

'Don't you worry about a thing. I've lots of savings we can use. Your mum needs me now. And I'll need your help now and again, to give me a break. The doctor said that was important. I'll be taking her back on Wednesday. You could come along?'

Andrew placed his right hand on his mum's face, trying to get her attention away from the blank, mirrored television screen. He could see that she momentarily saw him, really looked at him.

As he rose to his feet, she grasped his hand, trying to get it back onto her face. She whimpered, 'Don't leave me as well, my beautiful boy.'

Oliver walked past the lounge window and saw that the curtains were still closed. He looked at his wristwatch and was surprised to see that it was lunchtime. He didn't think Monica would still be in bed at this hour. He reached her door and gave it a timid knock. It remained shut, but the door of the house next to hers opened and the woman from last night stepped out, looking in a better state. She wasn't swaying this time. 'Hello, Robyn, isn't it? I was hoping to see Monica.' He thrust out the bouquet, as if presenting them to her instead.

'I'm afraid that I was worse for wear last night and not thinking straight. Sorry.'

Oliver remained quiet, not wanting to embarrass the lady by agreeing with her.

She continued with, 'Monica has gone to a retreat for the weekend.' She teased and left the statement hanging, expecting Oliver to say something like, 'What, with monks?'

Instead, he surprised her by saying, 'Yes, she spoke about that a few months ago. It's run by another bereavement charity. I think it'll do her the world of good, being with other mothers who have lost a child. It sounds healing. It's in Perth, isn't it?'

'That's right. It completely slipped my mind last night. But don't rush off. Graham phoned in sick today and I have the day off.' She opened her door wider, 'Come in and have a bite to eat with us, we'd love for you to join us. We don't get to meet many of Monica's friends.'

Oliver stepped over and placed the flowers towards Robyn and was pleased to see her reach out her arms for them. 'In that case, these are for you.'

Robyn dazzled him with her pearly-white teeth, 'They are so lovely. I'll put them in my special vase and show them to Monica,' She gave him a naughty wink, 'I have a feeling that you'll be buying a fresh bouquet on Sunday night. I know what time her bus gets in the station.'

Oliver grinned back and followed her into her home. Judy came running up to him and danced on two back paws and scrabbled at his legs with her front paws. He picked her up, drew her to his face, and allowed her to shower him with licks. He giggled at the tickling sensation.

Robyn watched them and chortled as she closed her door, blocking out Jeanie's view from across the square. 'You've just earned the seal of approval from Judy. She's Monica's best friend.'

Judy's ears pricked up straight at the mention of her pal next door, and her head turned immediately to the lobby in anticipation of her chum walking through. Then her attention was turned back to Oliver as he reached the soft spot in her ear that he was gently stroking.

The engaged dial tone repeated on a loop, much to the disgust of Corrina. She really needed to offload her thoughts about last night to the charity head office.

Adam, seeing her seethe with rage and not wanting to be inadvertently on the receiving end of her anger, had gone out for a stroll. He wished that he'd had the company of a dog. Instead, he had taken his wallet and had decided that he could afford thirty minutes in the local café. During this time, he had composed and sent a brief e-mail to the support group charity outlining his disgust at Roland's claims and explaining that they would not be returning.

He took a different route home. He found himself drawn to the address on the business card that Roland had slipped him last night. He stopped on the busy road and looked across to the shabby looking building. A crystal ball sat in the window and Adam had visions of the fraudulent Roland waving his hands mysteriously around the globe whilst an expectant and gullible client sat enthralled at his every word. Adam resisted the urge to go in, grab it, and throw it to the floor to shatter it. He wondered who even makes such things. Had he gone closer, he would have seen various tarot cards placed strategically around the windowsill.

He almost spat across the road as he saw the proud sign which boasted, 'Roland, your happy psychic medium and clairvoyant.' Small white lettering boasted his range of 'skills and qualifications,' which ranged from tarot card readings, past life regression, spiritual healing, life-coaching, personal horoscopes, tea leaf readings, angel cards, crystal healing, hypnosis, empathetic ear, and healing hands. Adam shook his head in despair, 'How desperate must some people be to come here?' he muttered under his breath.

As if reading his mind, a thin old lady, hair wrapped in a mauve scarf, paced to the window. She used a metal cane to support herself. She peered in nervously, cupped her hands around the pane of glass, trying to see into the building, walked two faltering steps away, stopped, turned back, and opened the door and was swallowed up from sight by the black drapes that prevented anyone looking in. Adam wished her luck and pondered what harmful lies she would be told as he made his way home. He hoped Corrina wouldn't still be seething, he just wanted a peaceful life with no dramas.

Monica was relieved to see a taxi in the rank and she walked up to it as another lady was running towards it. They reached the open window of the cab at the same time. Monica took a step back, 'You have this one. I've enough time to wait for the next.'

The breathless woman looked relieved, though a little embarrassed. 'That's kind.' She rattled off an address to the driver, and he nodded in acknowledgment. The woman went to open the back-passenger door and was surprised to see Monica still stood there.

'I couldn't help but overhear where you are going.' Monica lowered her voice, 'Are you there for the retreat?'

The woman looked surprised, 'Why yes.'

'So am I. May I share your taxi please?'

The woman nodded vigorously as she opened the door, 'I'm so relieved. I hate travelling alone and going somewhere strange. You pop in first, there's plenty of room for our cases. These traditional taxis are so much roomier than those firms that make their drivers use their own cars, don't you think?'

'Yes. I'm Monica.'

'Hello Monica, I'm Beryl. Let's get settled and we can have a chinwag during the drive.' She too heaved her suitcase across the taxi and closed the door. 'Thank you, driver.'

'No problem ladies, it's about a fifteen-minute drive. There are some roadworks on the way I'm afraid.'

'That's not a problem at all,' reassured Beryl as she then turned to Monica and told her of her loss and her hopes for the retreat.

Monica leaned back in her seat, nodding at the correct places, and offering words of consolation as Beryl spoke about her dead son. As she listened, she wondered if she might have a phone charger with her.

Regroup

Oliver ran through the shopping centre, not caring about the brightly lit shops to either side of him with their tempting displays. He only had eyes on avoiding the crowds of shoppers who were intent on an early Christmas bargain and gifts for their loved ones.

A bouquet of flowers was closely guarded to his chest, and he slipped several times on the highly polished flooring. He wore his best shoes and their soles had little grip. His favourite tie flapped over his shoulder as he sprinted. He'd not allowed time for the busy car park and had counted himself lucky to get a space on the seventh floor. But the lifts were broken today. He'd seen an engineer try to scratch his head through his safety helmet in puzzlement as to the cause. Instead, Oliver had flown down the stairs, not even stopping to help the young mother with a child in a buggy wondering how she was going to get to the only chemist in the city that sold the teething gel recommended by the health visitor. He'd felt guilty over that. But now his thoughts were on reaching the bus station that had been built to the side of the shopping centre but had no parking for cars and didn't allow vehicles, other than their proud fleet, to enter.

He turned the corner by the camping shop and mobile phone accessory store and bumped into a beefy man walking hand in hand with his young daughter. She had a tail-wagging, golden retriever by the leash in her other hand. Oliver looked first in puzzlement as to why she had been allowed to take her dog shopping, and then in disappointment as he saw how squashed his flowers now were. Then he looked up in embarrassment as he apologised to the stranger for not looking where he was going.

The man brushed a stray petal from his jacket and laughed, 'No harm done, mate.' He looked down at the flowers, 'I hope she's worth it. Come on Ruby and Annabelle, let's get your mum her necklace.' He strode off, led by his daughter, with the golden retriever trotting happily away.

The shopping centre floor sloped and through the glass doors at the end of this narrower corridor Oliver could just make out the bus station. He glanced at his watch and saw that he had a few minutes to spare. He checked the flowers, shrugged, and walked the last part of what seemed to him a marathon. He wanted to cool down. He wiped beads of perspiration from his forehead and rubbed his hand dry on his trousers, not caring that several people were watching him idly as they queued by the newspaper vendor for their favourite Sunday paper.

The glass doors opened automatically as he stepped towards them, and he welcomed the rush of cold air that sent an appreciative chill through him and halted his sweating. He stretched out his elbows, like a bird flapping its wings, to try to dry the damp patches under his armpits. Oliver sauntered over to the lit-up timetable and scrolled his eyes down the screen, seeing that the bus was due in any moment at terminus three. He walked towards it, his heart racing, and he could feel himself still panting from the exercise and from the butterflies that were in his stomach.

'Meeting a girlfriend?' enquired the old lady sat on the metal bench by the terminus. She was wrapped up in a long wax jacket, like those worn by gamekeepers, and a cosy looking scarf covered her neck. She had sensibly worn a green flat cap with a feather tucked in the side.

'I hope so!' enthused Oliver as he sat down and tried hard not to shiver. The cold December late afternoon was biting at him now that he wasn't exerting himself. He hoped he didn't smell. He shouldn't do, not after all the bottles and sprays Harriet and Mitch had dropped off this morning.

She snorted, 'You won't impress her much with those. Half the petals are off them.' She flicked her head to the dustbin, 'You should put them in there, or give them to me.' She looked on in expectation.

Oliver looked down with disappointment. She was right. Most of the colourful blooms had been deposited on the shopping floor. In his haste, he had left them for the cleaners to scoop up. He felt more guilt.

A fat bus appeared to glide towards the pavement like a space shuttle docking, and came to a halt, millimetres away from the kerb. The cargo side panels slowly released its lock and raised automatically, revealing rows of assorted cases and large rucksacks. The front door hissed open and passengers stepped off and made their way to the luggage compartment or went straight into the shopping centre. Monica wasn't one of them.

'It looks like you've been stood up,' grunted the woman. She was all but rubbing her hands in glee at Oliver's misfortune.

But then his eyes shone in the subdued lighting as he saw Monica speaking to the driver. She was handing him a banknote. The driver was grinning back and there was much nodding of heads.

Oliver took several steps towards the bus, his legs suddenly feeling like jelly. Not from the running, but in anticipation and fear. He ploughed on though and soon found himself at the foot of the steps, just as Monica turned from the driver.

'Oh, Oliver! What are you doing here? How did you know I would be on this bus?' She took a hesitant step down.

Oliver stretched out the squashed flowers, 'I bumped into a big man. Sorry! I was running and not looking where I was going.'

Monica scooped them up as if they were the crown jewels. She looked expectantly at him.

'I loved the kiss!' he blurted. 'I love you, Monica! I've grown to love you with each passing group meeting. You are such a special lady.'

She grinned and almost jumped the last step and then embraced him, not caring that the flowers were getting further crushed. She felt the desperate, loving embrace of Oliver, relishing the closeness. It was not a cuddle of consoling a grieving mother at a support group. It was a closeness of two lovers who savoured intimacy as if melding into one. 'I love you too, Oliver, I really do. I'd always hoped that you felt the same way. My battery died.'

'Eh?' he exclaimed in pleasant confusion.

'My phone went blank after reading your e-mail. I'd forgotten to charge it, and I hadn't taken a charger with me. The retreat was full on and I hadn't time to ask around for one.' She paused for breath.

Oliver laughed, a carefree, joyous chuckle for the first time in years. 'It doesn't matter. You are all that matters.' He broke off the hug and took her hand, relishing her warmth and softness. 'Let's grab your bag and get inside.'

They turned around and found the bus driver was standing by Monica's small case, as if guarding it. He extended out its handles and wheeled it towards her. As he handed it over, he grinned, 'The best of luck to you both. You've made my day.'

'Thank you,' murmured Monica as Oliver took ownership of the case. 'My afternoon just got a lot better!'

Beryl walked up her garden path, lit by solar powered lanterns that her son had installed last year. He had been a gifted gardener and would have been disappointed to see the rambling roses and feral hedging. Large weeds sprouted between cracks in the crazy paving. She vowed that tomorrow this would all change. She'd prune back the dead wood and apply weedkiller; it was time things changed. The retreat had taught her that. It was time to get out and face people once more. But not tonight. It had been a long journey home and two coach trips, with an hour wait between connections. It was midnight and long past her bedtime. Tonight, she would wean herself off the herbal tablets she'd bought from a local practitioner. She hadn't realised how addicted to them she'd become. Thank goodness one of the volunteer speakers had been a doctor and patiently answered their health questions. No topics were off the menu. She hadn't realised how harmful some ingredients could be to her liver. She'd been advised to reduce the dose over a few weeks, otherwise she'd get awful withdrawal effects like stomach cramps and muscle pains. She had to look after her health now that she'd applied to be a volunteer.

She put her key in the lock and thought about the training course in the Spring. She hoped Monica might be there; she seemed a lovely lady, and Beryl was so pleased that they'd exchanged phone numbers. If only she'd also thought to bring a charger, then Monica could have put it into her contacts. But no matter, she was confident that they'd keep in touch. It was nice to have a friend again. The retreat had taught her she wasn't alone in losing her friends because of the stigma surrounding suicide. One poor man, only in his late forties, had been ostracised by his father, mother and two siblings. All because his son had taken his own life. How heartless some people could be; and how sensitive others could be. She's heard stories of friends watching mums and dads around the clock until the grieving parents were strong enough to stand on their own two feet again. They cooked meals, cleaned, did the gardening, walked the dogs, and attended their hospital appointments with them. It had warmed her heart, and the kindness of the volunteers was priceless. She couldn't wait to get trained.

The morning sun shone across the cobbles, giving them a glittering shine, and lit up the communal square. Jeanie was out, brushing away imaginary dust from her doorstep. Robyn gave her a cheery wave as she and Judy popped next door.

Monica opened the door, a joyful countenance upon her, but she dropped into a frown as she saw her pal's expression.

Robyn shook her head at her chum and reached forward and flicked her hair around. She tutted, 'This won't do at all. No, no, no,' she chided to Monica. 'But fortunately, I have the answer!'

Monica creased her eyes tight and wondered if her friend had lost the plot. 'What on earth are you talking about?' She stepped back and ushered Robyn and Judy in out of the cold. The sun was deceptively teasing and had no warmth. It was Monday morning and Monica had spent most of the night talking to Oliver. He left at one-thirty and she'd only just got up. She had a splitting headache from all the emotion yesterday, and she desperately wanted a coffee or two.

'You. Have you looked in the mirror?' Robyn walked Judy through into the lounge and suddenly halted. She was staring at the alcove. 'She's there!' she cried joyously. She turned to her pal and cuddled her. 'Your Josephine is out for you to see.' She broke off her embrace, 'She was such a stunner, look at her cheeky smile.' She walked over to the alcove and picked up the photo frame and pointed to the seashells glued along the bottom of the wood. 'I love what you've done with it!'

'There were arts and crafts afternoon at the retreat. It was mostly us ladies. The men went off to sit in the woods and talk in a circle. It broke the ice and split up the couples, so that we could all talk freely. I wasn't the only one who'd lost a daughter. I wasn't the only one

244

who had found looking at photos painful. But it was good. The facilitators gave us some expert advice and tips. Each of them had lost a child. One had lost both her children to suicide, can you imagine?'

Robyn shook her head, 'No, I can't. But you and Oliver!' she shrieked. 'What a lovely man.'

'That was so naughty of you to arrange our meeting at the bus.' She eyed her friend, 'But thank you!'

Robyn waved her hands over Monica's hair and down her body. 'But this sister, this has to change. It's my day off, and I'd arranged a hair appointment, getting my nails done and a facial, now my other gift to you, and Oliver, is that you are coming with me and you'll be taking the appointments, and then we'll go shopping. It's my treat.'

Judy yapped her approval and was rewarded with a pat on the head by her favourite aunt. She then jumped on the sofa and got cosy on her blanket.

'I don't need all that,' she turned to her mirror and cradled her face, 'Do I?'

'Trust me, you do. I love you to bits, but you've let yourself go. I'll make you a coffee whilst you get ready and then I'll call a taxi.'

'Not for me, I've some fruit and porridge growing cold in the kitchen. I'll just have a glass of milk, or water. I must get a shop in and order some decaffeinated tea and coffee.'

Robyn did a double-take, with mouth agape.

'I drank too much caffeine. It made me wired. It doesn't help to promote a healthy sleep pattern. We had a brief talk about it, by a doctor. I'll have a stinking headache for a few days, I might even be crabby, but it'll be worth it.'

'Wow! Maybe I should meet some monks on a retreat too!' joked Robyn as she followed her pal into the kitchen.

Oliver walked up to Harriet, tipped her a wink, then strolled off to the lift with a bounce in his step. He left her mouth agog, but unable to press him for information as she was busy serving a customer. Oliver whistled as he waited for the lift, watching her with amusement from the corner of his eye.

Adam strolled slowly along the edges of the pond. He stopped at the gentle flowing waterfall as he watched the water glide down the three long steps. He idly beheld a twig drift by, taking a moment of mindfulness to recalibrate his mind. He'd had a reply from the charity and was satisfied with their intended action. In his mind, he drew a line under the events of the last week. But he was out for another walk because Corrina was still shouting down the phone to the unlucky administrator.

'Your aftershave did the trick, Mitch!' enthused Oliver.

Mitch held out his palm and the friends high-fived.

'Now can I stop smelling like a Greek God?' kidded Oliver as he idly rifled through that morning's post.

'Yes. I'll have them back, boss. Do you know how much some of them cost?'

Oliver shook his head ruefully, suddenly serious. 'I have an important call to make. I'll do it now and get it over with. Monica said she'll be ringing them too. You'll never guess what happened to us? I'll fill you in later. When you tell your mum, she'll think you are pulling her leg. I still can't believe it myself.' He wandered down to his office, leaving the post on Mitch's desk.

The younger man wondered what his boss was talking about, but remained at his desk, he'd learn all in good time. He grinned, Monica and his boss, who'd have thought.

'Okay. I give in. Let's go to the appointments. But remind me to make a phone call. I'll tell you all about it in the taxi. Something mind-blowing happened at group?'

Robyn looked to Monica, 'Is it serious? Oliver eluded you had a dreadful night there. But you left so early on Friday. I haven't had a chance to catch up with you. I tried ringing you several times.' She was about to tell her she heard her wails through the thin walls; but thought better of it. Her friend needed privacy now and again. She handed Monica her hairbrush.

Monica accepted it, putting her body at the disposal of her pal, knowing that she would smarten her up for her first proper date with Oliver. He was taking her to a plush hotel in the city for a meal. She'd have preferred some of Harriet's home cooking. She absent-mindedly wondered what he'd have for his lunch and whether he slept better last night.

'Well?' demanded Robyn. 'You can talk and brush at the same time. Our cab will be at least twenty minutes.' She listened, mouth and eyes growing wider, as Monica recounted the tale of Roland and Nancy.

Oliver sucked in his breath, 'I see,' was all he could bring himself to say. He still felt angry and didn't want to take it out on the charity founder. Such was the seriousness of his call that the administrator had put him through to her home number.

'I'm so sorry that this has happened to your group too, Oliver. We've been inundated with complaints from up and down the country. The Edinburgh group deputies came to see me personally. They said that Roland all but held a seance. I've had to seek legal advice, and this has prevented us from banning him from all groups straight away. He's still a grieving sibling and Nancy a grieving mother, so we trod carefully. But we've also had to factor in the feelings and safety of our groups. I founded the charity to help those touched by suicide. I hate the thought of this man lining his pockets at the expense of our members. But please be assured that our lawyer has sent him an injunction, banning him from attending any meetings. They have served the same legal papers to Nancy today.'

Oliver nodded his head, then remembered he was on the speakerphone. He leaned closer to the microphone. 'Thank you, Silvia, and bless you for founding the charity. Up to now, it's been a great comfort to my pals and I.'

'I hope you'll all find a way forward and attend meetings once more. We have paid the rent to the church for a few months more and I'll personally ensure it's paid till the end of the year and beyond.'

'I have the group members e-mails, except for one elderly man who doesn't use computers, but I have his phone number. I'll contact them and put their minds at rest. Thank you for acting so quickly.'

'I'm only sorry our legal team couldn't have worked swifter. It's not something they've encountered before.'

'No. It was a shock to us all as well.'

'I can only imagine. Nancy seemed such a sweet, old lady, always eager to help. Now we know why. She told me that no one wanted to be deputies, that's why she travelled so far to your city.'

'That's not right, Silvia. I've certainly been asking for about a year to do the training.'

'Ah. Again, I can only apologise. I have had this issue with some other groups she attended. As a result, I had to ask our trainers to work additional weekends to emergency train new deputies and facilitators.' She paused as she turned over a few sheets of paper.

Oliver waited patiently as he heard the sheaves turn.

'I know that it's getting near Christmas and people are busy, but do you think you could come here at the weekend? We'll pay your travel and hotel costs. Ideally, you'd need two deputies and a new co-ordinator for your group.'

Oliver grinned, 'If you've two spaces for this weekend, I have someone in mind who I know will say yes when I see her tonight. If you could please book two rooms, I'll take time off and drive us down. I'll let you know about a third. She might be on babysitting duty. Don't worry about travelling costs, I'll meet those and any expenses at the hotel. In fact, leave the accommodation booking to me, it'll save the charity some money.'

'That's so kind of you, Oliver. Every penny matters. Few people want to fundraise for a suicide charity. I hope to break this stigma one day.'

'I'll let you go now Silvia, thank you for taking such swift action.'

'I'm only sorry your group has been troubled by this man too. I've been taking calls all week. Bye Oliver. I'll see you at the weekend.'

Doctor Munro rolled her chair further to Adam, not quite wanting to believe what he was telling her. She leaned forward, as if trying to listen closer. 'He did what!' she thundered.

Adam looked abashed, 'We didn't realise that it was him you warned us about in our first consultation after we lost Fraser.'

'We didn't put two and two together, our emotions were all over the place,' insisted Corrina.

'Neither of you has anything to apologise for. If I had known that she was his mother, I would never have sent you to the support group. I've often wondered why none of my patients have come back and told me about it. I should never have sent you there.'

'We won't go back,' declared Adam firmly. 'I don't want any dramas.'

'There won't be,' insisted the doctor. 'You leave this with me.'

Robyn looked at her pal curiously, as if not quite believing what she'd just heard. 'You're pulling my leg!'

'You know I wouldn't use my group as a joke or prank. He went around them all, merrily dishing out business cards as if he were the Messiah with all the answers. You saw how vulnerable I was after losing Josephine.' She looked across to the alcove and smiled at the photo.

A dark cloud momentarily seemed to pass over Robyn's expression. 'I thought I might have lost you as well. You got really ill, not just physically.'

'I know. Sorry.'

'Don't you be sorry, I'm glad you came through it. I'd have been distraught if I lost you.' Robyn interlaced her fingers through Monica's, feeling just how bony her friend had become over the years. 'Now let's get you tarted up for tonight!'

Judy barked, jumped off the sofa and sat by the front door. Her little tail was thumping from side to side in anticipation.

'Okay,' sighed Monica, her little resistance all gone. 'But don't go overboard, will you?'

Her pal winked to Judy, 'Trust us!'

Monica groaned. She knew what that cheeky look meant. 'And I must make a phone call at eleven. Isobel and Oliver will have made theirs by then. We all agreed on the right course of action.'

That afternoon, Isobel picked up her phone for what felt to her for the hundredth time. She walked over to her lounge curtain, pulled aside the fabric, and looked to her front step. She then guiltily checked up and down the street. She half expected mother and son to be there. She thought back to what Wendy had said, took a deep breath, and pressed down hard on the numbers. She half-hoped that it would be engaged, but the ringtone sang out and she committed herself to her deed.

Oliver paced the chequered tiling, under the awning of the hotel that protected its guests from sunshine and rain. He wove between the doorman, who was splendid in a deep burgundy greatcoat with shiny buttons and a top hat, and the nearby office workers who just wanted to get home after a fraught Monday. He watched as each taxi pulled up, spilled its human cargo, and drove off. So intent was his scrutiny, he failed to see Monica walk across from the nearby bus stop. She was shrugging out of her overcoat. She crossed safely, put her fingers to her lips to warn the doorman not to give away her position, and then tiptoed, as carefully as she could on her new heels, far taller than any she'd ever worn before, to Oliver. He turned mid pace, and then froze as he took in the sight of his new girlfriend, 'Wow!' he exclaimed.

'A good wow, I hope?' she asked timidly.

'A brilliant wow! I sense Robyn has been helping. You look even more beautiful than when I last saw you. I love what you've done with your hair, and your dress. Wow! Your face is glowing!'

She looked at him coyly, 'You scrub up well yourself.' She leaned in for a kiss and was delighted to find that he'd omitted to put on that awful smelling aftershave.

The couple lingered over the kiss, not caring that the world continued around them. Then they broke off into a tight embrace, as if each feared the other would go.

Monica looked up to the revolving doorway and wondered why they had a doorman who didn't need to open doors. She assumed, correctly, that he was in fact a security guard and luggage porter, employed to keep out undesirables. 'I've never eaten here?'

'Me neither, though I've always wanted to.' He leaned out of the embrace and looked to her eyes for a reaction, 'I hope you don't mind, but I invited a friend. He's already at our table.'

Monica looked at him quizzically. She thought she'd have him all to herself, 'Oh,' was all she could manage, hoping that she didn't show her disappointment.

Roland held up the ripped documents. He'd sellotaped them together after his rage this morning, but he'd torn into them in fury again. He was reading them for the fourth time, not quite believing the cheek of the charity, his and his mother's charity, their groups. His anger had prevented him from seeing into his crystal ball, and his favourite crystals were doing little to soothe his rage. He'd tried to read the tarot, but his shaking hands had dropped the cards and they channelled little spiritual energy. He'd thrown them across the room in disgust and was shocked to see The Seven of Cups, the card that portended doom, uppermost on his carpet.

Nancy sat quietly in her lounge. The silence enchanted her, and the stillness brought her some inner peace. The last week had been heady and this morning's post was the icing on the cake. She'd failed them. Roland, with her help and guidance, could have saved so many souls, but they couldn't see it. She walked back to her computer screen, under the lounge window. Her curtains were open, and she could see out into the dark night. She hadn't bothered with the lounge lights, just the glow of the terminal. It afforded little illumination to the keyboard. She reluctantly put on the main light and drew the curtains. Then she interlocked her fingers and stretched them out, preparing herself physically and mentally for the e-mail she had composed earlier that day. Only one name was missing from the list she'd copied from Oliver's last round robin. He had omitted to blind carbon copy the recipients, and she had harvested the addresses from the CC section. It was her duty; she had to try one last time. She hit the send button and then switched off her PC. She'd read any replies in the morning. Her energy had been depleted. She missed her groups.

'The cheek of the woman!' blurted Andrew as he read his e-mail. He continued reading, uttering oaths under his breath. 'She's claiming that she was only trying to help, and that Roland had aided many people and used his counselling skills to heal them.' Andrew read the e-mail to the end; his fingers were busy scrolling through paragraphs heaped with unworthy praise for Roland. Andrew pressed down on the screen and vanquished it to his trash, where it belonged. He wouldn't bother his dad with it. He looked across to his mum. He expected her to be rocking and hadn't noticed that she had stopped her low-level humming. It surprised him to see her wagging her index finger at him, like she did when he was a naughty child.

'You mustn't swear, darling,' she stammered, just loud enough for Andrew to hear above the noise of the television.

It seemed like the sweetest words he heard all day.

The maitre d' nodded and silently showed Monica and Oliver to their table. Monica followed, hand in hand with Oliver, feeling like a prom queen on her maiden date. It was difficult to see in the candlelight, and she strained to see which tables had a solitary diner.

'Give me that, I want to read it for myself!' demanded Bella, all but snatching the mobile phone from Irvine. She swore loudly as she read with disbelief. 'I hope I never set eyes on either of them again, I'll knock their blocks off.'

Irvine grinned, his feisty old Bella was back, and he couldn't be happier.

Isobel looked to her mobile, and then turned back to Coronation Street, not caring that it was making pinging noises, one straight after the other. Someone somewhere was building up a head of steam.

Adam copied and pasted Nancy's e-mail address and added it to his list of blocked contacts. 'There we go, no more dramas!'

Monica saw the bald head, with tufts of growth along the sides, and recognised him immediately. His broad, slightly stooped back also gave him away. She squeezed Oliver's hand and murmured, 'You thoughtful, lovely, man. What a wonderful thing to do.'

The third guest stood up as he heard them approach, turned around, took in the sight of his friend, grinned and offered, 'You look amazing Monica.'

'It's so great to see you, Barry.' She gathered him in for a hug, not caring if her make-up got smudged. 'I've been so worried about you.'

The maitre d' gave a small cough, pulled out a chair a few inches and waited for Monica to let go of Barry and take a seat. He pulled it slightly forward as she sat. He then reached for her napkin, unfurled it with gusto, like a magician performing a stage trick, and laid it on her lap. He ignored Oliver; he'd already unfolded his napkin. 'May I take your drinks order, madam? Wine?'

'Not for me, I'm detoxing. But I'd love a glass of water.'

'Beer for me,' insisted Barry.

'Just water for me too, I'm driving.'

The maitre d' sighed and left them perusing their dinner menus.

'How have you been, Barry?' asked Monica with a concerned lilt to her voice.

'Oh, so, so,' he offered with a deep sigh. 'Oliver has been ringing me every day, several times at the weekend. That's helped. Roland really shook me up, I don't mind admitting.'

'Yes, please tell me you've not let him talk to you on the phone. You haven't given him your address, have you?'

'No, Oliver came round though. We had a good chat, then went for a walk. It cleared my head. I was believing the nonsense Roland was spouting. How daft was I?' He shook his head ruefully.

'Not at all. I'd give anything to speak to my Josephine, but it can never happen. I know that.'

'As do I now. Oliver showed me how to block Roland's and Nancy's numbers on my phone. He also encouraged me to go to my doctor. He came with me this morning, took time off work, just to help me.'

'It was nothing, I was glad to do it.'

'I'll be seeing a specialist, at the doctor's surgery, she's a counsellor. That's the right person for me to relive my experiences. The doctor thinks that I may have to be referred to someone in the psychiatric hospital as well.' He looked to Oliver, 'I'll try to gather strength to go. I don't have anyone else to ask, my friends have all passed, at my age, it happens every few years.'

Monica reached out for him and held his hand with her free hand. The other was delicately and discretely holding Oliver's under the tablecloth. 'You have us, and the other members of the group. You will come back, won't you?'

'I know, you're all wonderful friends, well, apart from those two,' his brow creased momentarily. He lightened up as he spoke again, 'And Bella, she reminds me of my Kimberly. I look forward to seeing her.'

'That's good. I can always come with you if Oliver can't get away from work.'

Barry looked surprised, 'You'd do that for me. Take time from your busy life.'

'Anytime,' confirmed Monica.

'Thank you.' Barry looked at his two friends, 'So, are you two stepping out?'

He had his answer when they both started giggling like two naughty schoolchildren.

Robyn stretched out on the sofa and gave a loud yawn, 'My work there is done. You should have seen her, Graham. I'd forgotten how gorgeous my Monica is.'

'That was some sacrifice, giving up your appointments for her. Especially at this time of year. Will you get another?'

'I hope so,' she flounced her hair. 'There's no way I'm looking like this at Christmas time.'

Graham leant down and kissed her, 'You look gorgeous as you are.'

'Correct answer!' She grabbed him by his shirt and pulled him down until he was astride her. 'And now it's time for your Christmas present.'

'This was such a lovely treat, thank you Oliver. Are you sure I can't pay for my share?' offered Barry.

'No. It's my pleasure. You've fed me well over the weekend, so this is to say thanks.'

'Bless you,' he hesitated, then continued with, 'mate.'

Oliver gave him his best smile. 'Can I give you a lift home?'

'No,' insisted Barry. 'I've played gooseberry enough. It's been a lovely evening and I've loved your company, but these old bones are ready for his bed! I'll get a taxi. The rank is just outside.'

'Will we see you at group? In January?' asked Monica eagerly.

'Yes, but who will lead it?'

Oliver hadn't chatted to Monica about it, so mysteriously answered, 'It's all taken care of Barry, by the charity.'

'Oh. That's good. I really couldn't face Roland or Nancy again.'

Monica thought back to her phone call this morning, 'They won't be back, ever.'

'That's good too. I wish I could have spoken to my Kimberley. Christmas is going to be so lonely this year.'

'No, it won't,' insisted Monica. She reached across to Oliver's jacket pocket and withdrew a pen. Then she rooted in her clutch bag for a scrap of paper. 'This is my address. I'll expect you at eleven o'clock sharp. You'll spend the day with us, won't he, Oliver?'

He smiled, he hoped she'd say that. 'Yes. But I'll pick you up and drop you off. Taxis will be too expensive on Christmas day, and you may not get one.'

Close to tears, Barry thanked them both for their kindness and bade them a goodnight. Just before he left, he surprised them with how insightful he had been at the groups, despite his anguish, 'She never named her child. Nancy, I mean. She never spoke Anthea's name. It seemed to me that she was ashamed. But you encouraged us all, and rightly so, to say the name of our lost children. It keeps their positive memories alive.' He then beamed, his eyes glistened with joy, rather than sorrow, 'You make a lovely couple. I could see that you were attracted to each other at group. I'm glad you finally got together.'

Monica blushed as she watched him totter off, stopping to thank the servers, and slipping them some coins.

Oliver broke her reverie with, 'That was so kind of you.'

'You don't mind.'

'Not at all. He's still fragile. He really thought he'd be able to speak to his daughter through Roland. I worked hard at convincing him that Roland was a fraudster.' He lightened the tone, 'Did you know Barry was a trained chef, before retiring? He worked at Balmoral, for the Queen. He baked me some scones and makes a light omelette.'

'I can see why you spent the weekend with him,' she teased.

They laughed in a sweet, carefree way, each taking delight in how the years seemed to fall off each other's faces.

'Shall we order coffee?'

'Not for me. At my retreat, I've decided to give caffeine up.'

Oliver looked at her in astonishment and felt her light touch as she reached out and closed his mouth.

'Have you work tomorrow?' she asked.

'Yes, but I'm in no rush to get home.'

'I'm tired, but I don't want to leave you alone. The lack of coffee is making my eyes sore with fatigue. What will you do when I go home?'

'I'll stay up for a bit,' mumbled Oliver.

'Something else I learned on my retreat is that we mustn't blame ourselves.'

'But I do.'

She gently asked, 'Why?'

'Because I was so tired,' he confessed. 'Emma made suicide threats all the time. I went to bed. I told her I loved her, and then we went to sleep. I didn't keep watch over her and she slipped away and ended her life, in our lounge.'

'But you had work, and no one can keep a constant watch on their wife,' reasoned Monica.

'I should have. It was my duty as a husband. That's why I've never dated since. I can't be responsible. I awoke in the early hours, felt her side of the bed. She wasn't there, so I went looking for her, to check on her. But it was too late.'

'It wasn't your fault, Oliver. Emma's mind was unbalanced. You couldn't work during the day and stay awake at night. You needed sleep.' She lowered her voice, 'Is that why you stay awake, until the hour when she passed has gone?'

'Yes,' he admitted.

'You must stop punishing yourself. It wasn't your fault. Can you see that? Like Barry has had to see Roland for the swindler he is.'

'Deep down, yes. But I've kept this secret from you all at group. I didn't want anyone judging me.'

She sighed, 'No one would have.' She raised her hand and waved to the nearest waiter. 'I'll pay the bill and then you are taking me to your house. No arguments,' she insisted as she saw him about to disagree. 'You can pay the next time. This has been lovely and what would be even lovelier is to see your home and to help you, like you've helped me. I put out Josephine's photo, the one on the shelf. It's on proper display now. I've even looked out some photo albums to show you. I thought we could do that together, tomorrow night. Bring your toothbrush.'

He looked up sharply.

Monica couldn't tell if she saw fear or surprise in his eyes, so reassured him with, 'Don't get any funny ideas. You'll be in the spare room. I want to help break this poor sleep hygiene. I want you to see that nothing bad happens if you go to bed early.'

'I'll bring my pyjamas then,' he quipped as the waiter brought over the bill on a silver plate with a selection of chocolate mints.

Barry opened his kitchen drawer, took out a small card, ripped it in half, then ripped these halves ever further, pressed his foot on a black pedal and consigned the shards to his bin. They fluttered down and were soon lost amongst the potato peelings, eggshells, and dried out tea bags. 'I'm still going to chat to you, Kimberly, but I know I'll never hear your voice again. I love you, sweetheart.' He picked up her school photo, kissed her forehead, and switched the light out as he walked towards the stairs still carrying the picture frame.

Monica stared up at the second-floor windows, 'What a lovely house, I hadn't realised that it was so big, Oliver.'

'Yes, Emma hoped to have a large family one day. I feel like I rattle around it some days. I really should sell it and downsize and let a new family enjoy it.'

Monica let the comment go. She felt it wasn't her place to suggest that he should. She was pleased when he opened his front door and ushered her in. Her dress was thin and not at all suited for this mid-December weather, even with her coat. She walked into the wide lobby, noting the mountain of post and junk leaflets piled on a small table. Oliver switched on more lights and it surprised her to see a towel draped over what looked to be a mirror. She pointed to it, 'Why's that there?'

He looked down at his feet bashfully.

She removed the towel and folded it and placed it by the neglected letters.

'I can't face myself. I cover all the mirrors,' he confessed, like a naughty schoolboy caught stealing in an apple orchard.

She cupped his face and gave him the gentlest of kisses. She pulled his face up and drew him to her, 'You are handsome. Over the years, I've seen how kind you are. You've fed and looked after us all at group. You make sure everyone is warm, you counsel those who are too distraught to stay in the meeting room, and you've ensured Barry's safety against that imbecile Roland. You've brought joy and hope back into my life. Emma was lucky to have you as a husband, and I know you did everything you could for her.' She led him by the arm to the mirror and placed him squarely in front of it. 'Now look at yourself and see all of that.'

Oliver did as she bid, but rather than stare back at himself, all he could see was how gorgeous Monica was. The dim restaurant lighting didn't do justice to her delicate use of make-up and the short bob of lustrous hair that curved around her cheeks. Its shine accentuated her high cheekbones, and the stylist had chosen this change of hairstyle well. She had a lovely glow about her. He took her other hand, 'I'm ready to go into the lounge now.'

Monica nodded and guided him to the doorway. She looked across to the kitchen and saw the chair with its back to the table. She guessed that this was where Oliver sat, probably looking at the lounge door in expectation. She would change this pattern too. She saw him take several deep breaths.

He opened the door.

Group

Layers of dust had settled on the cream carpet, making it a dull grey colour. Their footsteps showed with each tentative tread. What little light glowed from the lobby highlighted the thick grime that clogged the furniture. Spider's webs clung to the ceiling and spread towards the light fittings. Several gossamer strands dangled eerily from the chandelier crystals, their delicate structures blending in and covering the glasswork.

Oliver stared at the sofa, still half expecting to see the imprint of Emma's body. He reached over and flicked on the lights and was surprised to see that they still worked. 'She was thoughtful until the end. She looked like she was fast asleep. But she was cold when I touched her.' He shivered as he relived that fatal night and pointed to the sofa, 'I phoned an ambulance straight away. But the police came too, and I've never set foot in here again, not since the family liaison officer led me away and helped me to pack a bag. They stayed for hours; the neighbours told me later. The police even bolted and padlocked the front and back doors to prevent anyway, including me, from entering until the Procurator Fiscal office had completed their investigations. You can still see the screw holes. I haven't filled them in yet. We are lucky, so people say, here in Scotland. They don't hold a Coroner's inquest, like in England, which can delay burials and hamper the grieving process.'

Monica clinched his hand, allowing him to talk and let it all out. She stood and listened.

'I've many happy memories in this room.' He nodded along the walls where photos could just be made out, despite the layers of grime and webs. 'Those are just some of our happy times.' He turned to face her, 'Thank you. I'll clean in here and start using it again. Now that I see there is nothing to be frightened of. But I think I'll donate the sofa to a charity or get someone to take it to the tip in their van.'

'I'll help you. If you like?'

'But not tonight. You're tired, and you don't want to get that beautiful dress dirty.'

'No. But I'm not going to leave you on your own. Pack a bag and stay a few nights at mine. I've the weekend off work. Shall we tackle it together?'

He nodded, then remembered the training course, 'How about next weekend, it'll give me time to arrange a man with a van to take away the sofa.'

'Thank heavens for that. Those spiders up there are giving me the chills. I want to make sure I've a long pair of gloves and hairnet on before I get my feather duster out.'

He laughed, looked around at the other chairs, the low table, the dust-laden television, and ornaments, 'I think we are going to need more than a feather duster!'

Graham selected a record, held the vinyl up to the light, checked it for dust and scratches, refrained from sniffing it, as was his usual

266

practice, least Robyn think him perverse, and then set it carefully down on his decks. He lifted the stylus and was soon lost in the first track.

Robyn was stood by the window of his lounge, peeking out from behind the thick curtains, over to her two cottages. Her gaze was set upon the furthest of the two houses and her vigil was rewarded, 'She's back! She's walking hand in hand with Oliver. That's so sweet.' She continued her commentary, raising her voice higher than normal to compete with the trumpeter, 'He's got a bag!' she shrieked in delight. 'They are going in. He's not saying goodbye. He's going in with a bag.' She let out a filthy chuckle, 'The dirty vixen!'

Oliver placed his bag on the lounge floor, feeling like a guest at a bed-and-breakfast. He looked around at how sparsely decorated the lounge was. There were few ornaments or pictures. Though he admired the landscape painting, it looked like it was an original watercolour, or perhaps oil, he wasn't sure. Then he glanced at the alcove and walked towards it for a closer inspection. 'She was ever so beautiful, your Josephine.'

Monica nodded, 'I feel stupid for not displaying her proudly. It's taken me years to face her again. Sometimes I was so angry with her.'

Oliver nodded sagely, 'Those who haven't suffered a catastrophic loss wouldn't understand the fury we can sometimes feel towards those who took their lives. There are just so many unanswered questions.'

'Yes,' was all she simply stated.

He turned back to the photo, 'How could you!' he yelled.

She looked to him in surprise, a look of hurt on her face. And wonder at what she'd done wrong.

He continued with, 'That was what I would shout at the lounge doorway in some of my darkest hours.'

Her shoulders sagged, and she looked to him with a mixture of pity and love. She was right, she thought. He did sit in the kitchen chair, facing the closed door. She resolved there and then to help him in any way she could. She would make him stay until the weekend, she'd put a wash on midweek, and cook some meals. She only hoped that her cooking was up to Barry's standard. She changed the subject, hoping to prevent Oliver from going further down a shadowy path. 'What a dark horse Barry is. Cooking for the Queen. What an honour.'

He turned, face brightened, 'I know! Right! His family must have been proud. Thank you for inviting him, and me, for Christmas.'

'It'll be fun. You might not thank me once Robyn comes over and starts on the prosecco.'

Oliver laughed, 'You'd better keep her sober until three in the afternoon. I have a feeling that Barry will want to watch Her Majesty give her speech.'

'I hadn't thought of that,' she giggled. 'I don't think I can keep Robyn away from booze until then, not at Christmas. It would be like showing a child her presents and not letting her open them. We must buy in some non-alcoholic drinks for us, anyway. We'll pretend it is prosecco and see if she notices. Let me show you to your room. Then

I'd like you to see my favourite photo album of Josephine. She turned it into a scrapbook.'

'I'd like that.' He wondered what Robyn would think of her friend, he'd seen her looking out of the window in the big house.

Shaun helped Cherie into her nightdress, trying not to look at how thin she'd become. He could see her prominent ribs as she put her arms into the air for the sleeves. As he rolled the fabric down her torso, he almost flinched at how much her empty breasts sagged, like two deflated floppy balloons. Once they were pert and proud, even in middle-age. He crouched down and gently took her ankles, 'Put your head on your pillow, love,' he sighed.

She did as instructed and felt her legs lifted and placed onto the mattress, and then the weight of the winter duvet seemed to crush her. She closed her eyes, hoping to never wake up again.

Shaun leant forward and kissed her forehead, like a parent would do to a tucked-up child. 'Goodnight love.' He waited momentarily for a reply, but none came, so he switched off her bedside light, walked to his side of the bed and changed into his pyjamas.

The next morning Oliver went to work as usual, but he spent the afternoon shut in his office, e-mailing each member of the group, and apologising for the unacceptable behaviour of Nancy and Roland. He voiced his regret at revealing their e-mail addresses and advising them to block her. He ended by hoping that they would return in the New Year and wishing them as best a Christmas as possible. It relieved him to see that by midday, he was getting replies from some of the members. He made sure that he replied to each individual concern.

He looked down at his paperwork, then at his screen, shrugged, switched off his computer, and left his office. He bade a surprised Mitch a goodbye and asked him if he would secure the office. He'd left instructions for Nick to take over his work for the rest of the week.

'Are you okay, boss?'

'I couldn't be better, Mitch! You make sure to leave fine and early each day whilst I'm away. You and Nick work too hard and need some extra time off.'

Mitch nodded, loving the transformation that had come over his boss since yesterday. It was almost like he'd suddenly come alive. He couldn't wait to tell his mum.

Wendy left the buggy on the doorstep and used the spare key to open the door whilst juggling a squirming Lindsay. She took a tentative step into her grandmother's house and shouted out, 'Are you in? Why are your curtains closed? There's still a lot of daylight left.' She was relieved when the lounge door opened, and Isobel peeked through.

'Oh, hello darlings, I wasn't expecting you.'

'You haven't been replying to my texts, I've been worried.'

Isobel held out her hands and a joyous expression lit up her face as she received Lindsay. She held her tightly and walked through to the living room and sat on the sofa.

Wendy followed her and threw open the curtains, allowing the December sun to light up the room.

Isobel jumped to her feet, gave Lindsay back to her mother, then tentatively walked to the window and looked up and down her street.

'Ah, I see what's going on here. Give me your phone.' She put Lindsay down on the floor and then held out her hand to her grandmother. 'It's them, isn't it?'

Isobel looked bashful and admitted, 'I haven't slept a wink. It's been one text after another. The phone has been ringing through the night. I fear checking my e-mails anymore. I switched the thing off in the end.'

'Right!' declared Wendy purposefully. She took the phone from her, switched it on, keyed in the passcode, the same number she used for hers, and whizzed about pressing buttons and swiping. 'That's them blocked. I've deleted their e-mails and texts. You don't need to be reading them. Though there is one from Oliver, you can read that later.' She nodded to Lindsay, who was poking her head out from her favourite spot under the Christmas tree, 'You have some cuddle therapy and I'll put the kettle on.'

Isobel looked back to the window and stared out at her doorstep, 'But what if they come here?' she asked in a shaky voice.

'I have a feeling Roland will be too busy to do that,' replied her granddaughter mysteriously.

'And what sort of,' the police officer struggled to find the most appropriate word and settled with, 'business goes on here sir?' He drawled the last word.

'Never mind all the questions, what about my window?' shouted an enraged Roland.

'Calm down, sir,' replied the younger of the two police officers in an even tone. 'We need to establish some facts first, for our records.'

Roland sat down by the table with the purple velvet covering. A solitary china teacup, metal tea leaf strainer, and a small china pot sat on the table. 'I'm a psychic medium,' he said proudly, chest puffed out.

'Really, sir,' intoned the male officer whilst giving a knowing look at his colleague. They had previously charged this man with harassing a bereaved family. He claimed to know who murdered their daughter. They had little time for him.

'Put clairvoyant down then, or counsellor, or life-coach if you must.'

The young officer nodded to the table, 'Or how about tea leaf reader? We've room in our notebooks, sir.'

'Yes, that as well,' insisted Roland. 'What are you going to do to catch the thug that threw that brick through my window?' He looked down at the shards of glass that he'd swept from the pavement. It had worried him that a dog may have cut a paw on them. Painted lettering could be made out in several of the larger shards in the dustpan.

The male police officer grinned to his sergeant, then addressed Roland. 'You've no CCTV, sir. We'll make enquires at the other businesses. Maybe they saw someone. We'll see if they have cameras. In the meantime, I'd advise you to get a joiner in, or a glazier if you can get one at such short notice. But you probably already know that. You'll have foreseen this, sir. In your -' he paused again, for effect, 'professional capacity.'

His sergeant looked on with approval, a mischievous glint in her eye. It was all she could do to stop herself laughing. She couldn't have said it better herself. It was just the right amount of respect, heavily laden with sarcasm and just above the law. She looked on, delighting in the misfortune of this man who had wasted so much police time in the past, whilst inflicting untold damage to a vulnerable family. And not only on her patch. She'd noted the files on the computer from forces throughout Scotland and even a complaint from the North-East of England. He had been a busy boy.

Monica sauntered out of her office complex, thinking of the bus journey ahead and wondering if she should walk home instead and clear her head. The lack of coffee was still causing headaches, but she knew this would soon pass. She'd slept through last night. The first time in years. Having Oliver in the room next door helped. She wondered how long she could respectably last before inviting him into her lonely bed. She weighed up the time the bus took and how quickly she could walk and still be in time to meet Oliver at home. She was already wondering what she could cook from the freezer and hoped that she had something special in. She heard a wolf whistle. She looked around her, expecting some arcane, lascivious builder to be ogling over a young woman. It surprised her to see that it came from Oliver. He was leaning on his car, fingers in mouth, aiming his whistle at her. She blushed. Then she scowled and made shushing noises, 'My friends at work will hear you.' Though she didn't care, she secretly hoped they would.

'Want a lift home, gorgeous?' he shouted across the full car park.

He spoke in a drawling American accent. Or at least she thought it was meant to be that. Or maybe it was Welsh. It was awful, whatever it was. And pleasant, at the same time. She made him feel like she was twenty again. 'Okay, but stop that noise and don't ever speak with that twang again,' she chided, though she smiled through her cross words.

He walked over to the passenger door and opened it for her. 'Sorry!' though he didn't mean it. 'I've taken the week off.'

'Oh!' she replied as she sat down.

'I'm all yours. What would you like to do?'

She looked up at the darkening sky. 'Do you have a warm coat in the backseat? I've a fun idea.'

'Why don't you go for another walk, it'll clear your head,' suggested Corrina. 'I've messaged Oliver again. Everything is sorted.'

Adam looked at her doubtfully, 'Okay. When will tea be?'

'The usual time. You can shout the children down when you come back.'

'All right. See you in about thirty minutes then.' As he left, he scooped up his phone from the charge point, leaving the cable for Corrina to recharge hers. He knew that her battery would be flat soon as she'd been messaging Oliver for what seemed the better part of the day.

He pulled on his hat, scarf, gloves, and thicker jacket. When he exited their house, he didn't follow the garden path to the pavement. Instead, he walked around his home and sat at his favourite bench, by the fishpond and water feature, and relished the gentle sound of the running water. He pulled out his phone, took off one of his gloves, and typed a reply to Oliver.

He wrote, 'I'm so sorry for the upset Oliver. I think it may have been me who inadvertently told the charity about Roland. I spoke to my doctor about him. He must have been on my mind. When we lost Fraser, our GP told us to be wary of a psychic medium who worked in our area. She warned us he would read the obituaries, research people on the internet, and then contact bereaved families claiming to have messages from beyond the grave. She said that he gleamed lots of information from social media accounts and used it to his advantage. Doctor Munro described the fallout she had to help heal and wished to prevent us from heartache and damage. No one contacted us and we put it out of our minds. We didn't even twig when Roland was making his outrageous claims. Had I been stronger minded, I should have spoken at the last meeting, rather than walking away. I'm sorry, but I think our GP complained to the charity. We

275

won't come back, and I truly regret any upset I caused. I wish you well and thank you for all the fancy biscuits. Adam.'

He re-read his message, then hit the send button and powered down his phone. He put back on his glove after pocketing his phone, grateful for the warmth it brought back to his digits. Adam sat at the bench, relishing the stillness of the night. 'No more dramas,' he said aloud, for the benefit of no one but his prized fish.

Monica hugged Oliver tight as they walked towards the Christmas tree, a veritable giant of a fir, donated by a twin town in Norway. She loved the way he had his arm wrapped around her waist, like two young lovers without a care in the world. The warmth she felt wasn't just from his body heat close to hers, but from the love and care she felt he gave her.

They stopped at the foot of the tree and looked up, marvelling at the giant bows, the sparkling lights and the shimmering globes hung from the thick branches. 'Isn't it beautiful! I haven't been here for years, Josephine loved seeing the switch on ceremony and then going to the lights on parade. She'd cheer and clap, and her delight was a marvel to watch. Especially when the Cairngorm reindeers came prancing down the street.'

Oliver kissed her, caught up in her enjoyment. 'It's a magnificent tree. I'd forgotten how big they are.'

'You should see the size of the one in Robyn's house. Graham surprised her with a delivery of a huge one, which just about fitted in. I helped him decorate it, but I didn't enjoy it.' She looked to him and rubbed noses with him, 'But now I can appreciate Christmas again, thanks to you!'

'The same here,' cheered Oliver, his breath dissolving in little white clouds.

She pulled him by the arm, 'Let's walk up the main street and see all the lights.'

He allowed himself to be taken joyfully by the hand, and he could have sworn that she almost skipped along beside him.

She had her head tilted back, eyes cast high above her, not caring that fellow pedestrians had to carefully weave and bob along the pavement. She delighted at the Christmas stocking, with strategically placed lights that showed its hem, awaiting delivery of toys. Then she pointed out the bright candy cane, whirled red and white stripes enticingly decorated this sweet treat. Even the bobbles that hung between the buildings and stretched high in the air caused her to whoop like a child.

Oliver neglected to look long at each. Instead he was relishing the miraculous change in his sweetheart and storing her glee into his memory banks. He was replacing emotional pain with that of pleasure, and he loved her more for it.

She spotted the Christmas village, down a side street, set up near to the University halls. 'Let's have a hot chocolate, with marshmallows and everything!'

He thought his arms would ache in the morning as she tugged him across the street, grateful that the traffic lights were red and the green walking man flashing away. He gave silent thanks to whoever had pressed the crossing button at just exactly the right moment.

They walked past the ride that sprung its fares to a dizzy height and then suddenly dropped them. Its passengers screamed like banshees. He had a worrying realisation that he'd be on that in about ten minutes. He laughed. He didn't care, so long as they were strapped in, side by side.

He watched as Monica chose their drinks and pointed to some over-priced chocolate treats that claimed to have been hand-baked in Germany. She was presented with a star-shaped and a love heart biscuit beside two steaming drinks that were slowly dissolving a mountain of whipped cream with chocolate shavings and sinking marshmallows. She handed over a twenty-pound note and told the freezing woman to keep the change. This provided sudden warmth to the young lady whose hat stretched down beyond her ears.

They took their wares and sat down, and Oliver let out a sudden breath, 'And rest!' he quipped.

Monica laughed, took a drink of her hot chocolate, burnt her tongue, put it down and looked up to Oliver. She had a blob of whipped cream at the end of her nose.

He was about to wipe it off her, but then saw the look of lust come over her eyes as she spied the frightening ride. His fate was sealed, so he left the splodge on for a bit longer.

She wondered why he laughed, but guessed he was caught up in the moment and joined him. Monica hadn't had such fun for years.

She bit into her biscuit and let out an audible, 'Mmm!' that was soon drowned out by a fresh set of screaming students behind Oliver.

Adam checked his phone as he was making his way around the house, checking that doors were locked, and light switches were off. 'It's like Blackpool illuminations here sometimes,' he muttered under his breath. Though he knew he wouldn't have it any other way. He wondered how difficult it would be for Corrina to have a fun Christmas for the sake of their other children, without Fraser. He tried to put this to the back of his mind and stopped by the bedroom door as he saw the reply from Oliver.

It read, 'Please don't worry, Adam. It was I who contacted the charity. Roland and Nancy were well out of order, and it is I who should apologise for putting Corrina and yourself in that position. The charity has employed a solicitor who has made sure they won't return to any meetings here, or the others around the UK. You should be able to talk to your doctor about anything. You have a good GP there, looking out for your family's welfare. I hope to see you at the next meeting and wish you as pleasant a Christmas as you can without your beloved Fraser. From your friend Oliver. P.S. Harriet will be delighted to hear that you loved her biscuits.'

Adam smiled, he was glad that this blossoming friendship would continue, besides Corrina still needed the support from the others. He powered down his phone for the night, ready for his mind's lights out as he felt his tablets already working their magic.

Christmas had meant many things to each member of the group. Oliver and Monica had enjoyed the presence of their friends but were glad when they left. Whilst Oliver drove Barry home, she prepared a special hot chocolate for them, and they took it to her bedroom. Both mugs lay neglected, their drinks long cold after their lovemaking.

Adam and Corrina had put on a brave face for their children, ensuring that Santa delivered a bumper load of presents this year. After they were safely put to bed, Adam broke down first, and each consoled the other long into the night.

Shaun had burnt the turkey and couldn't get his batter mix to rise, but the Yorkshire pudding was the least of his concerns. Andrew had announced that he was ready to return to education, and Cherie has spent the day rocking and moaning to herself. Shaun felt lonelier than Ebenezer Scrooge before his transformation, and he saw the goodness of people. He thought to his dwindling nest egg and hoped it would be enough to support his son through University and his wife through life.

Barry had resolved not to cry and instead he cherished his new friends and came alive in the company of Robyn, especially when she stood to rigid attention for the Queen. He had enjoyed toasting Her Majesty's health with the special fizzy drink he couldn't pronounce.

Isobel had sung, danced, and laughed with Lindsay and her family. Then, alone, with only Call the Midwife for company, she let her tears flow until the cosy happy ending warmed her soul. Darren and Wendy had enjoyed a closeness that being away from the fish factory smells brought and would soon have delightful news for Isobel.

Nancy had spent Christmas on her own. Her foul moods had frightened off her second husband, who sought solace with the spinster down the road. Nancy barely left her house for fear of village gossip.

Roland had found vulnerable souls and had paid them 'house visits' on Christmas day and returned home with a fat wallet.

Bella had lightened the heart of her future mother-in-law and put at ease her soon to be father-in-law as she found gladness in the day. They loved her gifts, but her new happiness with their son was the greatest present Bella gave them.

Mitch proposed to Rachel, and Harriet was over-joyed and over-come and had left Jude to finish the cooking. She cried many tears of happiness.

Shelagh took morning service and prayed hard, especially for the bereaved and for lost souls.

Mathew and his wife missed the company of dogs when they shut their café for a few days and vowed to get one of their own as soon as the re-homing centre opened in the New Year.

Graham fingered a small box that he kept in his pocket for the right time. He hoped to have Robyn all to himself at Hogmanay, or perhaps he'd leave it until Valentine's, if he could contain his excitement for that special day. He was glad that next year wasn't a leap year. He so wanted to be the one to ask the question.

Christmas trees were reluctantly taken down throughout the city homes after the New Year celebrations, and the Council workers gathered in the festive lights from the main street. The spark seemed to go out of the granite buildings and a hush almost fell on the population.

Oliver was contemplating group and how cold the hall would be. He looked at the clock in Monica's kitchen and then at the two boxes with red bows.

Monica came in and wrapped her arms around him. 'Let's go early. I could do with a drink beforehand. There is a friendly pub along the street.'

Oliver broke off the embrace and looked at her in bewilderment. She had been teetotal throughout Christmas and Hogmanay. He merely nodded. He could always leave her for ten minutes and nip into the church hall and turn up the heating.

They drove in silence towards the group, Monica was deep in thought and Oliver didn't want to disturb her. He drove alongside the hall, in the place he usually parked, but wondered if he should instead take a space nearer the pub. Instead, he compromised and parked between both buildings.

Monica stepped out of the vehicle first, as if in a rush to go somewhere. Oliver left the tissues, biscuits, milk, sugar, tea, and coffee in the car, locked up and had to run to catch up with her. He wondered why she needed a drink so badly. He drew alongside her as she swung open the bar's door. 'Are you all right?'

She looked beyond him, towards the bar counter and nodded. 'You find us a quiet table. I'll get your favourite.'

'Okay,' he drawled, wondering what was wrong with her. She seemed distracted. He was about to walk over to the seats that afforded the best view of the church hall, but then he saw a familiar figure at the bar and smiled.

Monica strode up to the bar, caught the eye of the barman and ordered three orange juices with lemonade and a large coffee. She turned and said softly, 'Hello Gregor, do you remember me?'

The unshaven man with the deep-set, red eyes turned to her and squinted to focus his vision, 'It's Monica, isn't it? I recall your kindness.'

'That's right.' Drinks were placed in front of her and she passed a note to the barman. 'Please keep the change, but can you bring another coffee in about fifteen minutes?' She discretely pointed to Gregor.

'You were at that group, weren't you?' offered Gregor, now fully recalling who she was.

'That's right, Gregor. It's our first meeting tonight. I'm the new co-ordinator and Oliver and Isobel have also been trained, to be deputies. It's a fresh start for us.' She pushed the tall glass of drink towards him and then lifted the mug and placed it alongside. 'These are for you.' She pointed to the two remaining glasses, 'I'm going to take these to our table and join Oliver. Then we'll be opening the hall in about twenty minutes. The meeting will start in about an hour. I hope you'll join us. It's a new year and a fresh start.' She waited whilst he pushed away his half-full pint glass and then took a long gulp of his gifted refreshing drink. She was pleased to see him nod.

Author's Note:

Thank you, dear reader, for your support and interest in my books, I love writing these novels and I hope they bring you much pleasure. If they do, it will help my writing career, and enable me to reach new readers, if you kindly left a review at Amazon and/or Good Reads. I've entered Group into a literary competition which judges on the number of reviews it receives. Thank you!

Learn more about me at www.cgbuswell.com where you'll find links to my @CGBUSWELL social media pages and a video of me with my beloved Lynne.

Join my clan at www.cgbuswell.com/newsletter.php and learn about free books, discounts and new releases.

Thank you, as always, to my dear friends Ray and Katherine for their advice and eagle-eyed proofreading. If you ever need expert, remote, IT support, Ray can be contacted at www.crudenbaytraining.co.uk or find him in his shop in the village Post Office.

My thanks to Amanda at Let's Get Booked for the lovely cover and formatting. You can see more of her talented book covers at www.letsgetbooked.com

Chris

Printed in Great Britain
by Amazon